GREEN
FOR
DANGER

Other Mystery Novels by Christianna Brand

GREEN
FOR
DANGER

CHRISTIANNA BRAND

Reader's
Digest

New York / Montreal

THE BEST MYSTERIES OF ALL TIME

GREEN FOR DANGER

To E.F.

We change our skies but not our
hearts who go across the seas

Author's Note

It will be apparent (I hope) that I could not have attempted the background of this story unless I had had some acquaintance with the inside workings of a military hospital; and it must surely be equally obvious that, under the circumstances, I would do all in my power to avoid portraying any one particular hospital. All such institutions, however, must have operating theatres and wards and corridors and be staffed by Royal Army Medical Corps officers, by Sisters and by Voluntary Aid Detachments, just as all characters must have a nose and two eyes and a mouth, with a very limited choice of colouring for their hair and complexion. I do implore my readers, therefore, *not* to be more clever than their author and see portraits where, quite honestly, none are intended.

C. B.

GREEN
FOR
DANGER

Chapter I

Joseph Higgins, postman, pushed his battered red bicycle up
the long ascent that leads to Heron's Park, three miles out of
Heronsford, in Kent. It had been a children's sanatorium before
the war, and now was being hurriedly scrambled into shape as a
military hospital. Its buildings stood out big and grey and bleak
among the naked winter trees and he cursed them heartily as he
toiled up the hill, his bicycle tacking groggily from side to side
of the country road. All this for a mere seven letters! Six miles
out of his way for a handful of letters that would probably not
even be looked at till the morning! He spread them out, fanwise,
in one hand, his elbow resting heavily on the handle-bar, and
examined them resentfully. The first was addressed to the
Commanding Officer. One of the new medicos, guessed Higgins
shrewdly, holding it up to the light. A nice linen envelope and
a Harley Street postmark; and doctors' handwriting was always
illegible. . . .

GERVASE EDEN HAD ALSO CURSED as he sat in his consulting-room, confirming to the C.O. at Heron's Park that he would report for duty, "forthwith." The last of his lovely ladies had just tripped off down the steps in a flutter of cheques and eyelashes and invitations to dinner, and already feeling mir*a*culously better for her *heavenly* little injection (of unadulterated H_2O). He could not flatter himself that the pay of a surgeon in His Majesty's Forces was going to keep him in anything like the luxury to which he was rapidly becoming accustomed; but there it was—one had put one's name down during the Munich crisis, and already it was becoming a tiny bit uncomfortable to be out of uniform. . . . At least he would be free of the lovely ladies for a spell. For the thousandth time he looked at himself in the mirror, looked at his ugly face and greying hair, at his thin, angular body and restless hands—and wondered what on earth women saw in him, and wished they wouldn't. He rang the bell for his pretty little secretary and asked her to post the letter. She immediately burst into tears at the thought of his going, and after all it was only common charity to spend a few minutes in comforting the poor little soul.

HIGGINS shuffled over Eden's letter and turned to the next in the bunch. A huge, square envelope, covered with a huge, square handwriting; a woman's handwriting, vigorous, generous, splashed across all the available space; one of the nurses, he supposed. . . .

Jane Woods had written two letters, one to an address to Austria, the other to Heron's Park. She finished off three sketches of delicious, though impractical, syren suits and posted them to Mr. Cecil, of Christophe's in Regent Street (who paid her three guineas apiece for them, and thereafter presented them as his own); and, consigning the rest of her work to the waste-paper-basket, she rang up the circle of delightful riff-raff who constituted her friends, and summoned them to a party. "Eat, drink and sleep together, my loves," cried Miss Woods, "for to-morrow we join the V.A.D.s!" She stood, glass in hand, before the low mantelpiece of her elegant little, modern, one-roomed flat, a big, dark woman of about forty, with a plain, rather raddled face, an enormous bust, and astonishingly lovely legs. "Jane, darling, we *told* you not to go in for those fantastic lectures!" cried the riff-raff, who were all going in for fantastic lectures themselves; and, "Woody, darling, I simply can't im*a*gine you, sweetie, I mean *bed*pans and everything!" and, "Woody, darling, what on earth made you *do* it?" She treated them to a tender little sketch of herself in the character of Florence Nightingale, hanging over the truckle bed of some suffering V.C. ("Is that you again, Flo, with that bloody nightlight?"); and, when at last she was alone, sobbed off her eye-black on to her pillow, because her intolerable conscience had driven her to this tremendous sacrifice; the sacrifice of all the fun and gaiety and luxury of her successful career, in blind atonement for a sin not even of her own commission; a sin, just possibly, not even committed.

The next letter, also, was in a woman's handwriting, a girlish hand, sloping downwards a little at the end of each line. "Sign of depression," said Joseph Higgins to himself, for he had read about that only a day or two ago in the Sunday paper. "Another of the nurses, I expect, and doesn't want to come, poor girl!" But here he was wrong, for Esther Sanson did, very badly, want to go to Heron's Park.

She stood with the letter in her hand, looking down at her mother and laughing, for Mrs. Sanson was deep in the latest drama of the Heronsford Women's Voluntary Service. ". . . but

Mummy she *could*n't! I mean, not *all* that baby wool into sailors' stockings for going under seaboots! I don't believe a word of it darling; you're making it up!"

"On my word of honour, Esther, every spot of it, one pair pale pink and the other pale blue. I couldn't believe my eyes when she showed them to me. 'But Mrs. Huge,' I said to her . . .'"

"Not Mrs. Huge, Mummy—her name *could*n't be Mrs. Huge?"

"I promise you, darling, Mrs. Huge, or something exactly like it, anyway. 'Mrs. Huge,' I said to her . . ." She broke off suddenly and all the light and laughter went out of her blue eyes. "Who have you been writing to, Esther? Is it the letter to the hospital?"

"I've said I'll go as 'immobile' V.A.D.," said Esther quickly. "I've said I can't leave Heronsford. I'll only be working at the hospital during the daytime."

"There could easily be an air-raid in the daytime, Esther. Supposing I were caught up here in a top floor flat, in an air-raid; absolutely helpless with my back so ersatz and rotten. . . .'"

"Your back's been much better lately, darling; I mean, look how you were able to go out to-day to the W.V.S. meeting."

"Yes, but it's aching dreadfully now, in consequence," said Mrs. Sanson, and immediately, with the strange inner magic of the true hypochondriac, blue shadows were painted about her eyes, and her face was all etched into delicate lines of pain. "Really, Esther, I do think, dearest, that you're sacrificing both of us, unnecessarily; after all, you're *needed*, here at home." She sat curled up like a kitten on the sofa, watching her daughter from under her long, soft, golden eyelashes; and tried on a little act that never had failed before. "Of course, my darling, if you really *want* to go . . .'"

Esther stood very still at the window, staring with unseeing eyes at the lovely Kentish countryside rolled out below her, and for the first time in her life she did not respond. She was twenty-seven, tall and too thin, with the narrow feet and slender hands that are supposed to go with good breeding; not beautiful but with the pure oval face and lifeless, leaf-brown hair of a madonna, descended from her niche in the wall of some quiet old church, to walk, gentle and reserved, through the tumult of an unfamiliar world. Unused as she was to opposing her mother's will, she knew that here was a matter in which she must make her own decision; and she said at last, slowly turning away from the window, standing with her back to the light: "It's not that I want to go; but I think I should."

"But, darling, *why?*"

"Because everybody's doing something, Mummy, and I must do my share. Besides, at least it will give me some sort of training, some sort of—well, *I* don't know—some sort of a life. If anything were to happen to you, darling, think how lost and helpless I should be. I wouldn't have any money, I wouldn't know anything, I wouldn't know anyone. But with this behind me—and I've always wanted to nurse . . ."

"Oh, well, as to that," said Mrs. Sanson, "you've got a terribly exalted idea of nursing, you know. I mean, it's horrid really, darling, honestly it is; nothing but dirt and squalor and nasty smells."

Since Esther had tenderly nursed her mother through several years of perfect health, there was not very much that she could learn from her on that subject. She merely smiled sadly and said that she would have to risk not liking the work. "I'm not going for pleasure, after all, am I? I shall probably scrub floors all day long and never even get as far as making a bed." She came over suddenly and sat on the floor, leaning her head wearily against her mother's knees. "Darling—be kind to me! Do understand. It isn't that I like to go, but I think I ought to. It's your sacrifice, too, Mummy dearest; we've both got to make it. You're always the brave and gay and strong one; be brave for us both this time, and let me go."

But her mother shrank away from her, curling herself up into a small, frightened ball in the corner of the sofa, covering her big, blue eyes with her little hands. "It's the air-raids, Esther. The air-raids! Supposing I were up here, all alone, helpless—and bombs began to fall! How should I manage? What could I do? Esther, don't go, darling, and leave me here alone; tell them you won't go, tell them you can't go—tear the letter up!"

But Esther got to her feet and dragged herself downstairs and posted it.

Higgins knew the handwritings on the next two letters. One was the crabbed old fist of Mr. Moon who had been surgeon in Heronsford as long as one could remember; the other was that of the local anæsthetist, Barnes. "I wonder if that means they're both coming 'ere?" thought Higgins, frowning down upon the two envelopes. "I'd've thought Barnes, at least, would've wanted to go somewhere else. Well, I suppose if they're in the Army they has to go where they're told."

Dr. Barnes said much the same thing to Mr. Moon as, having posted their letters, they walked up the hill together to their several homes. "I've applied to go to Heron's Park so that I can give my father a hand with the practice now and then; but we're in the Army now, sir, whether we like it or not."

"I think I do like it," said Moon, trotting along beside him, but, thanks to conscientious early-morning runs, not puffing at all. He was a stooping, plump little man like a miniature Churchill but with all the pugnacity gone out of him; with soft pink cheeks and fluffy white hair, exceedingly thin on top. His blue eyes twinkled with kindness and he talked into his boots with little exclamations and chuckles, like a character out of Dickens, though with none of the foolish softness of Dickensian benevolence. "I think I do like it; I like it very much."

"It'll make a change," said Barnes.

"I can do with a change you know, Barney," said Moon, with a little twist of his kind old face. "That house of mine—now that I've got a chance to leave it, I wonder how I've endured it all these years. Fifteen years I've lived in that house, all by myself; and I don't think there's been a day that I haven't lifted my head suddenly and listened, thinking that I heard my boy laughing . . . thinking I heard him come clattering down the stairs. Well, well—I can find it in my heart now to be grateful, I suppose; now that the war's come, I mean. He'd have been of age, you know; I'd have had to send him off, to see him go off to France or the East or somewhere. . . . I'd have had to wait and hunger for news of him; he might have been posted missing, perhaps, or killed, and without any news of what had really happened. It's that telegram business. . . . I don't think I could have borne that. I don't think his mother could have borne it, if she'd been alive. The gods act in their own mysterious ways, don't they, Barney? Who would have thought in all these years that I could ever have found it in my heart to say that I was glad that my boy had been killed?"

Barnes was silent, not from any lack of sympathy, but because he was a man who could not easily put his feelings into words. He was in his late thirties, not very tall, not very good-looking, but radiant with the charm of absolute integrity; sensitive, modest, rather shy, honest to an almost painful degree. He, too, was glad to go into the Army. "That Evans girl," he said; "the one who died under the anæsthetic last week—I've had an anonymous letter about her to-day. I think it's a good thing I'm getting out of the practice for a bit; I shall be Brave Lieutenant Barnes, serving his King and Country, and by the time the war's ended the whole thing will have blown over."

"But, my dear boy, the death was no earthly fault of yours."

"Well, we know that now," said Barnes, shrugging his shoulders, "but I couldn't account for it at the time. I got it into my head that I'd seen the tubes crossed during the operation—the oxygen and the nitrous oxide, you know; it must have been my imagination, but I was worrying about what could have gone wrong, and I kept getting a sort of vision of the two tubes crossing instead of being separate. I went into the theatre and asked them to check up; everything had been put away by then, of course, but nobody had noticed anything wrong . . . only the staff are mostly local people and my asking must have put ideas into their heads, and I suppose they talked. The mother came to me after the inquest and accused me of murdering the girl. It was— oh, it was horrible! Of course they decided that the findings at the inquest had been cooked, to protect me. She said they would get up a round robin or something or other, and hound me out of the town. They could too, you know; that kind of mud sticks in a one-horse place like Heronsford. It's fortunate for me, really, that the war's come when it has, if it had to come; my father can carry on the practice while I'm in the Army, and by the time it's all over the affair will have fizzled out."

"The panel patient is a strange animile," said Moon, pacing along beside him thoughtfully. "When you think of all that you've done for this town, you and your father, Barnes. . . ."

"I wonder if T. Atkins is going to be so very much different," said Barney pessimistically.

TWO MORE LETTERS; BOTH FROM women. One very neat and correct, a pretty round hand, a pretty grey-blue notepaper, the stamp stuck neatly in the corner; the other on a cheap, white envelope, addressed to the Matron, the Sisters' Mess—the handwriting sputtering across the paper, uncertain and ill at ease. V.A.D. Frederica Linley, and Sister Bates of Queen Alexandra's Imperial Military Nursing Service, reporting to Heron's Park Military Hospital. . . .

FREDERICA'S father who for thirty years had been a legend in some outpost of Empire, had subsequently settled down in Dinard, where he could by no means be got to appreciate that the inhabitants had not only never heard of the legend, but had never even heard of the Outpost. The war put an end to this embarrassing state of affairs and, on a nightmare voyage to England, he met and affianced himself to a wealthy widow with a proper respect for the pioneers of the East. Frederica received the news with her habitual calm. "I think she's too frightful, Daddy," she said, "but it's you that's got to sleep with her, not me," and she absented herself from the new home upon a series of lectures, and finally wrote off to Heron's Park that she would be arriving for duty on such-and-such a day, as instructed. Since a blowsy trollop of fifty cannot be expected to care for competition from an exquisite, self-possessed little creature of twenty-two, the ex-widow was not sorry to see her go.

The reaction of Sister Bates to her transition from civilian to military nursing was simple and forthright. She thought: "Perhaps I shall meet some nice officers!" and lest anyone be tempted to despise such single-minded devotion to the opposite sex, it may be pointed out that this innocent aspiration was shared in a greater or less degree, by twenty future members of the Sisters' Mess, and at least fifty V.A.D.s.

SEVEN letters. Old Mr. Moon and young Dr. Barnes, and Gervase Eden, surgeon, of Harley Street; Sister Marion Bates; Jane Woods and Esther Sanson and Frederica Linley, V.A.D.s. Higgins shuffled the envelopes together impatiently, and wrapped them round with a piece of grubby tape and thrust them into his pocket, plodding on, wheeling his bicycle up the hill. He could not know that, just a year later, one of the writers would die, self-confessed a murderer.

Chapter II

1

Sɪsᴛᴇʀ Bates stood before the shabby plush curtains of the hospital concert hall, singing "Trees." Her pretty, foolish face was blank with fright, and her hands hung at her sides like lumps of raw, pinkish meat. Every now and again she turned the palms towards the audience with a little, baffled gesture of emphasis or appeal.

The three V.A.D.s sat at the back of the hall because Frederica was on night duty and would have to slip out before the concert ended. "Freddi," said Woods, "I'll murder you when we get out. Here's Bates singing 'Trees' and dressed from head to toe in solid uniform; and you swore to me that she was going to sing 'Ave Maria' dancing a hula-hula in a grass skirt with her stomach showing!"

"Not both together, you idiot," said Esther. They broke into the muffled squeakings and sobbings of those who laugh in holy places.

Major Moon and Major Eden and Captain Barnes sat in the front row, but as far as possible away from the Colonel. "Wait till

I get hold of those girls," said Eden. "They promised me faithfully that Bates was going to wear a hula-hula skirt and have her stomach showing. That's the only reason I came."

Major Moon thought it was too bad of Eden to make fun of poor Sister Bates, who was reported to be madly in love with him, but he could not help laughing, all the same. He burst into a perfect pandemonium of giggles at the thought of her exposing her abdomen in a Hawaiian get-up.

Gervase Eden turned his ugly head to grin fleetingly at the success of his joke. He felt a bit of a rotter, but honestly, Marion was like a millstone round one's neck. In the early days at Heron's Park, when it had all been so dull and uncomfortable, miles from anywhere and no work to get down to, he had flirted mildly with her, very mildly, only just enough to keep them both amused. He ought to have known better; women with sticking-out-teeth were always too hot to handle. And now there was this complication of Freddi Linley. . . .

Captain Barnes did not laugh. He thought Sister Bates was pathetic, standing up there making a fool of herself in a last desperate attempt to impress Gervase Eden and thought, to be honest with oneself, Eden seemed to make no earthly effort to attract women, they all seemed to fall for him and it gave him a sort of responsibility towards them. Bates was obviously unhappy, poor silly girl. "You can't help liking the fellow," thought Barney to himself, "but . . ."

But even Frederica seemed no proof against that casual charm. Barnes had fallen in love with Frederica at his very first sight of her; had promised himself that he would wait patiently for three whole months until she should have a chance to get to know him; and in the third week had finally broken down and told her, at a

Sergeants' dance of all places, that he did not quite see how he could get through the rest of his life without her. She had put her little hands into his, and promised to marry him, "some day." "Not yet, Barney; not for a little while . . . but one day I will." Her eyes had strayed to where Gervase Eden was trying to disentangle himself from the choking blandishments of Sister Bates.

Frederica. Right across the hall, Barney could see her, sitting with Esther Sanson and Woods. Her hair was dark gold, curling heavily under her V.A.D. cap; her face, clear as a cameo, with limpid grey eyes and a little, determined round chin, the whole head tilted adorably on the slender, golden throat. Beside her Woods looked like a Piccadilly flower-seller, with her plain, round face and twinkling, shrewd dark eyes, her arms folded over her deep bosom, under the short, red-lined cape. You expected her at any moment to cry out, "Buy a flah, kind gentleman," and thrust a bedraggled carnation under your nose. Between them Esther Sanson seemed drained of all colour; she was a very different person now from the haunted, broken creature that she had been after her mother's terrible death but—Barney whose own heart ached for something that his beloved would never quite satisfy, was sensitive to the pain in other hearts.

There are about half a dozen songs which can be relied upon for a good reception, however abominably they may be sung, and "Trees" is (unfortunately) one of them. The audience applauded vociferously and Sister Bates blushed with happy pride and would straightway have broken into "Song of Songs" had not the Compère interrupted. He was a corporal in the Company, and nobody knew whether his dress suit was or was not intentionally funny. He held up his hand for silence and announced gloomily: "The Commanding Officer."

Every new Commanding Officer begins his reign by having something repainted. It starts him off with a reputation for efficiency. ". . . and, my dear, he hadn't been two *days* in the place before the beds in St. Elmo's had all been enamelled white!" Colonel Beaton had created quite a furore by having the word "Rubbish" on the bins in the corridor, replaced by the word "Salvage" in huge black and white letters, and at the moment his popularity was at its height. He reminded one of a bottle with the cork driven in too far. One longed to get hold of his head and pull it out sharply so as to give him a bit more neck. The bottle contained a certain amount of froth and very little else. He made a jolly little man-to-man speech.

". . . sorry to break up this happy party, but as you may have noticed, there's an air-raid on! These entertainments are allowed strictly on the understanding that if things get too hot, we must close down." He explained earnestly: "If so many of the personnel were to be killed or injured at one time, it would make things very awkward," and everybody thought this silly and unnecessary because it was perfectly obvious and they all knew it quite well. "Now, I'm afraid there's been a bad show in Heronsford. The Air Raid Precaution centre has been hit, among other places, and there are a lot of casualties. The Cottage Hospital is filling up and we're taking some of the people in here. I want everybody to go to their posts at once." He added automatically: "Without panic," though anything less like panic it would have been difficult to imagine; and continued with a little duck towards Sister Bates who still stood uncertainly at the side of the stage: "We've all enjoyed the 'play' very much indeed; now it's time for work!" He scrambled down from the platform and hurried off out of the hall.

"*I* didn't see no play," confided the up-patients to each other, quite bewildered.

The hospital was built in the shape of a gigantic wheel, its spokes forming the different departments and, above and below ground level, the wards; its hub a great circular hall, not unlike Piccadilly Circus Tube Station both in shape and purpose, and general appearance of seething activity. The lift ran straight up through the hall, the staircase curling round it in a slow spiral. The main operating theatre was on the ground floor, easily available to all the surgical wards; the emergency theatre in the basement was used only during raids.

Marion Bates was theatre sister at Heron's Park. She scurried down to see that the emergency night staff was prepared, and her mind was the strangest jumble of surgical instruments, "Song of Songs" and Gervase Eden. She knew that her poor little effort at pleasing him had failed. "Thank God I didn't do the dance," she thought as she dived between the swing doors of the operating theatre. "He wouldn't have liked it. He'd only have laughed." The cold sweat broke out on her forehead at the thought of her madness in ever having supposed that it would impress him. If it had been Frederica Linley, now—but she knew that Frederica would never for a moment have considered so demeaning herself. Anyway, he was not with *her* this evening. Linley had gone back to her ward and Gervase was strolling across the circular hall with Woods. Woods was forty if she was a day, and she had a face like the back of a cab. "Forceps, retractors, scissors, knives," muttered Sister Bates, checking over instruments in the hot, bright, green-and-silver security of her own domain; "forceps, retractors, scissors, knives. But Woods has marvellous legs!" Outside, the guns thundered and rolled, there was the scream of a bomb and the occasional noisy rattle of machine-gun fire; even down here, twenty feet below ground, the room shook with the crash of every gun. "I wonder what he's saying to Woods," thought Bates, automatically separating the jingling instruments. "I wonder if she's still in the hall with him. I think I'll just slip up and see. . . ."

Frederica had gone back to her ward with Esther who happened to be on day duty there. "I'll stay and give you a hand," said Esther. "There are two empty beds and they're sure to fill them up with casualties. It's already as much as one person can manage in here, now that we're so short of orderlies."

The relieving V.A.D. was glad to see them. "The Orderly Officer hasn't made his round yet, Linley. Sister says when he comes will you ask him for some morphia for the two hernias and the appendix that were done to-day, and to say can he give you something for the asthma in number seven. She's gone down to St. Cat's ward."

"Oh, all right; thank you, Jones. I'll tell him."

"Blast these air-raids," said Jones cheerfully, struggling into her ugly blue outdoor coat for her dash across the grounds to the safety of her shelter. "They keep the men awake."

The ward was on the ground floor, opposite the main operating theatre; a long, high room, the tall windows now blacked out for the night; fifteen beds were ranged down each side, with an aisle down the centre, its narrow tables denuded of their bowls of flowers. The open lockers were tidily packed with the little miscellaneous possessions of the men; on the lower shelves their uniforms were folded into precise, square bundles and their overcoats and caps hung on hooks at the bed-heads. A corner of the ward, near the door, had been partitioned off into a small square "bunk" for the sister, furnished with a desk and some chairs; here notes were kept, reports written up, discussions held with the medical officers, endless cups of tea consumed, and a good deal of more or less surreptitious entertainment carried on. A large pane of glass had been let into the side facing the ward, so that all that went on there could be seen from the bunk. It frequently escaped the attention of the occupants that, especially when the light was on in the bunk, everything that went on there could be seen from the ward.

The air-raid was becoming very heavy. The droning of aeroplanes overhead was incessant, and the building shook and shuddered with the thundering of the guns in the neighbouring fields, and now and again with the sickening thud of a bomb. The men moved uneasily in their beds and made foolish, defiant little jokes. "Cor that was a near one! Nearly scraped me 'air off, that one did! They've 'eard about the pudding we 'ad to-day, nurse, and they're trying to kill the cook!" The hospital humorist sat up in bed and every time a bomb fell tapped himself on the back of the head and made his false teeth shoot out.

"You have no business to have all these lights on," said Freddi severely, and went round clicking them off.

Night Sister appeared in the doorway. "Oh, Nurse Sanson— are *you* here?"

"I said I'd stay on and help Nurse Linley, Sister, if that's all right?"

"Yes, of course. I expect she'll be very thankful. I shan't be able to help you much to-night, nurse; we've got four bad casualties in St. Catherine's. . . . However, if you need anything you must send for me at once. They've just rung through from Reception and there's a man coming in with fractured femur; get him into bed, will you, and just keep him quiet and warm; don't do anything about the leg. Major Eden will be along in a few minutes to see him. Let me know if he wants me." She hurried off again.

"What a flap!" said Frederica calmly, watching her go.

Two civilian stretcher-bearers appeared, carrying a grimy bundle on a canvas stretcher. "Is this right, Miss? The old gent in Reception asked us to bring him straight down here, as he hadn't got any orderlies to send with him."

"Yes, that's right: this corner bed, please. Esther, will you deal with this, while I get the rest of the ward settled? I think that'll be the best way to manage it."

The stretcher-bearers helped to lift the man on to the bed. "Wouldn't they take him in the resuscitation ward?" asked Esther, rather surprised at his condition.

"No, it seems they're filling up there, and he wasn't as badly shocked as some of the others. They've had two deaths there already. Never should have taken 'em in, really, but we thought there might be half a chance. The A.R.P. Centre's been hit, and a pub out at Godlistone, and various other places. They're still digging one chap out. Rescue squad they was, waiting to go out on a job. Looks as if he'd needed a bit of rescuing himself!" said the stretcher-bearer cheerfully. He put out his hand and pushed the damp hair off the man's forehead, with the rough, crude gentleness of all his kind. "Poor old boy!" he said, and picked up his stretcher and, whistling softly, went away.

Poor old boy. He lay pathetically still under the blankets, packed in with hot-water bottles, his hands lying loosely at his sides, his eyes closed, his face covered with dirt and dust and grime. His leg was bandaged to a long wooden splint. His boots had been torn off by the blast and his clothes were cut to ribbons, but she made no attempt to undress or wash him till the warmth and rest should have strengthened his pulse and brought back depth to the flickering respirations. She put her hand to his mouth, however, to feel the cold breath on her knuckles, and he must have been unconscious of the gesture, for he moved his head a little, laying his grimy cheek against her forearm with a gesture of trust and dependence, infinitely touching. Tears filled her eyes. "Don't worry. Just lie still. It's all over now. You're safe now. You're going to be all right."

He opened his eyes and she turned away her head, for she knew all too well the expression she would see there. It was only six months since her mother had died. For two days and two nights she had waited in anguish while men toiled unceasingly at the mountain of rubble that had once been a tall block of flats; had torn with her own helpless hands at the beams and girders and concrete that, having proved so frail a shelter, now heaped themselves into so deep a tomb. At the end of the second day, the foreman had come to her and wearily wiping the filth and sweat from his face, had broken it to her that it was useless to go on; at any moment the building would collapse, burying his men with those already dead. The following day the systematic demolition of the building had begun, and after another day and night they had brought her mother out. As they carried her past, she had turned her head very slightly on the stretcher, and her eyes had met Esther's; there had been no smallest gleam of recognition in their depths: only pain and bewilderment and terror and—could it be?—reproach! And so she had died, Mummy who had been so pretty and sweet, so gay and funny, whose little faults of selfishness and petulance had endeared her to a selfless heart, immeasurably more than nobler qualities might have done. Alone in the world, she had gone like an automaton through the heartbreaking details of identification and burial; had sought ease for her aching remorse in the hard, rough, satisfying toil in the wards at the hospital; it was through these first bewildering days when she walked through her work in a dream of hideous unreality and lay, sleepless and haunted through night after endless night, that Woods and Frederica had first come to be her friends; against Freddi's passionless sanity no less than Woody's fond, maternal clucking, she had dashed out the first agony of her mother's death. . . . "But I was a fool to come back here," she thought, standing with the old man's cheek against her arm. "I was a fool ever to think that I could forget the way she looked, when I see it again and again in the faces of strangers. . . ." In her heart, she reverted unconsciously to the formula of her childhood prayers. "Poor old man. God help him and make him get well."

Frederica came down the ward. "Esther, it's nearly ten and I've just realised I haven't had anything to eat. Could you possibly hold the fort for another ten minutes or so, while I rush out and get something? It's all such a muddle to-night, and the orderly's helping with stretchers, and I probably shan't get another chance and I shall be starving by morning?"

"Yes, of course, darling. Don't hurry. I can cope."

Freddi departed. Gervase Eden, who was Surgeon on Duty, came into the ward. "Sister here, nurse?"

"No, she's on one of the other wards. Shall I go and get her?" Outside the hospital, Eden was Gervase to Esther and Freddi and Woods, but she added the regulation "Sir."

"No, never mind. She's probably snowed under with casualties. Major Moon's just admitted a man . . ."

"Here he is, sir, in the corner bed. The Emergency Post label said, 'fractured pelvis'; he was given a morphia injection two and a half hours ago while they were digging him out. They don't give his name; I suppose they haven't found out yet who he is."

"You haven't cleaned him up?"

"Well, he was still very shocked when they brought him in, so I left him to warm up. That was right, wasn't it?"

"Yes, perfectly right," said Eden. He bent over the man's body, feeling with short, thin fingers deep into flesh and muscle and down to the bone. The man shrank and groaned. "It's all right, old chap. I won't be long now, and then we'll give you another dose of something and send you off to sleep. It isn't very serious. You're going to be all right." He straightened himself and moved away from the bed. "Fractured his femur all right. Everything else seems to be intact. There's no internal injury." Sister arrived while he was washing his hands in the lavatory outside the ward. "I don't think we'd better touch him to-night," he said, explaining the state of affairs to her there. "He's too badly shocked, and anyway we've got all we can cope with. They've fixed him up with a splint at the Emergency Post and I think we'll leave him undisturbed and have him up to the theatre in the morning. He'll have to be X-rayed first . . ." He consulted a list. "Major Moon's doing a duodenal ulcer at half-past nine; could you have him ready after that?"

"Yes, sir, of course; it'll just give the X-ray people nice time."

"Well, that's what we'll do then. Leave the leg as it is, nurse; clean him up a bit, but don't worry him; and then you can give him a shot of morphia and I'll see him again in the morning."

"Put a couple of screens round him, nurse," said Sister, "so that the light doesn't disturb him; I'll leave out the morphia for you. Oh, and Major Eden, will you let me have something for the appendix Major Moon did today, and those two hernias? And the man in seven, Captain Newsome's cartilage, you know, he's developed a very troublesome asthma . . ." She drifted away with him, towards the bunk.

2

FREDERICA returned, still swallowing the last crumbs of her meal. "It's too heavenly of you to have stayed on like this, darling. Have you coped all right?"

"Yes, nothing's happened except a visit from Gervase." She repeated the gist of his instructions. "I'll stay and finish this fractured femur for you. You carry on; I'm perfectly all right."

Frederica whisked off up the ward. The lights flickered with the thudding of the guns. A bomb fell somewhere close. The old man stirred and groaned, "Bombs! Bombs! The bombs!"

"No bombs," said Esther reassuringly. "Only guns; not bombs."

He lost even his feeble interest in the bombs. "The *pain!*"

"Just bear it for a little bit longer," she said, her hand on his wrist. "Just while I get your clothes off and clean you up a little bit; and then you shall go off to sleep and forget all about it." Standing with the basin balanced on her hip, towels over her arm, she looked down at him pityingly. Poor old boy; poor, frightened, broken, pitiful little old man. . . . She wrung out a piece of gauze in the hot water, and began gently to wash his face.

3

NIGHT Sister had left out four quarter-grain tablets of morphia on a tray in the little bunk. Frederica looked up the prescriptions book. "Three 'stat' and one 's o s.' Will you give them, Esther? One to your man, and one each to the hernias; the appendix seems to be dozing off, so we'll leave his s o s till he seems to want it. I'll deal with this asthma question. Yes, all right, Wilson, I'm coming!"

Esther lighted the tiny spirit lamp, dropped one of the tablets into a teaspoon, added sterile water and resterilised the whole over the flame, mixing in the dissolving tablet with the needle of the hypodermic syringe; sucked up the solution into the syringe and carried it over, with a piece of iodined gauze, to one of the hernia patients. "There you are," she said, smiling at him, dabbing at the tiny puncture with the gauze. "That'll set you up till the morning!"

He smiled back at her hazily. "Thank you, nurse."

She gave the second injection to the other hernia, and a third to the fractured femur. He was becoming increasingly conscious, muttering wildly to himself: "Bombs! The bombs! All gone . . . all of us gone this time!"

"This will ease the pain now, and make you go to sleep."

"All of us gone; all my mates gone. . . . All sitting there and the whole place came down on top of us." He struggled up from his pillow, muttering wildly: "It's going to hit us! It's going to hit us . . ." and after a pause began to mumble softly to himself: "The effete and spineless remnants of Churchill's once-great England . . . cowering in their rabbit holes from the might of the German air force. . . ."

Frederica came and joined her at the foot of the bed. "What the dickens is he talking about?"

"He seems to be quoting something; I suppose he's a bit light-headed."

"All gone," insisted the man, moaning to himself. "All gone and me the last!"

Frederica was the perfect nurse. If she was moved by the sight of suffering or sorrow or fear, she gave no sign of it, and her dry, matter-of-fact little manner often brought balm where more gentle methods failed. She said now, softly but quite brusquely: "You mustn't talk any more. Give yourself up to the morphia and let yourself go to sleep. Try not to look forward, try not to think or worry. . . . Everything's going to be quite all right. Just lie still and let yourself go to sleep." The monotonous repetition, the level voice, soothed and comforted him. He relaxed against his pillow and did not speak again. She clicked off the remaining lights in the ward and arranged a couple of screens round him, leaving him in almost total darkness; on the centre table a lamp shone in an unshadowed pool upon the layer of fine plaster shaken down from the ceiling by the guns and bombs; she passed a cloth over the dust, and five minutes later it had settled there again. The men moved restlessly, resigning themselves to the long night; there were still one or two to call out: "Good-night, nurse! God bless, nurse! Aren't you coming to kiss me good-night, nurse?" Outside the guns grumbled and reverberated round the base of the hill, a flare hung, dripping stars, in the shell-splintered sky, the drone of the bombers was rent now and then by the frightened scream of a falling bomb. . . .

4

ESTHER replaced the syringe on the tray, blew out the spirit lamp, and wiped the teaspoon clean. "Well, darling, I think my work of mercy is over for the night."

"Yes, and thank you a thousand times, sweetie, for all you've done. They're expecting another in from Resuscitation, and I don't know how I'd have managed without you."

"You're sure you're O.K. now?"

"Oh yes, perfectly, now that I've finally got the ward under control. That's the worst of these blessed air-raids; they do un-settle the men."

"I suppose Woody and I will have to plunge down to that mouldy shelter. The one and only advantage of night duty is that you *can* stay above ground. Do you think we dare just go to bed and see if we can get away with it?"

"My dear, last time Joan Pierson and Hibbert did that, the Commander routed them out and drove them down to the shel-ter just as they were, and now everybody knows that Hibbert goes to bed in her vest and knickers."

"Well, *we* don't go to bed in our vests and knickers. Com's welcome to drive me forth in my Jaeger pyjamas. I hope Woody's got some tea."

"Have some here, Esther, before you go."

"No, no, I'd better go over to quarters; she'll be wondering what's happened to me. Good-night, darling. God bless!"

"Happy sheltering," said Frederica. She added, with rarely spoken sympathy: "You do look tired, my dear; and I'm afraid it's my fault!" and came over and gave her a brief little peck of apology and gratitude.

5

It was long after ten. Esther departed, and Frederica made her-self the inevitable cup of tea and settled down to innumerable small jobs left over from the evening's work. A shadow fell across the table. "Hallo, Freddi."

"Oh, hallo, Barney; I wondered if you would come. I saved some tea for you; it's only just made."

"I need it," he said wearily. "We're having a rotten time. Perkins is on his seven days' leave and there's no one else to give anæsthetics, so we've just been working all out in the emergency theatre. Some of the casualties are awfully bad; they've had two deaths already in Resuscitation. You've got another fellow to come in here; did you know? Compound fracture of the tibia and fibula. They've cleaned up the wound and put on an extension; he'll be along very shortly. I thought I'd slip along and see you while we had a little lull." He put his tea down carefully and came round the table and took her into his arms. "Frederica—I just get through my days, waiting for this moment!"

She returned his kisses lightly and pushed him gently away. "You ought to be concentrating on your work, Captain Barnes, not thinking of your young woman!"

If he was hurt he did not show it; but after a moment, as he sat stirring his tea, he said suddenly: "Frederica, you would never let me down? Would you?"

"Of course not, darling," said Freddi; but a little too lightly; a little too readily.

He sat staring at his tea, speaking more to himself than to her. "That would be too much cruelty," he said slowly. "I—I couldn't bear that. Cruelty and dishonesty—those are two things that I just can't stand . . ."

"Sometimes a person has to—has to choose between them. I mean, sometimes if you don't want to be cruel, you have to tell, or act, some lies."

He went very white and stood up suddenly, looking down into her wide, grey eyes. "Well, Freddi—always remember this: I'd rather have cruelty than dishonesty. I'd rather be hurt than deceived. . . ."

Something broke in her, and she went up close to him, grasping at his coat sleeves with her little hands, straining herself against him as though both giving and taking comfort. "Oh, Barney—I'm sorry, darling. Don't look like that, my dearest; you break my heart, I'll never hurt you *or* deceive you, Barney, honestly I won't, I swear I won't. . . ."

He looked down at her sadly, at the lovely little face and deep, deep into the limpid eyes. "Oh, Freddi," he said, "my little love—don't frighten me! The bare thought of ever losing you, makes me sick and dizzy. . . . You're mine, Freddi, aren't you? Promise me you'll always be mine, Freddi, *prom*ise me. . . ."

She closed her eyes, pressing her forehead against his shoulder. "Yes, darling, I promise you; always, all my life."

A man called from the ward. "All right. I'm coming. Look, Barney, you must go, dearest. The tib. and fib. will be in soon, and I must get all this cleared off. . . . (Yes, all right, nurse is coming!) Good-night, my love."

The appendicitis case had woken and was in some pain. She gave him the last injection of morphia and went back to the bunk. The casualty in the corner bed was moaning softly; she shone her torch for a moment on his face, but his eyes were closed, and she went back to her work; but again there was a step at the door and Gervase Eden came in. "Hallo, Nurse Linley, my lovely one!"

"Oh, hallo, Gervase," she said uneasily.

"You look like an orchid, Frederica, sitting there with the light shining down on your hair. How do you manage to be so full of colour when you're wearing a plain grey dress?" He saw the look that lit up her eyes and added hastily: "I got that out of a book!"

"And you've been going round looking for a female in a grey dress ever since, to try it out on," said Freddi, laughing; but her heart did a foolish little somersault in her breast.

"Why the devil can't I just ask for Night Sister, and not go and make jokes that they take too seriously?" thought Eden, exasperated with himself. He hastened to ask where Night Sister was.

"On one of the other wards; do you want her?"

"Not a bit," said Eden, and Frederica smiled again. "For a moment, Gervase, you looked at me as if I was Sister Bates!"

"My dear—have I got a special look for Sister Bates?"

"Gervase, of *course* you have! You look at her all cross and withdrawn, like this!" She assumed an expression of hideous ferocity, screwing up her lovely little face, drawing together the delicate eyebrows, pursing her full, red Burne-Jones mouth, in an effort not to laugh. "Do I look funny, Gervase? Do I? Do I look like you looking at Sister Bates?"

"Oh, Freddi," he said, "you don't look funny at all. You only look adorable. . . ."

Something shivered between them as real and potent as an electric shock; and she was in his arms, pressing her body against him, reaching up to him for kisses that he could not restrain. "Oh, Freddi—Oh, God! Oh, Freddi. . . ." But in a moment he had pushed her away from him, unfastening her hands from his shoulders, shifting away to the other side of the table, nervously fingering his tie. "I'm sorry, my dear. I—I lost control for a moment. I'm sorry; I shouldn't have done it." He stood silent, violently pressing his forehead against the back of his hand. "I feel such a rotter, Freddi. Do forgive me and forget all about it." He ignored the fact that, of the two, it was she who had most completely "lost control."

"There's nothing to forgive, Gervase. But as for forgetting. . . ."

He refused to recognise the significance in her tone. "Just let's pretend that it never happened, Freddi. I feel so rotten about it." He said deliberately: "Rotten to Barney, I mean," and added, smiling shakily, "You must obviously never make funny faces again!"

She stood in stricken silence, staring at his face; and, at a step in the passage, escaped into the ward. Sister Bates came into the bunk. She said, spitefully, sick with jealousy and anger: "Oh, there you are, Major Eden! I thought I should find you here!"

"I'm making my rounds," said Eden, who had finished them half an hour ago.

"Do you kiss the nurses in every bunk, when you're making your rounds?" she said furiously, blurting it out in her pain and despair.

"No," he said coolly. "Only the sisters."

He had not meant to say it, like that; he had not meant to refer to the past when she had been on night duty, when she had followed him round from ward to ward, when she had "happened" to be in every bunk he arrived at. He had only just meant to pass it off as a light joke, to protect Frederica from her jealous curiosity. He said apologetically: "I'm sorry, my dear; I didn't intend any wise-cracks. But I was not making love to Freddi Linley, and, to be honest, I don't know what business of yours it would have been if I had."

She looked at him bleakly. "Oh, Gervase—how can you say such a thing?"

"My God!" thought Eden; but he said, kindly and patiently: "Look, Marion—we must have this out, once and for all. You and I had a little affair. I never pretended to you for a moment that it was more than that. These things can't last for ever, and they don't. It was charming and it was delightful and I'm very grateful for all the fun we had together—but now it's over."

"It isn't over for me," she said desperately. "After all you said to me, Gervase—all you promised me: you can't just leave me flat like this."

"I never said a word to you that you could have taken as a promise of any sort."

"You told me you loved me . . ."

But he interrupted her, saying sternly: "I never said those words to any woman in all my life."

"Oh, words!" she cried passionately. "Who cares about words? Men think that they can do what they like, can treat you as they like, and as long as they don't say those three magic words, 'I love you,' they're free of all responsibility in the matter. Well, you aren't free, Gervase. Kisses can be promises and—and just looks and silences. . . . Whatever you may have said about loving me, you let me love *you;* and now I'm not going to be thrown away because you've gone and fallen for a silly little chit like Frederica Linley. I shall go to Barnes and tell him about it. I shall tell him he must put a stop to it, that it's ruining his life and mine. . . . I won't let you go, Gervase. I can't; it would kill me. I'm not going to. . . ." She broke off and cried, wretched and helpless: "You *can't* be in love with her!"

"I'm not in love with anyone," he said steadily.

"You're in love with Frederica Linley. I suppose you want to marry her. . . ."

"You know I'm not in a position to marry anyone, Marion," he said impatiently. Once, long ago, one of the lovely ladies had been importunate, and he had not then acquired his skill in evading desperate situations. He had not seen her for several years, but she formed a shield against similar assaults upon his liberty.

"But you don't love *me* any more?"

"Oh, Marion," he said wearily, "do let's not go over this again. Men fall in love and fall out of love, and that's all there is to it." You could not explain that you had never even fallen in love, that the worst you had done was to accept attentions flung at your defenceless heart. "I—I want to remember our little affair with affection and gratitude; let me do that, my dear. Don't spoil it all by trying to hold on to something that's gone, past recall."

But she looked at him with blue eyes, stupid with pain and misery, defeating her own hopes by her uncontrollable need to put those hopes into words. "All the same, Gervase, I won't let you go; I'll tell everybody how you've treated me, I'll tell everybody how you're letting me down for that Linley girl, I'll *make* you stay with me. . . ."

He caught her by the wrist, staring down, grim and angry into her frightened face. "Don't you *dare!*" he said.

"I will, Gervase, I swear I will. I'll—I'll sue you for breach of promise. . . . I'll make it so that everyone thinks what a rotter you are. . . . All those women in Harley Street. . . ."

He flung her away from him in disgust and marched off out of the bunk and into the hall; she stayed for a moment, leaning against the wall, sick with the realisation of her own behaviour; and then crept out after him; neither of them gave a backward glance towards the ward.

Frederica had retreated into the dark recess of the screens round the newcomer's bed; she came to the door and stood there, staring after them. "My God—supposing she does tell Barney!" Their unconsciously raised voices had reached her clearly through the thin partition. "Supposing she tells Barney—he'd never speak to me again; he'd never love me again! I should lose him, and all for a man like Gervase Eden. . . . Gervase would love me for a week

31

or a month, and then just let me go. 'I want to remember our little affair with affection and gratitude, Freddi; be a little darling, my pet, and let me go!' He has every woman in the place running after him, and he doesn't want any of them . . . any of the others. But he does want me! It was only because of Barney. . . . Oh, my God! Barney, why don't I just stick to you, when you're so decent and sweet and you love me so much more than I deserve . . . but the moment Gervase comes along—he doesn't say anything, he doesn't *do* anything, he never even touched me before to-night . . . but my heart turns over and my knees go to water . . . it's disgusting, really it is, it's nothing but sex, that's all! It's just my misfortune to look like a blinking machine and all the time be a raging furnace underneath. Oh, well!" she shrugged her little shoulders and smoothed down her apron and settled her starched white veil. "I suppose I'd better stop having inhibitions and look to my suffering patients." The man in the corner bed said something and as she went over to him, taking his hot hand in her cool and gentle one, she thought: "Anyway, thank goodness Esther and Woody don't know!"

6

ESTHER had just arrived back from the ward and was sitting in their quarters with Woods, discussing Frederica's infatuation. A benevolent providence had placed a small row of labourer's cottages at the main gates of the park, and here the V.A.D.s were accommodated, three or four to each little two-roomed house. The cottages were small and dark and inconvenient, but the plumbing was adequate and each had a tiny kitchen with a gas stove; to three girls unused to community life and especially to life among sixty women of greatly varying ages and drawn from every imaginable class, their cottage was a haven of privacy and relaxation and peace. Frederica, being on night duty, did Box and Cox with Esther in the room upstairs; Woods had a camp bed in the communal sitting-room.

The whole place rocked with the deafening roar of the guns, but the bombs seemed fewer and the flares were dying down. They sat very comfortably with their feet on the fender, drinking cups of cocoa, in defiance of all orders that nobody was to remain in their quarters after black-out, during a raid. Esther said thoughtfully: "What people can see in Gervase, I never could understand. I mean, he's nice and he's funny, but he's as ugly as anything, so thin and grey and, well, he must be at least forty. . . ."

"Thanks very much," said Woods.

"Well, I don't mean that, darling, you *know* what I mean. He's not a glamour boy; and he never seems to try and make women like him."

"Ah, but you're a lady icicle, Esther."

"Well, I must be, because I seem to be the only female in the hospital who can see Gervase Eden without swooning at his feet. How did the great Act go to-night?"

Woods grinned. "Not bad at all. I caught up with Casanova as he came out of the concert, and I put on a terrific air of indifference and tried to look anxious to get away, and it was such a change for him, poor lamb, that he fell for it like a log."

"Mind you don't fall yourself, Woody. That would be a laugh!"

"I should say it would," agreed Woods, cackling with ribald mirth. "However, it would do no harm, Esther, and the effect would be the same. Frederica would see that some other female has only to whistle and off he goes like a shot."

"She must know that anyhow; look at poor old Bates."

"Ah, yes, but it's one thing for Gervase to sicken of Bates and turn his attentions to Freddi; and quite another for him to start running after fat old Woody, right in the first stages of his affair with Frederica!"

"Are you so sure it's an affair, darling?"

"Well, Freddi goes round looking like a love-sick hen all the time he's about; and love may be blind, but if it gets any worse, Barney's bound to see it. Barney wouldn't take a thing like this lightly, you know, Esther. It would break his heart, but he'd just write Freddi off for ever: he loves her too much and too sort of *deeply*, for her to try playing fast and loose with him. It's as much for Barney's sake as Frederica's that I want to put an end to it if I can."

"I hope this won't get you into a mess though, Woody," said Esther, still not satisfied.

Woods sat staring into the fire, a shawl clutched round her bosom, her exquisite legs stretched out towards the blaze; the lines of laughter ironed, for a moment, out of her face. She said slowly: "My dear, I'm past getting into messes. I've led a bit of a comic life, Esther, one way and another, getting in and out of messes and not doing any harm to anyone, that I could see; except perhaps to myself; and even then I don't know—I don't think I'd have it any other way if I could do it all over again. Freddi's different. She's so young and she's so pretty and attractive; she must settle down with Barney, Esther, and run his house and have lots of lovely babies and be a little Madam . . . the charm about Freddi is that she's so cool and sure and—well, sort of pleased with herself; isn't she? Not in a nasty way, I don't mean, but just rather funny and sweet. If she went and got herself a past, she'd lose all that; she'd lose her faith in herself, and, you know, I don't believe she'd marry Barney. She wouldn't be able to deceive him, and yet she wouldn't be able to confess her weakness by telling him. I don't know. I may be all wrong; I'm rotten about knowing people's characters . . . but anyway, if I can prevent her from going off the rocks with this Don Juan of hers, by fair means or foul, I will. I don't think there's the earthliest chance of my getting hurt in the process, but if I do, well, I've been hurt before and I can take it again." She belched vigorously and patted her chest. "My Godfathers! That stew!"

"Well, I hope it works, Woody, and I hope you ever get any thanks from Frederica, if it does!"

"I don't want any thanks," said Woods calmly; and Esther, looking at her, sitting there bundled up in shawls, fat and jolly and rather common, with her made-up face and shining, shrewd, dark eyes, said to her lovingly: "No, darling, you never do."

Chapter III

1

IT WAS always a miracle, after a heavy raid, to look out in the morning and see one's world still intact about one. Esther walked across the grounds with Woody, wrapped in her short red-lined cape against the cold, dawn air. "I believe there's a new crater in the field over there . . . that must have been the one that fell at about ten. I could have sworn it was nearer."

"Stick of three," said Woody comfortably, in the familiar jargon of life under the blitz. "Look, there's another one, up in the woods—you can see where it's broken the branches of the trees. Good thing it wasn't a bit more to the left or the third would have given the Sisters' Mess a conk. That would have shaken them up!"

"Never run, except for a land mine!" said Esther, mimicking Matron.

The fractured tib. and fib. was agreeably surprised to see her, on the ward. "Hallo, I haven't met you before!"

"I've met *you*," she said, smiling, not pausing in her assault upon his person with a large wet flannel. "I saw you last night being wheeled across from the theatre, but you weren't taking much notice at the time."

"I can't have been," he said grinning.

He was a young man, a slim, blonde, smiling young man with bright blue eyes and something pleasant and clean and reliable about him. Esther was profoundly bored with dependable young men, but she recognised in him something a little different from the ordinary run. She said kindly: "How are you feeling to-day?"

"Oh, I'm not too bad for seven o'clock in the morning. They say I've fractured my tibia and fibula or something. What does that mean?"

"It means that you've broken the two bones running down the front of your leg; they generally get sort of—overlapping, you know, and you have to have them pulled apart so that the bones can meet and have a chance to unite again. I expect you'll be strung up like this to an extension frame for a little while— several weeks; but it won't hurt, not very much; and then they'll fix you up in a plaster and you'll be able to hop about, and when it comes off it'll just be a matter of getting the leg strong again and you'll never know the difference. It'll take a long time and it isn't exactly heaven, but that's the worst there is to know."

He looked at her intently. "Are you just telling me this?"

"No," said Esther. "I don't 'just tell' people things. Give me your other hand."

"Are you going to hold it for me?" he asked, laughing.

"Only as long as it takes to wash it; and don't try to flirt with me—I don't like it." She pulled down his pyjama sleeve with a jerk and picked up the basin and towels.

"I'm sorry," he said, surprised and rather hurt.

"That's all right." She looked at the remains of his clothing folded away in the locker, at the shoes beneath it, which, though cut and scratched by debris, were of the rich, chestnut colour that only comes of polishing beautiful leather. "Are you a civilian?"

"No, I'm a simple Able Bodied in the Navy. I happened to be home on leave and I was helping out with my old job."

She did not inquire as to what his job had been, but the word "home" caught her attention. "Do you live in Heronsford?"

"Just outside. I—well, you know the big brewery out at Godlistone?"

"Good gracious—don't tell me you're a brewer?" she said, laughing.

"I'm afraid I am; does that astonish you?"

"Well, no, not exactly; but you don't—well, you don't *seem* like a brewer, that's all."

He looked at her with a quizzical smile. "You mean I talk like a pansy?"

She had not met many men in her sheltered life with her mother, in their little flat; not on equal terms, not in easy badinage. She was a little embarrassed and said doubtfully: "No, of course, not that. But . . . well, one thinks of brewers as large men with brawny arms and red noses."

"Well, I don't know about brawny arms," said the tib. and fib., laughing, looking down at the muscles bulging under the thin sleeve of his hospital pyjamas. "The red nose is only a matter of time, I expect. I have to explain that I'm the sort of King Brewer. I own the place, you see."

"Yes, I see," said Esther.

"So, if you ever want any free beer, you know where to come."

"Well, I'm not very fond of beer," said Esther apologetically.

"That's a pity," said the fractured tib. and fib. He added: "Because you're going to see an awful lot of it in future," but he did not say it out loud.

The sister on day duty came bustling in from the bunk where she had been in consultation with the retiring night sister. "Everything all right, nurse?"

"Yes, Sister, thank you."

"You know number eight is going up for operation at half-past nine?"

"Yes, Sister."

"And the fractured femur after that." She went to the corner bed where the screens had now been moved aside. "Good morning. How are you feeling?"

"I had a terrible night," said the man briefly, opening his heavy eyes and looking at her resentfully.

"Is your name Higgins?"

"Yes, it is," said the man. "Who wants to know?"

"Well, we all want to know. They couldn't find out last night. You're a postman, are you?"

"Yes, I am," said Higgins; "at least I was. It doesn't look as if I'll ever be able to do it again."

"Oh, nonsense, of course you will," said Sister brightly. She said to Esther as she hurried on round the ward: "He seems very low. You'd better have a talk to him about his operation while you prepare him for it, or he'll start refusing to have it done or something. By the way, I believe the police rang up to inquire for his wife; if she comes, you'd better let her sit with him before he goes up to the theatre."

"Yes, Sister."

"And you'd better go up with him, Sanson, and stay there and bring him back. By the way, there's that duodenal being done before him. Would you like to watch it? Have you seen any abdominals?"

"Well, no I haven't, Sister. I *would* like to see it, if I could."

"Yes, all right, then. The other two can manage in here for an hour or so. You can take Higgins up early. It'll keep him from lying here upsetting the others by getting nervy and also get rid of the wife if she turns out to be trying."

Mrs. Higgins turned out to be very trying. She objected to being sent out to the bunk while Barnes came round with his stethoscope, checking up on the patients due for anæsthetic that day; and again while Gervase Eden made a second examination and sat for a little while talking to her husband at his bedside. At nine-thirty, by which time, in a hospital ward, the day seems well advanced, Esther transferred the old man to a trolley with the help of an orderly, and pushed him out of the ward and across the great, circular hall towards the theatre.

2

THE modern operating-theatre is no longer a dazzling white, trying to the surgeon's eyes and inclined to tricky shadows, but a restful, rather dark green. The theatre at Heron's Park was a large, square, green-tiled room, with glass cabinets and shelves of metal sterilising drums ranged round its walls; the table was in the centre, under a huge, circular metal lamp, lined with innumerable mirrors so angled that the surgeon's hands cast no shadow across his work. The table itself was of light, strong metal, white-enamelled and hinged at either end; it stood on a thick, central pedestal so that no legs or cross bars should get in the surgeon's way, and was fitted with pedals and handscrews for raising or lowering the whole or either end. It was covered with a thick pad of sorbo rubber, wrapped in a linen sheet. The stretcher was placed over this, and steel supports removed, leaving the patient still lying on the canvas of the stretcher, so that as little lifting as possible need be done after operation. To the patient's right were two small trolleys, presided over by the theatre sister, one with a selection of instruments appropriate to the operation on hand; the other with open troughs of knives and scissors, needles and catgut and swabs. To the left of the table was a tray on a single tall leg so that it could be pulled across the patient's body, to receive the instruments used or still in use; a basin of antiseptic stood ready for rinsing the hands, and a couple of buckets to receive the blood-stained swabs. In a corner of the theatre, a red rubber sheet was spread out on the floor, where the swabs could be counted over and checked and re-checked with a slate hanging on the wall over the sterilising drums from which the swabs were taken. The temperature of the room was kept very high by means of radiators hidden in the walls, and over all was the strong, sweet, sickly smell of ether.

Barney was sitting at the head of the table getting the first patient under, when Esther arrived wheeling Higgins. His trolley stood to his left, a sturdy metal affair with the big iron cylinders of gas and oxygen strapped to one side of it, the water in the glass jar, through which the anæsthetic must pass on its way to the patient, bubbling merrily away at the top. A thick red rubber balloon, in a black net bag, inflated and deflated regularly with the patient's respirations.

Higgins had had his pre-operative injection of morphia and atropine in the ward, and was feeling drowsy and more or less at ease. "You'll have to wait a little while, Higgins," said Esther, wheeling him into the anæsthetic-room, and putting up the catch inside the door to keep him safe from interruption. "Just lie here and keep quite quiet. Do you feel all right?"

"I feel a bit thirsty, miss," said Higgins, licking his dry lips.

"I'm afraid you will; that's the atropine. Now, will you be all right for a minute or two, while I go and get a gown?"

"Yes, I'll be all right, miss," said Higgins indifferently.

Woods was the theatre V.A.D. She and Sister Bates were both in the washroom in long green gowns, tied at the back of the neck and waist with tapes. Woods had a small oblong of green gauze hanging by its strings round her neck, ready to be pulled up over her mouth and nose when she went into the theatre; but Sister Bates wore a more elaborate mask, a sort of yashmak that covered her whole head, and tucked in under the neck of the gown; her eyes, acknowledging Esther through the slit, looked very big and blue against the green. "Get yourself a gown, nurse, if you're going to stay." The mask was sucked in and blown out over her mouth as she spoke.

Major Moon turned away from the washbasins, holding out dripping hands. He was dressed in a white cotton singlet and wore a pair of shrunken white duck trousers and huge ankle-high rubber boots. Woods handed sterile towels and a green gown for him to shuffle his way into, his own hands held stiffly away from his body; she fitted a little round green cap on to his head, and fixed a small head-lamp on a band round his forehead. Woods chucked Esther a gown and an oblong mask like her own, and hurried to pick up the battery attached to the headlamp; she followed Major Moon into the theatre, carrying the battery at the end of its long flex like a page with a bride's train. Major Moon wriggled his plump little hands into thin brown rubber gloves.

The patient was breathing quietly, his eyes closed, his head lolling a little to one side. Gervase Eden, already masked and gowned, stood at his side, waiting with curbed impatience to get on. Major Moon went over to the sister's trolley and stood looking down at the instruments there. As Esther pushed open the door into the anæsthetic-room to make sure that Higgins was all right, she heard the old surgeon say, in his mumbling voice: "What a rotten collection of stuff we've got in this place; we could do such a lot more if we only had better equipment."

Woody adored Major Moon. He reminded her of Mr. Churchill, and Mr. Churchill was the idol of all Great Britain. She quoted, looking back over her shoulder as she stood at the door of the anæsthetic-room with Esther: "Give us the tools and we will get on with the job!"

Sister Bates bridled. Honestly, these V.A.D.s! Who did they think they were, joking with the officers? After all, V.A.D.s were only "other ranks." She said indignantly: "Be quiet, please, nurse! You're not here to . . ."

But she never finished her sentence, for there was a wild cry from the anæsthetic-room, and Higgins was struggling up to a sitting position on his stretcher, clinging to Esther, staring at the doorway into the theatre, and mumbling over and over and over again: "Where have I heard that voice? Oh, my God, I can't remember! I must remember! Where have I heard that voice . . . ?"

3

MAJOR Moon looked up astonished. He said sharply: "Who's that?"

Woods let the door swing to behind her and leaned back against the wall of the theatre; she said hurriedly: "It's only that

man Higgins, sir; the fractured pelvis, your next case. He's—I expect he's excited by the morphia, or something." They could hear
Esther's voice in the other room, calming the old man down.

Moon and Eden shrugged their shoulders and went to the patient, now well under the anæsthetic, on the table. Barney pulled
down his mask to say kindly: "You look very shaken, Woody.
Did he startle you? Are you all right?"

"Yes, yes," she said hastily, "I'm perfectly all right," and, with
a glance of purely professional inquiry, stepped forward to pull
back the blankets from the patient's body, folding back the grey
flannel gown on to his chest, unwrapping the bandages, removing the sterilised towels, and leaving the abdomen bare.

Eden picked up a brush and idly sloshed iodine over the gently heaving patch of flesh; Major Moon came and stood opposite
him, and together they arranged the rubber sheets and sterile
green cloths across the body, leaving only a naked, yellow-painted
square. They looked for all the world like two women helping
each other to make a bed. Eden said, grinning: "I regret to inform
you, sir, that the patient has a pimple right in the line of fire!"

Moon smiled absently, standing turned a little away from the
table, pushing with bunched fingers at the slack stomach. He
nodded to Barnes. "Yes, he's very nice," and, without further
ado, picked up a knife and made a long, slow, deep slash, apparently at random, across the yellow square. The flesh gaped,
fatty white, turning to deep red against the dark green of the
surrounding cloths: opening out after the point of the knife like
the wash in the wake of a ship. Eden took forceps from Sister
Bates' hand and clipped up the blood-vessels, holding each for a
moment while Moon tied it off with gut, before dropping it and
passing on to the next. There was no flow of blood, but swabs

and instruments became stained in ugly patches. Barnes forced open the man's mouth and thrust in a short, red rubber air-way to keep clear the breathing passages.

Moon worked steadily, freeing the adhesions from the slack, veined balloon of the stomach with little half-scraping, half-paring movements of the knife, plunging his whole hand into the wound to feel his knowledgeable way about. He might have been a woman washing out old and fragile lace—his hands moved with the same delicate care, the same scrupulous attention to detail, the same cool competence and freedom from hesitation or strain. When the stomach was finally exposed, they wrapped it up carefully in a wet, green gauze and left it, bubbling pale pink and faintly blue, out on the abdomen, at the edge of the wound. Moon said to Barney, in the voice of a man asking for a little more butter on his bread: "Let's have him a bit slacker, will you?" and Barnes fiddled with a tap. The patient gave a little grunt as though in response, and was silent again.

Major Moon rinsed his hands in the saline at his side, already discoloured with blood from his rubber gloves. Sister Bates said: "Change the basin, nurse." It was an education in itself to watch her handing the instruments, each held so that it presented itself most readily to the surgeon's fingers. Major Moon exposed the duodenum.

Woods tipped blood-stained swabs on to the rubber sheet in the corner of the theatre and began sorting them out. She said, out of the corner of her mouth, to Esther as she slipped back into the theatre: "How's the old boy now?"

"Oh, he's quietened down again. He thought he'd heard your voice somewhere."

"So I gathered," said Woods drily. She crouched on her hams, busily separating swabs with a pair of long-handled forceps, holding them well away from her spotless gown. "How are you liking your first abdominal?"

"I feel a bit sick, to be honest."

"Well, you can't be sick here. You look rather green I must say; it's the heat, I expect. Why don't you sit down?"

Esther moved over to a stool and sat down quietly. Barney looked at her over his mask and raised an eyebrow; he had fastened the rubber mask over the patient's face with wide red rubber bands, which gave a somewhat unattractive, snout-like effect. "They look as though they were slaughtering a pig," thought Esther, revolted.

Major Moon, bending over the body, suddenly straightened himself. "There it is! See it? It was an ulcer, all right. . . . Just give me a little swab, Sister, will you? Want to have a look, nurse? Wait a moment while I swab. There! You'll never see a prettier example of a duodenal ulcer than that!" Woods peered over his shoulder into the wound. Esther shuddered.

Woody came over and stood beside her, glancing into the anæsthetic-room *en route*. "Your old boy's all right; lying quite dopey and quiet. Didn't you want to see the ulcer?"

"No, I can't take it to-day. It's the heat in here."

"Won't be long now. You'd better wait outside while they're doing Higgins; he won't be very interesting anyway." She clumped off in her big, white rubber boots. Sister Bates broke open little glass phials and threaded up needles with gut. Eden fished out a bluish-pink coil of intestine, holding it clamped to the stomach while Moon cut and stitched. They packed it all into the belly at last and tucked it neatly away. "Won't be long now, Barney. Retract please, Eden. Harder if you can . . ."

It was over. Major Moon threw the last of the forceps on to the tray and stood looking down at the patient, peeling off his gloves, with an expression of calm satisfaction in his faded blue eyes. All gone off nicely; no strain or fuss; and as pretty an ulcer as he had ever seen. He went out to the washroom, followed by Eden. "I *thought* it wasn't a diverticulum. . . . Crossley seemed to think from the X-ray that it might have been a diverticulum . . ." Sister Bates and Woods bound up the yellow abdomen with its rough, red, five-inch wound all puckered together with stitches and metal clips, tossed aside the rubber sheet and pulled down the blankets, leaving the mouth and nostrils free to the air. Barney tidied up his trolley, got to his feet and stretched himself and went out to the washrooms. Woods scurried about the theatre clearing away swabs and dressings, placing a new basin of saline for the surgeon's hands, staggering across the room with a fresh cylinder of gas clasped like a large, black baby in her arms; tidying away the used tubes and scraps of gauze from the anæsthetist's trolley and placing a fresh airway tube in an enamel bowl. Esther went out to the anæsthetic-room and wheeled Higgins into the theatre; they lifted him on to the table, and slid away the metal poles of the stretcher, leaving the canvas under him, ready for lifting him off again. He stared about him with frightened and clouded eyes.

Barney came over to him and took his hand, speaking to him gently and soothingly. "You're going to be quite O.K., old man. I'll just put a mask over your nose and you'll breathe in and out quietly and you'll soon be fast asleep, and when you wake up you'll be in your bed and it'll all be over. . . ."

Higgins turned his head on the pillow. "Nurse! Nurse!"

"Yes," said Esther. "I'm here. I'm with you."

"I'm going to be all right, nurse, aren't I?"

"Yes, you'll be fine, Higgins, honestly. It's only quite a little operation, hardly anything at all."

"What are they going to do to me?" he said piteously, his eyes roving round the theatre, shying away from the instruments laid out in readiness.

Barney had a fad about using the anæsthetic-room. He preferred to start the anæsthetic with the patient already on the table; but he acknowledged the extra fear and distress involved and he now explained, kindly and gently: "It's really only a very small thing, Higgins; hardly an operation at all. You've broken your femur, that's the thigh bone, and we're going to put a little thin steel pin through, above the knee, to pull the bone into place. That's all there is to it. It won't take very long and it isn't serious a bit—is it, nurse?"

"Not a bit," said Esther.

"There isn't any danger, nurse? I'm going to wake up all right?"

"Oh, Higgins, of course you are. There's nothing to be frightened of."

"Promise me, nurse?" he insisted. "*Promise* me?"

"Yes, Higgins, of course; there's no danger—I promise you."

"You'll tell the missis, will you, my dear?" he said anxiously. "She's waiting in the hall outside, and she'll be fretting a bit. Tell her there isn't any danger will you, my dear?"

"Yes, all right, Higgins, I will. As soon as you've gone off to sleep."

He relaxed on the pillow, comforted. "Thank you, my dear. God bless you, my dear." He gave her a little, rather pathetic smile, and Barney put the rubber mask down, gently, over his mouth and nose.

The water bubbled gaily in the little glass jar at the top of the trolley bracket, through which the gas and oxygen pass. "Breathe quite normally, old boy. Don't worry. Relax and breathe gently. No hurry . . ." Barney's voice was quiet and soothing, but the mask was pressing down more heavily on Higgins' face. "Just quite quiet, old man; nothing to worry about . . ." Woods stood beside the table, ready to hang on to kicking legs or flailing arms. Major Moon and Eden came back again from the washrooms, pulling on fresh rubber gloves.

4

SOMETHING was going wrong. Higgins' face was turning from blue to a dark plum colour, showing on the cheek bones and at the edges of the mask. He breathed noisily and under the blankets his limbs jerked convulsively. The line of bubbles in the jar altered as Barnes cut down the gas and increased the oxygen: he looked rather troubled.

Two minutes later the man was still a bad colour, and the red rubber bag in its black net heaved in and out with the heavy, stertorous breathing. Only the oxygen showed bubbling now in the jar. Major Moon said anxiously: "He's an awful colour."

"I can't make it out," said Barney, his eyes flickering over the apparatus for signs of anything wrong. "He's having nothing but oxygen now."

"There doesn't seem to be any obstruction," said Eden, watching the heaving bag.

"I'll just slip an airway in, to make sure." He caught up the tube from the trolley, dabbled its rubber end in a pot of lubricant, and, removing the mask for a moment, thrust a gag between the teeth to keep the mouth open, and forced the tube down Higgins' throat. Blue lips closed over the metal mouthpiece and Barney replaced the mask. After another half minute the man's breathing changed. The respirations became light and shallow and irregular. The jerkings gave way to little twitchings and jactitations and the livid colour was replaced by a leaden grey, infinitely more horrible. Barney said, staring down at him: "He's collapsed!"

Major Moon flung back the blankets and started artificial respiration, pressing down upon the ribs and relaxing them with a slow rhythmic movement that yet was pregnant with urgency. Barnes plucked open a little bottle and filled a syringe: as he plunged the needle under the rib into the heart he said briefly to Woods: "Give some coramine—intramuscularly."

Even the shallow respirations had now ceased. Major Moon worked on, slowly pressing and relaxing. Barnes stood by help- lessly. He said after a minute: "Shall I try more oxygen?"

Eden shrugged his shoulders. "I should shove in some more coramine, intravenously," said Moon, not pausing in his work. He added gravely: "As a last resort."

Barnes found a vein and thrust the needle in. "It's no use, I'm afraid. . . ."

Moon took no notice. It was horrible to see him working so rhythmically, working with that air of panic-stricken calm, on a body now beyond all help. After five whole minutes more of it, he straightened himself and stood erect, his hands on his aching back. "It's no use. . . . We can't do any more. . . ."

Esther stood frozen with horror at the foot of the table. "There isn't any danger, nurse? I'm going to be all right?" and she had promised him: "Of course you are, Higgins; there's nothing to be frightened of." "You'll tell the missis, my dear, will you? Tell her I'm going to be O.K." "Yes, Higgins, I'll tell her as soon as you've gone off to sleep." "Thank you, my dear," he had said. "God bless you, my dear. . . ." Those were the last words he had spoken; and he had smiled at her and turned his head on the pillow, satisfied to give himself up to the unknown since she had promised him that he would come through "all right." "Thank you, my dear. God bless you, my dear." The last words he had spoken. Joseph Higgins was dead.

Chapter IV

1

NOT many surgeons remain unmoved by a death "on the table." The patient may die on his feet if he will, or in his bed, or even on the trolley bringing him up to the theatre; but to die in that shining little room, with the hot, bright lights beating down upon him, is to cast a gloom over a group of comparative strangers; to clutch icily at hearts that will not be warm again until a succession of straightforward, everyday cases has brought back reassurance and strength. Major Moon said sadly: "First time this has happened since I've been here," and pulled up a blanket over the dead man's face.

They stood round in stricken silence, gazing helplessly at the quiet form. Eden's thin, grey face looked more grey than ever. Barney was white and miserable, Sister Bates' blue eyes round with horror over the green mask; there was a small black speck on the bosom of Woody's gown, and she picked at it with nervous fingers. Moon, who was a Catholic, crossed himself with unobtrusive simplicity and said a little prayer. Two big tears gathered in Esther's eyes and rolled down her cheeks. "Thank you, my dear. God bless you, my dear. . . ." She could not forget the little smile.

Major Moon pulled himself together. "Eden, perhaps you and Barnes would get him on to the trolley for the girls, would you? Will you be all right, nurse, after that?"

"I'll take him," said Woods, glancing at Esther's face. She added perfunctorily: "If that's all right with you, Sister?"

Bates pulled the mask up over her face and head; she looked very pretty with her ruffled fair hair. "Yes, very well. Sanson can stay and clear up in here." Her tone boded ill for V.A.D.s who were too squeamish to wheel a dead man down to the mortuary.

"We'll close the theatre for to-day," said Moon abruptly. "If there's anything else urgent we can take it to emergency. I—I hope there won't be." He looked very old and shaken.

Woods wheeled the body away without a backward glance. As Bates and Esther went out to the washrooms, the men gathered about the anæsthetic-trolley. Barney said desperately: "I checked up on everything. . . . There doesn't seem to be anything wrong; and yet—the old boy was all *right*. . . ."

"He was pretty badly shocked when they brought him in last night," said Eden.

"Yes, but he was quite over that. I went over him this morning with the stethoscope and he was as sound as a bell. He should have taken the anæsthetic without turning a hair." He said again, wretchedly: "There doesn't *seem* to be anything wrong."

"What *could* be wrong, old boy? The tubes aren't crossed. I looked at them several times while we were working."

Coloured rubber Y-tubes led from the cylinders of nitrous

oxide and oxygen and the (unused) central cylinder of carbon dioxide; but there was nothing out of order at all. Barney said: "God knows what went wrong. *I* don't."

"These things happen, Barney," said Eden. "They seem to be perfectly O.K. but they pip off for no rhyme or reason and you never know exactly why; I don't know why we're all getting quite so het up about it!"

"Such a bother," said Major Moon, suddenly rather careless and offhand. "It will have to be reported to the Coroner, of course, in the ordinary way of things; and it'll mean an inquest and all that. What a pity! These things create such a stink!" He was full of funny little schoolboy expressions, surprising in a man of his age.

"Stink'll be just about the word, as far as I'm concerned," said Barney bitterly.

"You mean because of that other case?" said Eden; and put his hand to his mouth as though he had said too much.

"Yes, I was thinking of that," said Major Moon. "It's all rubbish, of course, because you couldn't be held responsible in either case, my dear boy; but the death took place before we'd even started operating—and people talk."

"Are you telling me?" said Barnes.

"Nobody outside need know anything about it," said Eden.

"My dear fellow—with the local police bumbling round asking the regulation questions! They'll probably all be cousins and brothers-in-law—everybody's related to everybody in a place like this. I was thinking, Barney—if there's an open verdict at the inquest, and there has to be any investigation, I'll ring up Cockrill for you. He's the high ding-a-ding at Torrington, and he'll see that there isn't a lot of undue fuss."

"How can a high ding-a-ding in Devon or Cornwall or wherever it is, be the slightest good to us here?" said Eden.

"Torrington in Kent, not Torrington, Devon," said Moon.

"I didn't know there was one."

"Well, there is. It's in the middle of the downs, and you never heard of downs in Devonshire, did you?"

"No, so I didn't," admitted Eden, laughing.

"Cockrill was on that murder case last year, at Pigeonsford . . . there was a terrific fuss in the papers at the time about it; you must remember it?"

"Well, for goodness' sake, this isn't a murder case," said Barney, summoning up a faint smile.

Major Moon turned away towards the washrooms, peeling off his gloves, lifting the head-lamp with a weary gesture, from his forehead. He said, looking back, raising a quizzical eyebrow: "I trust not! The circle of suspects would be rather a narrow one, wouldn't it?"

"What nonsense you two are both talking," said Eden, laughing, following them out.

2

Detective-inspector Cockrill, arriving at the hospital two days later, could not have been in more entire agreement. "Don't see what all the fuss is about," he grumbled to Moon, fishing for papers and tobacco in the pockets of his disreputable old mackintosh. "Just another anæsthetic death. You doctors slay 'em off in their thousands. However, I know young Barnes' Papa quite well and I happened to be over this way, so I thought I'd look in myself. I suppose you can give me some lunch?"

The Mess Secretary was with difficulty persuaded that rations for twenty might, without positive hardship to anybody concerned, be stretched to supply twenty-one. Afterwards Inspector Cockrill made a tour of the hospital, popping his head into wards and operating theatres in his darting, bird-like way; small and brown and irascible, his shabby old felt hat crammed sideways on his head in the familiar, Napoleonic fashion; Sergeant Bray following ponderously in his wake, keeping a weather eye open for anything gorgeous in the shape of V.A.D.s. "There's nothing much to be done here, Moon," said Cockrill at last briefly. "I want to get back before the black-out, so I'll just see the widow first, as she seems to be clamouring for audition, and then I'll buzz off home and report that the death was just the private misfortune of the gentleman in question, and that they may as well let the thing drop." He stumped off to the small and dusty office that had been put at his disposal for the afternoon, and, rolling himself a wispy cigarette, flung his hat and mackintosh into a heap on the desk and sat down before it and composed himself to give ear.

A large round black bundle was led in by a stony-faced corporal and dissolved immediately into a flood of tears. "Never a cross word," sobbed Mrs. Higgins, standing patiently with out-thrust behind until somebody should put a chair under her. "Never a cross word in all our thirty-seven year of married life. Thirty-seven year and every year as happy as the year before; and all to end like this, first of all that 'Itler and now this 'ospital, first of all them bombs and now this sinful neglect of my pore old man. For sinful neglect it was, Inspector, and you can take my word for it; the things I've seen in this 'ospital, well you wouldn't believe; the goings *on!* And now there 'e is, lying there dead in a nasty mortuary, a thing I couldn't abide even to pass, let alone go into one; and all cut up and poked about by a lot of prying people that don't know their own business and wouldn't if they saw it. Thirty-seven year of married life and never a cross word, Inspector, and all to end like this!"

"It's very hard on you, Mrs. Higgins," said Inspector Cockrill, who knew better than to try and stem the flood before the first spate had exhausted itself.

Mrs. Higgins gave a perfectly dreadful sniff. "Hard! Hard it is indeed, Inspector, and worse than hard! Here's my pore old Joe, took in this 'orrible way, and me a widder and my fatherless orphans cast upon the world and what is the Government going to do about *that* I should like to know?"

As Mrs. Higgins would have a pension from the Post Office where her husband had worked for many years, and as her fatherless orphans were grown men and women, making a nice little thing out of various aspects of the war effort, it was not likely that the Government was going to do very much. "Anyway, I'm glad to have a few words with you, Mrs. Higgins," said the Inspector, crushing out his cigarette without much regard to table, office, Army clerks, for the use of, and immediately lighting another; "I'd like to know if you have any particular complaints to make, or if you know of anything which you think might explain your husband's death . . ."

Mrs. Higgins had spent a profitable hour at her husband's bedside on the morning of his operation, listening to the account of the sleepless night he had passed. "Goings on, sir! They shove 'im in a corner bed, right next to the little room where them nurses sits; and the goings on in that little room, you wouldn't 'ardly believe." She related them in detail and the Inspector believed about

half of it. "'Eard every word, 'e did, and saw everything that went
on. Nurses and sisters and all—flirting away with them doctors in
a way I wouldn't like to describe," cried Mrs. Higgins, describing
it in detail all over again. "Call themselves nurses, indeed! Sluts,
more like! And cruel—well! Left 'im lying on 'is bed half an hour
or more before they even washed the dirt off of him; never give
him a nice cup of tea or anything; just a nasty prick with a needle
and told 'im to go to sleep. Sleep! Much sleep he could get with
all them goings on to be watched through the window of that little room. And the next morning! Five o'clock they had 'im up and
washed his face all over again, as if he could of got dirty, laying
there in a nice clean bed; and one miserable cuppa tea, and nothing else till 'e went for 'is operation. I wish I'd of known, I'd of
smuggled 'im in somethink, but of course how was I to know he'd
have the operation, and it's my belief he'd of been a lot better off
without it, anyway; always cutting bits off of you, these doctors
are. I don't 'old with it, myself. So there 'e was, 'ungry as a 'unter,
pore old boy, and no bloody wonder, well, excuse my language,
Inspector, but you know what I mean. I 'adn't 'ardly settled down
to have a nice chat with him, when a whole lot of men come in
and starts giving him an X-ray, or some such, a nasty looking
lamp affair they had with them, and I don't know what all; then
they put a lot of screens round him and started getting him ready
for the operation; no sooner than I sits down again, and it's one
of the doctors comes and wants to listen to 'is chest; and 'e was
just going to tell me somethink, I don't know what, and then another one comes and there's a lot more screens put round 'im and
I'm turned out again; and two minutes later I'm told, 'You'll 'ave
to go now, Mrs. 'Iggins!' 'Well, all right,' I thought to meself, 'I'll
go, but I won't go far,' and I stood in that round hall place outside

the ward, and I watched them wheel him out on a stretcher thing, all covered up with blankets and 'is pore old face quite red, laying on the piller. That young 'ussy was wheeling him, that Nurse Samson, they call her; a cruel girl she is, cruel hard to the patients, Inspector, I can tell you that. 'Well,' I thought, 'that's a nice thing,' I thought, 'leaving my pore old man in charge of a chit like that,' and I was just going up and say somethink about it, when another one come up to her, the night nurse, Lingley or some such name. 'Oh, 'allo, Nesta,' she says . . ."

"Esther?" interrupted the Inspector, leaning forward with a gleam of interest. "Esther Sanson? Is *she* here?"

"Well, Esther or Nesta, I don't know and I don't care," said Mrs. Higgins, not pleased to be checked in the narration of her history. " 'Oh 'allo, Nesta,' she says, or Esther, if you like, and she stops and says, 'Who's this?' she says, 'is it 'Iggins?' she says, and she stoops down over him and she says, 'Pore old 'Iggins,' she says, 'but don't worry,' she says, 'you're going to be all right,' she says, quite kind like, and then she goes on and she says, 'Oh, Nesta,' she says, 'I'm so tired I don't know what to do with meself, I've been wandering about ever since I came off duty trying to make myself want to go to bed. It was a terrible heavy night last night,' she says; 'but I wanted to tell you that I've taken over our laundry so you don't have to bother about it,' or something of that sort; and then she has another word with Joe, 'don't you worry,' she says, and then off she goes, and the other one wheels him away into the operation theatre and that's the last I see of him. . . ."

"Very sad for you," murmured the Inspector, devoutly hoping that this was the last he would see of Mrs. Higgins.

". . . and the next thing is they comes and tells me he's dead," said Mrs. Higgins, beginning to weep again. "And the next thing is they'll have to inform the Coringer. 'I'm not going to 'ave any nasty inquests on my old man,' I says: 'I'm not going to 'ave 'im cut about and that's flat!' 'I'm afraid we can't prevent it,' they says, 'any case of death under annersetic has to be reported to the Coringer, and if he orders a poce mortem there's nothing we can do about it.' So the next thing is there's the inquest, and the next thing is I come up here to find out what's what, not being satisfied with the Coringer's Verdick myself: and now here's Scotland Yard, narking and questioning and bullying and me a pore widder thirty-seven year married and . . ."

"And never a cross word," finished Cockrill, and bowed the lady out without further narking or bullying.

3

A LITTLE group met that afternoon in the central hall of the hospital. "We saw you trotting the Inspector round, Major Moon," said Woods. "What did he say? Is he going to arrest us all for murdering poor old Higgins?"

"Really, Nurse Woods, the way you do talk!" cried Sister Bates, who did not care for this kind of conversation even in fun.

"He looked rather a sweet little man," said Frederica.

Inspector Cockrill was anything but a sweet little man. Major Moon was about to explain this, though carefully exalting his many and genuine virtues, when he was interrupted by one, Sergeant McCoy, who, coming out of the reception-room, hesitated, saluted, and stood respectfully silent until given permission to speak. "What is it, McCoy?" asked Moon.

Sergeant McCoy was Orderly Sergeant on night duty in the reception-room, where, among other things, various keys were kept. He had been greatly excited by the rumour that a detective was going round the hospital, and he now had a tale to relate of which he proposed to make a great deal of capital, though, in his heart, he believed it to be entirely without significance. On the night of the blitz, the night of Higgins' admission, that is to say, a figure, masked and gowned, had come into the reception-room, taken the key of the operating theatre off its hook, and silently glided away: returning sometime later, unseen, and replacing the key on the hook. His expression added: There now! What do you think of *that?*

Major Moon thought very little of it. "Well, what about it, McCoy? You must often have people in their gowns coming in for the key."

"But this was the key of the main theatre, sir; and it wasn't being used that night."

"Well, somebody in the emergency theatre wanted something and sent up for it. Didn't you see who took the key?"

"No, I didn't, sir. I thought it was just one of the nurses, like you say; and then I was busy, sir, with the blitz and all, and so many admissions, and I didn't see anyone put it back."

Sister Bates was up in arms at a fancied reflection on her staff work. "I'm sure there couldn't have been any need to send up from emergency. In fact, I asked the night staff afterwards and they said everything had been quite all right. They'd have told me if they'd had to borrow anything from the main theatre. . . . I even went down myself and checked up on everything before operating started, though I wasn't on duty; I'm sure there was nothing wrong."

"What about you, nurse? You weren't on duty either, so I suppose you wouldn't know?"

"Well, no, I wasn't, sir," said Woody; she looked at Barney, also standing by. "You would know if anything had been sent for."

"I don't think anything *was*," said Barnes.

Sister Bates marched to the telephone and rang across to the Sisters' Mess. "No, definitely nobody left the emergency theatre," she announced triumphantly, rejoining them. "Sister Gibson was on duty and she says they had everything they wanted."

"It seemed a bit funny, sir, being *masked*," said McCoy, disappointed by the prosaic turn his blood-curdling story was taking.

"It would if it were any key but the theatre key," said Moon impatiently. All the same it was odd. "What time was this?" he said.

McCoy had no idea what time it had been, but he had noticed the key back on its hook when he went to his meal at midnight. "Was it a man or a woman who came for it?" asked Barney, rather impatiently.

"I don't know, sir," said McCoy, giving it a rather eerie emphasis. "You don't know?"

"Because of the mask," insisted Sergeant McCoy.

4

WHICH of the two bombshells it was that kept Detective Inspector Cockrill at the hospital that night, he never knew; or at any rate never acknowledged. He had one leg already in his car when Major Moon arrived to tell him about the first, and when the second crashed, without benefit of air-raid warning, in a neighbouring field. The sirens broke belatedly into their unearthly howl; a flare dropped slowly over the downs, out towards Torrington, splitting the early winter darkness with its gradually brightening gleam—and where there are flares, there are very soon going to be bombs. Inspector Cockrill was interested in bombshells and he did not like bombs; and there was a fifteen-mile drive home in the general direction of those flares. "I'll stay," he said briefly, and withdrew his leg and marched back to his dusty room. Sergeant Bray, rejoicing, made tracks for the Sergeants' Mess.

Sergeant McCoy was astonished beyond measure at the effect of his recital, and hastened to spread the extraordinary news that the detective (who was naturally immediately promoted to Scotland Yard) had actually turned back and was staying for the night; the story lost nothing in the telling and by seven o'clock that evening the original author would have been puzzled to recognise it. The sinister word "murder" licked through the hospital like a forest fire, and an agitated Commandant summoned the Inspector to the V.A.D. Mess, to calm her young ladies down.

Sixty faces turned towards him through a fog of Irish stew as he made his way to their dining-room and solemnly mounted a chair. He stood before them, completely unselfconscious, his mackintosh hanging in folds about him, his felt hat crushed into a bundle under his arm, ceaselessly rolling a chain of untidy cigarettes, and made them a little speech. He knew how to be charming when he would, and now shamelessly exploited this gift. "You all look like sensible, responsible (and very delightful) young ladies," was the burden of his song. "I'm here on a perfectly ordinary, uninteresting, regulation inquiry into the death of a patient in the operating theatre, and I look to you not to talk a lot of nonsense about it; or better still not to talk about it at all." The unit beamed back into his bright old eyes, and vowed in their hearts that no word about the matter should ever again pass their lips; subsequently, by their mysterious deportment, spreading rumours like wildfire round Heronsford. In response to a further appeal, half a dozen girls who could claim to having had some connection, however slight, with the patient in question, gathered outside the Commandant's office to speak to him; and the rest retired bitterly regretting having had none.

Esther and Frederica and Woods, who usually carried their food to their quarters and there reheated and consumed it, had been obliged to have their supper in the Mess, on account of Cockrill's visit. They assembled with the two V.A.D.s on duty in St. Elizabeth's, who on account of a superficial resemblance were commonly known as Chalk and Cheese; and one, Mary Bell, who had been in the Reception Room when Higgins was admitted. Cockrill saw this lady first, while the others lounged on the bench outside the office complaining about the smell of Irish stew and languidly discussing the case, to the virtuous indignation of Chalk and Cheese, who sat with sealed lips until they should be called in.

Mary Bell emerged from the office. "What's he like?" asked Chalk and Cheese.

"Well, rather an old pet actually; not at all terrifying. There wasn't much I could tell him."

"Why did you volunteer? Because you were there when Higgins was admitted?"

"Yes, I thought I'd better. Of course I didn't even see him actually; Major Moon took him in and sent him straight down to St. Elizabeth's by the outside stretcher-bearers who brought him in the ambulance. Nobody knew his name; we didn't even get it till early in the morning when they rang up asking if any such person had been brought in here. His wife arrived about seven, and I had to cope with her, poor old dear. I was as late as hell going off duty."

"What else did the detective ask you?"

"Well, he wrote down my name and address and he asked me if I'd ever seen or heard of Higgins before, and of course I never had. He said again that there wasn't the slightest suspicion of foul play, as he rather divinely called it, but that he just had to fuss round and see that mistakes weren't being covered up or anything like that. What did you think of the Little Talk?"

"All done by mirrors," said Woody promptly. "He took one look at us, sized us up quite correctly as a horde of sex-starved women, and exerted his doddering masculine appeal to lull us into a false security."

"Sex-starved yourself!" said Mary Bell, and laughed and went away.

"*Definitely* not the murderess," said Freddi.

"No, definitely not. Personally I think it was Chalk and Cheese."

Chalk and Cheese were now closeted with the Inspector. "Why on earth them, Woody?" said Esther, laughing.

"I think they gave Higgins the wrong pre-operative injection."

"Oh, nonsense, darling; how could they?"

"Well, I don't know, but it's just the sort of thing they *would* do."

"No, truly, Woody, you underestimate Chalk and Cheese. They're not bad at all, really they aren't. Besides, the poison cupboards and things were checked directly after Higgins died, and ours were certainly quite all right, because I was there. They couldn't have given an overdose, if that's what you mean; and, anyway, it wouldn't have acted like that on Higgins. . . ."

Chalk and Cheese emerged from the office and closed the door behind them. "My dears, he's too divine; no, honestly, he's a perfect lamb, isn't he, Elsie? He asked us our names and addresses and if we'd ever seen Higgins before, and of course we told him we'd never set eyes on him in our *lives*, and he asked us if we'd nursed him while he was in the ward and of course we said we'd hardly even spoken to him, because as it happens we were off duty by the time he came in, and in the morning you looked after him almost entirely, Sanson, didn't you? and prepared him for operation and all that. . . ."

"So what was the point of your going to the detective at all?" asked Frederica.

"Exactly what *he* asked us!" cried Chalk and Cheese, much struck by the coincidence.

Cockrill came out of the office. "Now then, who's next? Why, hallo, Esther, my dear? I heard you were here. . . ."

"Hallo, Cockie," said Esther; she went a little white, for Cockrill had known her mother, and immediately a host of tiny memories clamoured for recognition in her sorrowful breast.

For Esther he shed his air of false benignity; he said nothing of sympathy or distress, but deep down in his arid old heart, there burnt a small glow of genuine pity. He took her quietly through the events of the night of the blitz, going with patient precision into every detail of the evening. "All right, my dear; thank you. That's very nice and clear. Send one of the other girls in to see me now, would you?"

"Bags I go next," said Woody, receiving this message. "I won't be long, Freddi, and he'll take hours asking you about Higgins in the ward, and I want to get ready for the party. You don't mind, do you?"

"I couldn't care less, darling," said Frederica, who, being on night duty in the ward, could not go to any party.

Inspector Cockrill was much amused by Frederica when at last she sat before him, tiny, erect, absolutely composed. She gravely related her share in the evening's proceedings up to the time that Esther had left the ward. "After that I went in and looked at Higgins from time to time, and sat by him for a bit now and then and let him grumble."

"Grumble? What about?"

"Oh, just patient's grumble," said Frederica indifferently. "I always let them do it. It keeps their minds off their real troubles. He was a dear old boy, really, but he couldn't sleep, and the pain made him fractious and crotchety. He got an idea into his head that they'd had no business to put him in a military hospital and that he was going to be neglected and would probably die—which seems to have been rather well-founded," added Freddi coolly. "He said the nurses were cruel to him, by which I presume he meant poor Esther because nobody else had looked after him; and who happens to be an absolute angel to the patients, much *too* kind actually; and he said there were goings-on and he would have it reported; I don't know who to, and I don't suppose he did either." Higgins had probably confided all this to his wife, and if anyone was going to tell the Inspector about it, it had better be oneself.

"What did he mean by goings-on?" asked Cockrill, smiling grimly at this transparent ruse.

"Well, I think he'd seen me kissing my fiancé in the sister's bunk," said Frederica, blushing faintly. She qualified this rather shattering confession by a description of the sister's bunk.

"Oh," said the Inspector. He turned the matter over in his mind for a moment. "Could he, in fact, have reported it to anyone? Is it quite the regulation behaviour to be kissing even one's fiancé in the sister's bunk?"

Frederica reflected solemnly upon this problem. "Well, if it was brought to the notice of the C.O. or Matron, I suppose they would have to make a song about it; but the trouble would be more that you let the patients see you, than what you'd actually done. The bunks are sort of ante-rooms; everybody meets here and talks and has tea and all that kind of thing. The sisters aren't above doing a bit of kissing there themselves, if they have anybody to kiss them, only most of them are such old battle-axes that they haven't."

This was something of a revelation, even to Cockrill, who had believed in common with much of the laity that the nursing services consist of all-powerful, omniscient, stiffly starched automatons, incapable of human emotion other than a rarefied compassion for their patients, and certainly immune from the doubts and fears and disillusions of the everyday human heart. Freddi elaborated, watching his face with a small, ironical smile: "People are—just people, aren't they, where ever you go? I mean, I look upon detectives as superhuman creatures who press buttons and waffle about with a little grey fingerprint powder for a bit, and have their case all solved in half a minute; but I suppose you're really just ordinary people with worries about having a clean collar and eating your breakfast too quickly and things like that; and so are we."

Inspector Cockrill could not imagine Frederica in any difficulty with clean collars or eating her breakfast too quickly, but he bowed to her superior ruling with a quizzical, small smile. Having thus effectively laid a smoke screen across the question of her having kissed anyone other than her fiancé in the sister's bunk, she answered the rest of his questions with serene despatch. No, Higgins had not made any particular accusations, except that there were goings-on. No, he had not told her anything about himself except that he was a postman and that the things people wrote upon postcards you wouldn't believe! Yes, she supposed she could have asked him his name then, but actually she had not thought of it; this had been in the early hours of the morning, and she had really forgotten that they did not as yet know who the old man was. Night sister had done a round at about four o'clock but Higgins had been asleep by then, and she had not disturbed him. She, Frederica, had not left the ward at all from the moment Esther Sanson had gone; an orderly had come on soon after the Surgeon on Duty had made a second round, at about a quarter to eleven (she blushed faintly again at this description of Eden's visit) and he could confirm that she had been there all the time. She raised her golden eyebrows at the necessity for any testimony on this point.

"So that nobody else saw the man until the morning? And then? I understand his wife arrived very early. . . ."

"Yes, she sat beside his bed till he went up to the theatre; he was on the Dangerously Ill list, or the Seriously Ill, I forget which."

Cockrill registered mystification. "The dangerously ill list," explained Frederica patiently, "as opposed to the seriously ill list. If you're on either your relatives can come and see you at any time, not only in the ordinary visiting hours; if you're on the D.I. they get their fares paid; if you're only S.I. they don't."

"It's all very complicated, isn't it?" said Cockrill humbly. She looked at him suspiciously, but there was no sign of a twinkle in his beady eye.

He kept her waiting for several minutes while he read carefully through his notes; and when she thought he had almost forgotten her, said suddenly, sharply, looking up from under his shaggy eyebrows: "What do *you* think of this case—eh?"

"Who—me?" said Freddi; she considered for a moment. "Well—I just think it isn't a case."

"Not a case?"

"Well, I mean I think Higgins died under the anæsthetic, that's all; and as for McCoy I think he's just talking through his hat."

"And as for me, I'm an old fuss pot," suggested Cockrill grinning horribly. He wagged a pencil at her: "Do you realise, my child, that if this does turn out to be 'a case,' you yourself are very intimately concerned?"

"Me? Concerned in the death of old Higgins . . . ?"

The Inspector looked down at his notes again. "Captain Barnes administered the anæsthetic," he said slowly, "so of course we have to put his name on our list; but apart from him, there were only—six—people in this hospital who had anything to do with the man; in fact, only six who knew that he was here. Major Moon admitted him; you and Miss Sanson were in the ward when he arrived; Miss Woods happened to be in the central hall when he was being carried through, talking to Major Eden and Sister Bates. You have told me yourself that nobody came into the ward after that; several people were in the sister's bunk, but Higgins' bed was in darkness and they couldn't have seen who he was. Nobody knew his name. Supposing for the sake of argument, McCoy's story is correct: between ten o'clock and midnight, somebody went into the main operating theatre where Higgins died next day . . . well, Miss Sanson left the ward a little before half-past ten; she went over to her quarters, but we don't know what she may have done in the meantime. . . . Sister Bates was free after she left the emergency theatre, Miss Woods says she was sitting in her quarters, but there was nobody there to tell us that this is true; Major Moon was in and out of the reception-room, Major Eden was wandering about the hospital, and Captain Barnes, though he was busy giving anæsthetics, was not doing that all the time, as you yourself know; besides, Captain Barnes is the anæsthetist, anyway. . . . I don't say that any of these people killed Higgins, of course I don't; I only say that *if* anybody killed him, it must have been one of these seven; and that includes you."

"Well, I never left the ward that night," said Frederica stubbornly.

"Except before Miss Sanson left, to get yourself some food." He said suddenly: "Where were you that morning—the morning Higgins was having his operation, I mean?"

"I was in bed in my quarters, of course," said Freddi impatiently.

He looked at her intently. "Oh, were you? In bed in your quarters? That's interesting," and added, not thinking: "Alone, of course?"

"Quite alone," said Frederica, and marched out indignantly, her golden head in the air.

5

BARNEY was also going to the party, and he was not best pleased at being approached by Inspector Cockrill with a request to demonstrate his anæsthetising apparatus. "Wouldn't you rather wait till to-morrow?" he asked politely.

"No, I want to get back to Torrington to-morrow; I wouldn't have stayed at all if it hadn't been for the air raid . . . and this business of Sergeant McCoy, of course," added Cockie hurriedly. The air-raid was still going on, rather mildly, over their heads, but it was one thing to be in a good solid building, and another to be bucketing along the country roads in a little car, with the guns going off all around you and Jerries overhead. He led the way imperiously to the theatre. "I won't keep you long; I just want to see what you do."

Barney's grave eyes questioned him uncertainly. "If there *was* anything cockeyed about the man's death, it does seem likely that it may have been connected with the anæsthetic, doesn't it?" suggested Cockrill apologetically. "It's really particularly for your sake that we want to get it straight." His own opinion was that it was all a lot of military flammery and red tape.

Barnes led the way over to his trolley, switching on the great overhead lights of the theatre; he sat down on the little round revolving stool and pulled the trolley between his knees. It was green enamelled, about twenty-four inches square, with a bracket across the top from which hung three glass jars; on one side of the trolley were five circular metal bands into which were set the big, cast-iron cylinders of gas and oxygen; two were painted black, two black with a white collar, and one, in the centre, green. Barnes flicked them with a finger nail: "Black nitrous oxide; black and white, oxygen; and green carbon dioxide."

Cockrill stood with his short legs apart, an unlit cigarette between his fingers, still in his droopy mackintosh with his hat on the back of his head. He hated to know less than the man he was talking to; and he had watched young Barnes grow up. He said at last gruffly: "Talk plain English."

Barney smiled up at him suddenly, that rare and charming smile of his, that lit up his face into good humour again. He said apologetically: "Sorry, Cockie; I was being difficult. I want to go to a party"; and elaborated more clearly: "Nitrous oxide is just ordinary gas, like you get at the dentist's. For longer anæsthesia we use it with oxygen; those are the two outside cylinders. The green one in the middle is CO_2—carbon dioxide; but we needn't bother about it, because we didn't use it on Higgins, and in fact it very seldom *is* used, except in special cases."

"Is that why there's only one tube of it, and two of each of the others?"

"Yes, that's right. There's a spare of nitrous oxide and a spare of oxygen; they're connected up, and in emergency you only have to switch on the reducing valve; but, again, they don't concern Higgins, because as it happens we were using fresh cylinders of both, so of course we didn't run short. Anyway, we didn't have time to run short."

"No possibility that the reducing valve wasn't turned off?"

"It wouldn't have made any difference; after all, they were still just gas and oxygen, and the flow is regulated up here." He glanced at the glass jar on the bracket. "But, anyway, they were both firmly turned off, because of course we went over the whole thing afterwards."

Cockie fiddled with his cigarette, longing to light it, but overawed by the formidable cleanliness of his surroundings. He said, rocking backwards and forwards slowly, from his toes to his heels: "What about all these rubber tubes and things?"

The Y-tubes led from the cylinders, black from the nitrous oxide, red from the oxygen and green from the central cylinder of carbon dioxide, to the first of the glass jars hanging from the bracket above the trolley; and each was controlled by a tap. Two of the jars were coloured, but the first was plain; it was half filled with water, and three metal tubes, each with a line of little holes, like a flute, stuck down into the jar and well below the surface of the water. Barney turned a tap and bubbles appeared from the first tube at the water line, and spread down to the bottom of the tube as the tap was turned more fully on. "The nitrous oxide," said Barnes. He left it bubbling and turned on another tap, and the third tube bubbled. "That's the oxygen. They mix above the surface of the water and pass along a single metal pipe to the mask over the patient's face. If we used the carbon dioxide, it would bubble out of the centre tube; but we didn't." He let a line of bubbles run up and down the centre tube for a moment, and then switched off.

"So only these two are being used," summed up Cockrill, pointing to the two outside cylinders with the toe of his shoe. "And only the corresponding outside tubes in the jar are bubbling?"

"Yes, that's right."

"And that's all that was used on this man Higgins?"

"Yes, that's right," said Barney again. He got up off the stool. "You sit down and try."

Cockie sat down, wrinkling his nose in disgust at the sickly familiar smell of ether and antiseptic, but concentrating deeply upon the trolley in front of him. He twiddled the taps for a minute or so, and bubbles played madly up and down the little tubes. "What about all these bits and pieces—bottles and jars and things?"

"Oh, those are mostly emergency stuff; adrenaline and strychnine and so forth; and the usual collection of gags and tongue clips and what-have-you. This funny short, fat red tube is the air-way; we put it down the patient's throat when he's well under, to keep it from closing up or getting obstructed. It's got a metal mouthpiece, you see, to keep him from biting on it and closing it."

"Charming," said Cockrill dryly. He looked at the rows of bottles and jars and instruments. "Which of these was actually used on Higgins?"

"Well, none of them until things began to go wrong. Then

I put in the air-way—that's why I mentioned it to you; and, of course, I used a gag between his teeth while I put it in. After that I gave an injection of adrenaline and after that we gave him a shot of coramine, intramuscularly; finally I gave him some into a vein; but it was all no use."

"And these are literally the only things that were used on him?"

"Yes, definitely; unless you count the injection of morphia and atropine an hour before the operation began?"

Cockrill considered. "No, for the moment I'm only interested in what happened here in the theatre."

"Well, that's absolutely all," said Barney, looking surreptitiously at his watch.

Cockrill observed the glance and grinned to himself; he made no comment on it, however, but continued steadily with his questions: "These injections—you gave them all yourself?"

"I gave the adrenaline, and the second lot of coramine, intravenously. The V.A.D. gave the other dose, into the muscle."

"Who, Miss Woods?"

"Yes, that's right." He pointed to a row of little glass ampoules, similar to those sold by tobacconists for filling cigarette lighters. "This is the coramine. You just break the thing open and suck the stuff up into a hypodermic."

"And the adrenaline?"

"In a bottle."

"Could there have been anything wrong with the bottle?"

"There could, I suppose, though heaven knows what or how; but I've used it since, and anyway the man was already collapsing when I gave him the first injection."

"I see. So that all that was used before things began to go wrong was really just the gas and oxygen?"

"That's absolutely all. I gave pure nitrous oxide first, to get him under. . . ."

"The black cylinder," said Cockie, scowling at it.

"That's right; and then added oxygen till the mixture was about fifty-fifty. . . ."

"The black cylinder with the white top . . . ?"

"Yes," said Barney again, grinning faintly at this naïve summary of his lesson.

"And they both passed through the water in the first bottle on the bracket, the clear glass one; bubbling out of the two outside tubes in the bottle, and mixing above the surface of the water and then passing along this big rubber tube to the patient."

"You'd better come and give the next lot yourself, Cockie," said Barney, laughing.

Cockrill made a little movement of irritation at this misplaced levity; he continued stolidly: "And all these tubes from the cylinders to the glass bottle—they definitely weren't crossed or mixed up in any way?"

"No, definitely not. Moon and Eden and I all checked them over till we were blue in the face. There was nothing wrong with the trolley."

Cockrill was silent, swivelling gently to and fro on the stool. He said at last: "I suppose you will think this is funny too—but would it be possible to have the wrong gas in a cylinder? Would it be possible to empty one and fill it with something else?"

Barney, far from being amused, was shocked to the core by such a suggestion. "Good heavens, no. It would be impossible. It takes terrific pressure to fill these things; that's why they're made so strong."

"Oh," said Cockrill, continuing to swivel.

"Even supposing it could happen—supposing you got nitrous oxide in an oxygen cylinder, for example—it wouldn't work, because the reducing valves of the oxygen and nitrous oxide cylinders are different. The things wouldn't fit and you'd soon find out what was happening."

"What about the green tube in the middle—the carbon dioxide?"

"Well, yes, that's the same size valve," admitted Barney.

"All right then; supposing, just for the sake of argument, that you somehow got carbon dioxide in an oxygen cylinder, a black and white cylinder . . . supposing the manufacturers made a mistake, for example. . . ."

"My dear Cockie, as if such a thing could happen!"

"I'm not saying it *could* happen," said Cockrill irritably; "do use your imagination: I say pretending for the sake of argument that it did happen . . . what then?"

"Well, the carbon dioxide cylinders are very often smaller than the others," said Barnes; "however, in our case, they certainly were all the same size. I suppose—yes, if such a thing happened, you would connect up the cylinder quite cheerfully, and go right ahead."

"And the patient would die?"

"Yes, the patient would die all right. Instead of getting nitrous oxide and oxygen, he'd be getting nitrous oxide and carbon dioxide; and he'd collapse for want of—well, for want of oxygen!"

"But all the little bubbles in the glass jar would appear quite normal?"

"Yes, obviously, because the cylinder would be in the right position with the proper tubes and everything duly connected up."

Cockrill considered again. "Couldn't you smell the wrong gas coming out of the cylinder if such a thing were to happen?"

"No, all the gases are colourless and odourless. . . ."

"I thought you said nitrous oxide was ordinary gas like you get at the dentist's?"

"Well, that doesn't smell."

The bare thought of it sent Cockrill into a sickly warm, swoony daze; for a horrible half second he was fighting against gas, great nauseating waves of it, strong and pungent and thick. . . . He said indignantly: "It smells like a thousand drains!"

"No, honestly. That's the rubber mask that you smell; nitrous oxide is absolutely odourless."

Cockie remained unconvinced. "It's quite true," said Barney, laughing.

"Well, all right, if you say so; I suppose you should know. And the others don't smell either?"

"Carbon dioxide gives off a little prickly feeling if you get it in a strong enough concentration; like sniffing a glass of soda water; but it doesn't smell."

"Did you sniff at the cylinders after Higgins' death to see if there was any prickly feeling?"

"No, of course I didn't," said Barnes. "The whole thing was properly fixed up, and though we seem to have demonstrated that you could kill a patient by getting carbon dioxide into an oxygen cylinder, the solid fact remains that it would be physically impossible to get the CO_2 into the cylinder in the first place."

Cockrill stood up and stretched himself. "Wouldn't it have been—I don't want to seem offensive, my boy, but other people will ask the same question if anything develops from this inquiry—wouldn't it have been a reasonable precaution to have taken?"

"No, it wouldn't," said Barnes, impatiently. "You couldn't

possibly tell by sniffing at a cylinder, what was in it . . . you have to have a very strong concentration to be able to detect CO_2 and smelling the mask or the cylinder certainly wouldn't give it to you. Besides, we were looking for accidents, not miracles; you don't expect an elephant to come out of a rabbit hole. Short of a mistake on the part of the manufacturers, which is out of the question, it would not have been possible to have had anything in the oxygen cylinder but oxygen, and that's flat. You can ask all the anæsthetists in Kent and none of them will say that he would have dreamed of examining the cylinders. Of course there was nothing on earth wrong with them."

"Were these particular cylinders used again?"

"I suppose they were, on the next patients; I don't know anything about that. The theatre staff are responsible for seeing that enough gas is ready on the trolley; we used hardly any nitrous oxide on Higgins, and only a certain amount of oxygen; so I suppose the cylinders will have been practically full, and we're almost sure to have just carried on with them."

"You talk as if I were accusing you of carelessness, my boy," said Cockie, gruffly.

"Well, it's so idiotic to suggest that I neglected to do something which it would have been sheer idiocy to *do*."

"I look at it from the layman's point of view," said Cockrill; it was not like him to be so humble.

Barney cursed all laymen under his breath; and Higgins above all for dying and letting him in for all this maddening heckling; and Cockrill for—for coming to the hospital and doing his best to stop ugly questions about himself! He tried to smile and appear a little more grateful. "Anything else?" The party would be in full swing by now.

"I don't think so. But on our way out," suggested Cockrill with a certain temerity, "you might just show me where the empty cylinders are kept. . . ."

Barney pushed open the door of a big cupboard. "The stock's kept downstairs in the Reserve Medical Store, of course; but we have a certain amount of stuff here for current use." A number of cylinders were ranged on brackets along one wall, and half a dozen lay rolled together on the floor. "These are sent back to the manufacturers for refilling," said Barnes, drubbing his toe against them. "Here's a list of what's in, what's being used, and what's actually been used. It all seems to check up O.K."

The swing doors closed behind them. "If this has been a penance to you, my boy," said Cockrill, fishing for paper and tobacco, rolling a cigarette and slapping his pockets noisily for matches; "it's nothing to what it's been to me." A light flared in the dim hall and he drew deeply on his first cigarette in more than half an hour.

Chapter V

1

A ROUTINE investigation into an anæsthetic death had seemed to the Commanding Officer insufficient reason for cancelling his seven days' leave; and when the C.O. took his seven days' leave, the Mess automatically threw a party. A large, rather dingy room called the Ladies' Room, was dusted and polished for the first time since the Colonel's last absence, a motley collection of buns and sandwiches was arranged on one of the tables, and a row of bottles stood on the piano top. There was the usual little difficulty as to whether the Sisters would kick up a fuss if V.A.D.s were invited, and the usual decision that this was only an informal do, and it didn't matter in the least whether they did or not; there was the usual mix-up as to who had promised to see about the french chalk, and the usual rejoicing on the part of a lance-corporal who was taken away from some more arduous duty to fix up the radiogram. The older members of the Mess retired to the ante-room and confided to each other that it was difficult to know whether one should shut one's eyes to this kind of thing or just mention it to the C.O. on his return and let him do any blinking that *he* thought advisable; and ended by agreeing that boys would be boys and, after all, there was no harm in it. As the boys concerned were all qualified doctors and surgeons and included Major Moon who was getting on for sixty, this would appear to have been a rational decision. The officers' wives arrived in full force and there was a little competition in condescension between themselves and the Sisters, for most of the wives were very young and took their husbands' pips or crowns with the utmost solemnity; while the Queen Alexandras, besides ranking as officers themselves, had the unquestionable advantage of being on their own home ground. The younger officers had brought V.A.D.s from their various departments or wards; Barnes, because Frederica was on night duty, had invited Esther; Gervase Eden had for so long produced Sister Bates upon these occasions that it had been impossible to alter his custom; and Major Moon, who steadily went the rounds asking a different person each time so that nobody should feel left out, had brought his own theatre V.A.D., Woods. Woody, in pursuance of her plan, took advantage of Freddi's absence to make hay with Major Eden. She sat on the arm of a chair and ran her hand provocatively from knee to ankle of one of her exquisite, silk-clad legs. He said, at last: "Don't do that; you're driving me crackers."

She stopped and turned towards him, the whole lovely line from ankle to hip exposed. "Am I? I don't see why?"

"Heaven help me!" thought Gervase. "Here I go!" His expression was the expression of a drowning man. He suggested: "Let's go out and get some air."

The black-out curtains were closely drawn, there was no

ventilation, and the atmosphere grew hot and full of smoke and the smell of beer. The guns still pounded outside, but the raid had not developed into anything serious. The wives, who had mostly come from a distance, leaving nannies and babies safe in the country for a single night, took advantage of the precious evening to flirt with their own husbands. The Sisters and V.A.D.s whirled round with their chosen officers, laughing and chattering and having a very good time. Marion Bates stood alone by the piano and poured herself out a very large gin. Barnes arriving, saw her there; he made his apologies to his own guest, Esther, who had arrived before him and was sitting with Major Moon, and went over to the mantelpiece. "Hallo, Sister! Aren't you dancing this one?"

"No, I'm drinking it," she said sullenly.

He took the glass out of her hand and put it on a corner of the piano. "It'll keep; come and dance with me."

She danced round in silence, but she was beside herself with jealousy and pain and after a few minutes she burst out: "Why doesn't he come back?"

"I should let him go," said Barney quietly.

She pulled a little way from him and looked into his face, though she continued, automatically, to dance. "How did you know who I was talking about?"

He smiled at her with gentle mockery. "It isn't very difficult to guess. He's only out in the garden, walking up and down with Woody; I saw them as I came in."

"I hate him," she said vehemently.

"There's such a delicate little line of difference between love and hate, isn't there?" said Barney, in his quiet voice. "It's like a sort of circle—you don't quite know where love stops and where hate starts."

"Gervase knows where love stops all right," said Bates angrily. She added, as though struck by an idea: "And he knows where hate starts, too. It starts at you!"

His eyes clouded over, but he said immediately: "Oh, nonsense; why should Eden hate me?"

"Most people hate anyone they do an injury to," she said shrewdly. "It's a sort of protection against their own conscience. And Gervase Eden is doing you an injury all the time. Don't pretend you don't know that."

"Well, never mind," he said. "Don't let's talk about it."

"You *are* a *fool*," she said, her eyes on the door. "You think it's nothing, just a mild little attraction, don't you? Well, you're wrong. I caught him kissing her in the bunk the other night; he swore he wasn't, but I know better—he was. And I saw his face. He never looked like that after he'd kissed *me*. I believe he really is falling in love this time; before you know where you are, he'll be asking her to marry him—and *then* will she stick to you?"

"I think so," he said gravely, though his heart was cold with dread; he could not bear to discuss it with her, but he felt impelled to argue: "Besides, he's a married man."

"Married my foot," said Bates, with vulgar contempt. "Do you think I don't know that old gag? Oh yes, I fell for it at first; every man who wants a little flirtation with you tells you that he's a married man: he hasn't lived with his wife for years, but the lawyers made a muddle of the divorce and here he is tied to her for life . . . and now he can't offer you anything but love, baby! Don't tell *me—I* know!"

He felt sorry for her, for she was not made to be ugly and bitter and vulgar. "Poor little you," he said, looking down at the foolish face and unhappy eyes.

"Poor little you!" she retorted roughly, still watching the door. "Don't you realize that he's rich and glamorous, he's got a marvellous practice in Harley Street. . . ."

"Well, I don't think I'm glamorous," admitted Barney mildly. "But I've got a good practice too, you know, and a nice old house and—well, I don't know, most things a girl could want." He added, laughing: "And anyway, what is all this nonsense about?—he's with Woody now, not Frederica."

The music stopped. He handed her her drink and got one for himself, and they lit cigarettes, and she stood there silently, watching the door like a dog; her fair hair curled itself up in little frizzy tendrils, round her white veil, and her foolish face was ugly with despair. The clock began to strike eleven and she seemed to be taking a resolution; as the last chime died away and still he did not return, she made up her mind. She said, as though casually: "Did you kill a girl last year, during an operation?"

Barney stiffened and went a little white. "I had a girl die under an anæsthetic, yes. I didn't know that anyone here knew about it."

"Gervase knows about it," said Sister Bates.

Eden had referred to it in the theatre; had put his hand to his mouth as though he should not have spoken. "How does he know?" said Barnes.

"Higgins told him," she said steadily, and her eyes were no longer on the door. "Higgins saw you in the ward when you came in to go over him with the stethoscope for the anæsthetic. Gervase examined him afterwards, before operation, and Higgins asked him if you were a doctor in the town, and Gervase said yes, he thought you used to be; and Higgins said that just before the war you'd killed the daughter of a friend of his. He said that it had all been rather forgotten, but that now he knew you were at Heron's

Park, they would write up to the War Office about it; he said that the people would hound you out of Heronsford and out of the army, too."

"The death was from natural causes," said Barney shortly. "Every anæsthetist comes across a few cases like that in his career; death was caused as much through the operation as through the anæsthetic, and the coroner exonerated both the surgeon and myself at the inquest. Nobody could say anything against me; they couldn't do me any harm."

"Gervase didn't seem to think that," said Bates. "I know because I went and waited for him outside the ward. He was talking to the man for a long time . . ."

"About *me?*" said Barney incredulously.

"Well, of course about you; what else? He'll have gone very carefully, naturally; he won't have said very much. But if Higgins had gone back into Heronsford and spread it about that one of the other doctors agreed that there had been some bad mistake about that girl—well, it would have wrecked your practice, wouldn't it?"

"What good on earth would that have done Eden?" protested Barney, whose mind reacted slowly to treachery and guile.

"Then you wouldn't have had 'most things a girl could ask for' to offer to your Frederica," said Sister Bates, and finished the rest of her drink.

2

ESTHER sat beside Major Moon on a sofa in one corner of the room. She wished she had not started on gin for it always depressed her and made her talk too much. She found herself telling him the long, sad story of her mother's death. "I'm sorry; this isn't much of the party spirit, is it?"

"Don't be sorry, my dear," said Major Moon. "It does us all good to speak of our troubles sometimes; and it's odd, isn't it? how often one feels like doing it to strangers . . . not that you and I are strangers, of course, but I dare say you can't often open your heart like this even to your more intimate friends . . . ?"

"They have their troubles too," said Esther sombrely; "one can't always be moaning about one's own. Freddi has no home to go back to after the war; her father's married to some awful, common woman, and all her life's sort of fallen apart. . . . She's engaged now, of course, but—well, I don't know . . ."

"Don't tell me anything is going wrong with that affair?" said Major Moon anxiously; his eyes went to Barney, dancing round automatically with Sister Bates, talking to her earnestly.

"Oh, I don't think so," said Esther hastily; and because she was afraid of having said too much about Frederica, she sought to cover it by saying more than she might otherwise have done about Woods. "Woody had a younger brother, you know, that she was terribly fond of; but really most *ter*ribly fond, not like you are of just ordinary brothers and sisters. He was abroad, on the continent when war broke out, and he's never been heard of since." While she was on the subject of Woody, she continued: "Inspector Cockrill has been asking her a lot of questions about the injection of coramine she gave to Higgins in the theatre. I suppose he thinks there might have been some mistake there. Don't you think that's nonsense—how could there have been?"

"There couldn't," said Major Moon promptly. "The coramine's put up in ampoules; there weren't ampoules of anything else on the trolley, and she gave it under Barney's instructions. Besides, the man was dying by then, if he wasn't already dead; we only gave it as a last resort."

"Of *course!*" agreed Esther, enormously relieved.

"He's being very thorough, is old Cockie," said Major Moon, confiding in his toe-caps. "He had every poison cupboard in the place turned out this afternoon, and generally behaves as though one of us had slain old Higgins of malice aforethought. However, the great thing is that, having proved that the whole thing was just a natural death, he'll see that there's no more talk about it; the local people would have bumbled on and poor Barney's name would have suffered. . . ." He suddenly noticed the time: "My goodness! Nearly eleven, and I'm orderly dog to-night. I'd better be going." He trotted off, round and rosy, muttering anxiously to himself about being so late. "However, they'd have sent for me if they'd wanted anything. . . ."

All was quiet in the wards. He left St. Elizabeth's to the last, in the hopes of a private word with Frederica; for he was thrown into a panic at Esther's hint that all might not be well between Barney and his love. He finished his round and sat himself down in the bunk, holding out his toes to the blazing fire. "What about a cup of tea, Nurse Linley, my dear, since I've left a party on purpose to come and talk to you?"

"Me and two hundred patients," said Freddi, laughing.

"Well, I had to do my round, dear, of course; it wouldn't have looked well to just make a bee-line for Linley's ward. . . ."

But with all his little jokes and friendliness, he found Frederica a difficult nut to crack. She sat dispensing tea in her gracious little way, serene and impersonal; friendly without being intimate, a tiny bit smug. He roamed for a long time over a multitude of subjects, before he dared to touch upon her own. "You've got a wonderful man there, Frederica, my dear; one of the very best. In all my experience, I don't think I have ever come across a fellow I liked and respected better than I do Barney."

"Yes, I know," she said soberly.

"He's the sort of a chap that only falls in love once," he went on, mumbling dreamily, staring into the fire. "Oh, he's had affairs, I dare say; he's a man of the world, of course, but there'll only ever be one woman in his life, and that's you, my child. You're a lucky girl: with all your loveliness and charm and—I know—great worth . . . I still say that *you're* the lucky one, to have the love of such a man as Barnes."

"I know," said Frederica again.

"You must never fail him," said Major Moon, lifting his head and looking at her almost appealingly, with his kindly, faded blue eyes. "It would be a terrible thing to see Barney lose his faith. I—I don't think I could bear it. But there," he smiled at her fondly: "I don't know why I even say such a thing; for I know you won't let him down."

"No, of course not, Major Moon," said Freddi politely.

In his effort to force her confidence he offered her his own. "A happy married life—that's everything in the world, Frederica, my dear. I—my wife—it wasn't an ideal marriage, but when my son was born that drew us together, and for a little while I knew what real happiness was, real, true actual happiness. . . . Of course that isn't everything; but I think as a general rule happy people are good people, don't you?"

"I didn't know you were married, Major Moon," said Frederica, evading this direct attempt to draw an opinion from her.

"Well, things are different now, Frederica. My—my little son was killed in an accident you know. He was everything we had, and we were inclined to cosset him. I persuaded his mother that we should let him make a man of himself, and we bought him a little bicycle, and after a bit he used to go out on the country roads on it. He was knocked down by a man on another bicycle; I saw it all happen, from the top of the hill. The man came tearing round a corner much too fast; he—well, my dear, the boy was flung off his machine and into the ditch. I saw the man pause and stare down at him, and then he jumped on to his own bicycle and rode on down the hill and out of sight. When I got to the corner my boy was dead. My wife—well, she didn't want to live after that. She felt it was my fault that the boy had been killed; she died very soon after. . . ."

"And the man?"

"I knew who the man was, but—I couldn't do anything; there was no proof. If he'd damaged his machine, he'd got it repaired before the police examined it. But I knew. I didn't see his face, but I saw the colour of his bicycle as he stood looking down at what he'd done before he pedalled off, leaving my boy to die like a dog at the side of the road. . . ." All the colour had gone out of his pink cheeks, and the blue eyes were clouded with tears. He said in his low, grumbling old voice: "I'm sorry, child. I didn't mean to say so much. It's all a long time ago. . . ."

She could be demonstrative only in passion; and now her habitual reticence was like a cage about her. She longed to put out her hand to him, to stroke the quivering old face, to wipe away those unashamed tears; but she could not. She sat rigid in her chair, polite, attentive, interested, and after a moment she said, in her crisp little voice: "And what was the colour of the bicycle?"

He got to his feet and blundered out of the room.

3

MARION Bates started back alone from the party, sore and angry. Eden and Woody had come back to the "ladies' room" towards the end of the evening looking a trifle foolish, and Eden had done his best to placate his legitimate partner; but Sister Bates now knew for certain that her hope was gone. It was not that Gervase loved Freddi—it was that he no longer loved *her;* anybody, even that ugly old Woods, was preferable to herself. Too much gin had inflamed her jealousy, and the genuine pathos of her disappointment was overlaid with an ugly spite. She grew loud and quarrelsome. Gervase, conscious of having been in the wrong in spending so much time away from her when she had actually come to the party as his guest, said, uncomfortably: "Come along, Marion, and I'll see you back to your quarters."

"Oh, I know you want to get rid of me," said Bates belligerently. "And I'm going all right—don't worry! But I'll walk back alone, thanks very much—not with you."

"Well, I'm sorry," said Eden briefly, for to argue would only mean a scene. "It was only that I thought you were supposed to be afraid of the dark."

"So I am afraid of the dark," said Sister Bates, who had used this plea often enough to engineer ten minutes alone with her beloved; "but I'd rather have the dark than *you.* . . ."

"I should be petrified of your hospital murderer popping up," said one of the officers' wives, who did not believe in the hospital murderer for one moment, but thought that this unlovely argument should end.

Sister Bates looked at her with tipsy cunning. "Oh, that doesn't worry me; you see I happen to know who the murderer is!"

"Christmas!" thought the officer's wife; "what have I gone and let myself in for now?" She said that in that case Sister Bates ought to rush off this *min*ute to the police and tell them all.

"You don't believe that there was a murderer, do you?" said Bates defiantly. "But there was. Higgins was murdered. I know."

"Oh, don't be silly, Marion," said Gervase impatiently. "Of course he wasn't. He just couldn't take the anæsthetic, that's all. Come on home like a good girl."

"Then what's a detective-inspector doing down here?" said Bates, ignoring the second part of his speech.

"He came down to get the whole thing properly cleared up, so that people wouldn't go round saying this kind of idiotic thing," said Woody coolly.

Sister Bates' tiddley dignity was affronted beyond bearing. "Kindly remember, Woods, that you're speaking to an officer and you're nothing but a private yourself!"

Woods stared at her for a moment and then went off into fits of laughter. "I'm sorry, Sister, but *hon*estly . . ." Words failed her. The officer's wife and her companion moved unobtrusively away. "This is what comes of mixing Sisters and V.A.D.s at parties," said Bates furiously.

"Yes. Next time we mustn't ask any Sisters," said Gervase.

It was too much. She swung round upon him, and her face was livid with rage. "You'll regret that, Gervase! You'll all regret it . . . my God, I'll see that you all regret it. . . ." She was sobbing with fury and wounded dignity.

Eden put out his hand to her. "I'm sorry, Marion. It was horrid of me. You're tired, my dear . . . we're all tired and cross and hor-rid. . . . Come on and I'll see you home . . ."

But she brushed his hand aside and went on hysterically: "You think there wasn't any murder, but there was, and I know who did it and how it was done and everything. . . . I'll go to the detective to-morrow and tell him everything. . . . I'll show him the proof of it. . . ." As Woods moved impatiently, she swung round on her. "Oh, yes, you think I haven't got any proof but I have! I've got it hidden away in the theatre. I kept it in case . . . in case I might want to use it. I'll show it to the detective, I'll take it to him in the morning and tell him. . . . *He'll* believe me, don't worry!"

Eden stepped forward once more pacifically; he saw that she was beyond her own control and he felt a brute. "All right, old girl—you go to him in the morning and tell him everything you know, and show him the proof and all the rest of it. In the mean-time it's after twelve and we all want to go to bed. Come along, and I'll take you back to your quarters. . . ."

But she tore herself from his grasp and flounced off by her-self, out of the Mess and across the road and into the hospital grounds. The Sisters' Mess lay at the other side of the park. "I'll go down the avenue," she thought; "and cut through the hospi-tal and get—it—and take it to my room with me. It'll be safest there." A shell burst in the sky and there was a booming of dis-tant guns; she almost wished there were flares—it was terribly dark and they did light up the place a bit.

Someone was following her. Someone was dodging from tree to tree of the long, uphill avenues of oaks; dodging quickly from tree to tree and then standing quietly, motionless, peering out at her. She flashed her torch round nervously, half terrified of knowing who was there, half terrified of finding out. She paused and called: "Who is it?" but her voice came out croaking feebly, and seemed to be suffocated in the breathless pounding of her heart. She hurried on, and at once there was a flutter of movement, a whisk of white, an almost soundless brushing of grass and breaking of tiny twigs. She flung herself, panic-stricken, against the huge, friendly, stolid bole of a tree and clung there, sick with dread, calling out again: "Who is it? Who's there? Who's *there?*" The very darkness about her seemed to hold its breath, listening for the reply; but there was no reply—only a creeping of dry leaf against dry leaf, and a stealthy, motionless silence that crawled with fear.

She did not know how long she crouched, her hands fluttering against the rough, hard bark of the oak; but just so long as she was motionless, nothing moved. When she started away from the shelter of the tree, the eerie rustling movement began again. "I must run," she thought; "I can't stay here all night with it; I must make a dash . . . I must run!" and she clutched her little grey cape about her and took to her heels, running for her life up the long corridor of tree trunks, with the pursuer, unseen, dodging after her through the shadows: catching her up, outstripping her, waiting for her in the gloom ahead. Her mouth was dry and her heart thundering in her bursting breast. She did not know whether she were running away from the enemy now, or towards it; she paused for a moment, trembling horribly, and for that moment all was still; she ran on again, blindly then, her high heels tripping and stumbling in the loose stones; her torch fell from her trembling fingers and crashed to the ground and its tiny light went out, and ahead of her something huge and menacing stepped out of the velvet dark and caught and held her fast—and she was in Major Moon's arms, choking out her terror and relief on his kindly shoulder.

"Good heavens, child," he cried, holding her safe and steady, patting and comforting. "What is all this? What's it all about? Afraid of the dark?—I do believe you were skedaddling up the avenue like a kid afraid of the dark!"

"There's somebody following me!" she cried. "Something's creeping after me. It's because I said I knew who the murderer was."

"The murderer?" said Major Moon.

"Yes, yes, I know, you see. I—I saw something. I didn't realise it at first. . . . I was just going over the things. . . . I just took it out to ask her what on earth it was. . . ." She pulled herself together a little. "Well, anyway, when I heard about someone having gone into the theatre the night before, I began to see what had happened. I didn't want to say anything, but after to-night— well, why should *she* have him? Why should other people have him? Not that I. . . . Well, I don't care, I'll go to the detective; I'll tell the detective. I think I ought to; I think it's my duty to go to him. . . ." She grasped at the old man's arms, muttering incoherently, looking back over her shoulder into the silent dark.

Major Moon smelt the alcohol on her breath. "Well, now, don't bother too much about it to-night," he said, soothingly. "You go to bed and sleep on it and to-morrow if you still think you have something to tell, you can go and see Cockie and talk it over with him. Meanwhile, I don't think you need worry; there's nobody about tonight, except the military police, and perhaps an occasional Jerry overhead . . . but we don't let *them* upset us, do we? I dare say you just heard Sergeant Edwards making his rounds, or Corporal Bevan or someone. . . . I'll walk over to your Mess with you."

"No, no," she said, frantically. "I must go into the hospital."

"Well, all right, I'll see you to the hospital. But you aren't going to spend the night there?"

"No, but—I expect I'll have a cup of tea with Night Sister on St. Cat's, or something. I don't want you to come with me."

"Well, I'll just see you to the side door," he said, pacifically.

Patients from the ground-floor and upstairs wards, who were not actually bedridden, slept on stretchers in the long corridor that ran through the hospital basement, so as to be fairly safe from bombs. She parted from Major Moon at the door, and made her determined way down this corridor to the central staircase, leading up to the hall. The men slept uneasily on their improvised beds, humped under rough brown army blankets, their arms, out-flung in sleep, lying supine across the dusty floor. Here and there a pair of bright eyes gleamed, open and aware; here and there a face was coloured vividly green or purple, where the skin special-ists were trying out some new treatment; once she almost collided with a blue-clad figure, its eyes dark hollows in a huge, white bandaged face. She began to panic again, picking her way among the stretchers, stepping over sprawling arms and legs, starting at the sound of a man muttering the name of his wife or his sweet-heart in his sleep. The stairs to the ground floor seemed endless in their dim, carefully shielded light. She took them two at a time, and was glad of the brightness and warmth of the reception room, where Sergeant McCoy sat drowsily over a paper.

She took down the key of the main theatre from its hook. "I won't be long, Sergeant; just going in to get something."

There was no reason why the Orderly Sergeant should ques-tion the theatre sister's right to enter her own domain. "O.K., Sister," he said, raising himself about three inches off his chair as a happy medium between sitting still and standing to attention when speaking to an officer. "Don't get yourself murdered!" He laughed briefly and went back to the *Kentish Mercury*.

Sister Bates pushed open the swing doors of the outer lobby of the operating theatre, felt for familiar switches, and unlocked the inner door. After the terrifying dark, the glaring light of the great central lamp, brought comfort and security. She went straight across to the poison cupboard and, unlocking it, took from a little-used lower shelf the proof of—murder; took it and thrust it into the front of her apron, and locked the cupboard door, quietly and carefully and without haste, and turned back, thankfully, into the calm and sanity of that bright, white overhead light.

A figure, gowned and masked in green, stood in the doorway, watching her, with something gleaming evilly in its gloved right hand.

4

Sergeant McCoy continued listlessly to turn over the abbreviated pages of the *Mercury*. "Death of Heronsford Man" said a small headline, and added that "Joseph Higgins had Given his Life for Others" in a recent air-raid. The sergeant shook his head over this (strictly inaccurate) sub-title, for he was a sentimentalist; he turned lugubriously to the In Memoriam column.

Nurse Woods put her head quietly round the door. "Oh, hallo, McCoy; I thought you were asleep. I—I just want the key of the theatre for half a second." She went over, all careless, to the board, but added sharply: "Good lord—it's not here."

"Sister Bates took it twenty minutes ago," said McCoy, rousing himself dismally from the post-mortem encomiums of Higgins' heartbroken wife, Gert, and of George, Arthur, brothers- and sisters-in-law, and little Ruby.

Woods dithered indecisively. She said at last: "Oh, well, don't bother. Don't mention that I asked you," and went out, but returned a minute later to say, a little anxiously: "There's no light in the theatre, Sergeant. I wonder what she's done with the key."

"She ought to have brought it back here," said McCoy angrily. "She's got no business to lock up the theatre and keep the key. As if there 'asn't been enough fuss over all this other business; I wish I'd never 'ave mentioned it now, the Sergeant Major 'aving me on the mat and seeming to think I ought to have seen more what was going on the other night and who took the key and all, as if I wasn't rushed off me legs, thirty-one admissions in the middle of the night, and the whole place upside down. . . . I wish people would be a bit more considerate, that's what I wish. I suppose I'd better go and see what she's done with the key; probably gorn off and never locked up at all. . . ." He got up, still grumbling, and went out into the corridor.

There was not a sound in the theatre; and when he turned on the lights in the lobby, still there was no movement or sound. The key was in the door to the theatre itself; and he gave an angry exclamation and turned it and took it out of the lock. "Going off and leaving it like that! I'll report this to-morrow, nurse, you see if I don't! Getting me into more trouble. . . . I'll report it."

"Perhaps she hasn't finished," said Woods, uncertainly. "She may be coming back or something. Ought you just to take the key away? She may be still there."

"What, sitting in the dark!" said McCoy derisively.

Woody thought it not impossible that Sister Bates might be sitting in the dark, even in the operating theatre; she might have lured Gervase there on one pretext or another, and be having a little petting party with him. She could not help grinning to herself at the thought of the happy couple being locked in to the theatre all night, and of the explanations next morning; but she said, loyally: "I do think you ought to just open the door again, Sergeant, and—make sure there's no one there."

"Well, if there is, why don't they say so?" said McCoy, crossly. He opened the door, however, and switched on the light and poked his head inside. "Nope—no one here. . . ."

But the words froze on his lips; for there was someone in the theatre, after all. Laid out ceremonially on the operating table, rigged up elaborately in a surgical gown and mask and gloves, with huge white rubber boots on her feet, Marion Bates lay very silent and still. There was a jagged tear in the front of the gown, its torn edges wet and sticky with drying blood: and thrust into her breast and deep down into her foolish heart, was the quivering, delicate blade of a surgeon's knife.

Chapter VI

1

COCKRILL, hastily summoned from his unrestful sleep on an army bed, scrambled into his trousers and a shirt, thrust the mackintosh over these and, issuing a string of instructions, rushed off to the operating theatre. Half an hour later, six cold, shocked and bewildered people sat uneasily round the little office, awaiting his return. Esther was white, with big circles under her eyes, Woody looked ten years older, Barney's grey eyes were desperately troubled, and Gervase sat with his hands between his knees, staring down unseeingly at his shoes. Major Moon was an old, old man, and his fingers trembled as he put his cigarette to his lips. Only Frederica was cool and serene as ever, neat and exquisite, every golden hair in place under her starchy white cap. Her placid little voice grated on their nerves as she said for the hundredth time that she wished the detective would come and get it over with, and let her go back to her ward.

"For God's sake, Freddi—the hospital won't fall *down* because you're not on duty!"

"But I'm worried about my drip saline, Woody," said Frederica plaintively. "He's awfully ill, and the orderlies are so hamhanded. . . ."

Barney put out his hand to her, wordlessly, and she took it and sat close against him, and he could feel her body tremble. "Only *I* know her," he thought; "only *I* know how much goes on under the offhand little air of hers. . . ."

"Give me another cigarette, Gervase, will you?" said Woods.

Eden raised his head and his ugly face was grey with worry and remorse, more purely emotional than anything he had felt for many years. He took a cigarette from his case and handed it to her in his fingers, hardly knowing what he did; she said, pityingly: "Don't take it to heart so much, Gervase. It wasn't your fault."

"Supposing it was suicide," he said.

"My dear, it wasn't suicide. Suicides don't dress themselves up in theatre gear and lay themselves out on the table!"

"You can't say what they do or don't do, Woody," said Barnes. "They do some very odd things sometimes."

"They don't stab themselves twice," said Woods.

"What do you mean—twice?" said Major Moon, looking at her sharply.

"She'd been stabbed twice; I saw it. McCoy left me there with her; I knew she was dead, actually, but I couldn't be certain, could I? I didn't know if I ought to try to get the knife out. I—I sort of bent over and looked at it. There was a big, jagged hole in the gown and you could see two holes under it, through her dress. She couldn't have done it herself, that's flat."

"But who—I mean, Woody, if she didn't do it herself, some-body else must have done it; it means that she was *mur*dered!"

"Well, what do you think, Freddi?" said Woods, impatiently.

"But Woody—but *Bar*ney—I mean, *mur*dered! Here in the hospital! It can't be; she can't have been!"

"You talk as if you'd never heard the word before, Freddi. What do you think the Inspector's been investigating all this time?"

"But *Woody*—you don't mean you think Higgins was murdered too?"

"Freddi, darling, don't go on and *on*," said Esther from her quiet corner.

"What I want to know is, what has it got to do with us?" said Barney. "Why should Cockrill get us all out of bed at this time of night? I mean, why us six? Why not Perkins, and Jones and—well, I don't know: Matron or whoever you like?"

"But that's just the point, darling," insisted Frederica. "That's why it's so frightful if it really was murder. Because it would mean that one of us had done it!"

Major Moon paused, lighting his third cigarette. "Oh, non-sense, child; you don't know what you're saying."

"But it's true, Major Moon. Inspector told me so, himself. At least I suppose if Sister Bates was murdered—and I honestly can't. . . . Well, all right, Woody, say she *was* murdered then! Anyway, if she was, then I suppose Higgins was too, and the same person must have done them both; and the Inspector told me this evening that if Higgins had been murdered it would have meant that one of us six had done it!"

"How the hell could he work that out?" said Eden.

"No, my dear, really, it's absolutely true; one of us must have. Nobody else knew that night that Higgins was in the hospital."

"Well, if that's all you're going on, you can leave me out," said Woods cheerfully; "I didn't know a thing about him until the next morning."

"But you saw him, Woody. You were talking to Sister Bates and Gervase in the hall when Higgins was carried past on the stretcher, being brought into the ward."

"Good lord, my dear, I saw a sort of bundle of filthy rags; and afterwards Esther told me you'd had a fractured femur in."

"Well, that's what you say, darling; but you *could* have seen who it was, and so could Gervase and Bates. The point is that nobody else even *could* have seen him except Esther and me, and Major Moon who took him in."

"And me," said Barney. "I didn't, actually, but I suppose I could have; I was in the bunk talking to you."

"Well, as it happens, you couldn't have, darling, because the corner bed was in pitch darkness, and with the light on in the bunk, you couldn't see a thing. I know, because to see if Higgins was all right, I had to use a torch. For the same reason, Night Sister couldn't have seen him, though she was in and out, and the orderly and people like that."

"Weren't they in the ward?"

"Yes, but Higgins was behind screens and neither of them went in to him . . . even the outside orderlies didn't see him, because he was brought straight down to the ward by the ambulance people."

"And nobody knew his name," said Esther, in a subdued despairing voice.

They all sat silent, appalled by the reality of this fantastic situation. "One of *us*—I can't . . . Well, anyway," said Woody generously: "It lets you out, Barney, dear."

"Actually, Inspector Cockrill said he would have to include Barney because he gave the anæsthetic and I suppose he could have killed Higgins quite easily without us knowing; and without any preparation."

"What do you mean, preparation?"

"Well, the point about us not knowing the night before is that if anybody really did murder Higgins they must have had it all fixed up somehow or other; I mean it couldn't have been done on the spur of the moment. . . ."

"I don't see why not," said Barnes.

"But how could it, darling? I mean, even supposing someone gave him an injection of something peculiar, I don't know what, but just pretend they could have, and that affected him under the anæsthetic—well, even so, it would have to have some preparation, you'd have to know beforehand. And as it happens, only us six did anything for him before his operation; the X-ray people messed about with him of course, and the orderly in the ward probably helped Esther get him on the trolley, and things like that, but it was only sort of last-minute things."

"You seem determined to keep it in the magic circle, Frederica," said Gervase, with a wry smile.

"Well, I'm only telling you what the detective said to me."

Esther had been deep in thought. She said suddenly: "Higgins was alone in the anæsthetic-room while the duodenal ulcer was being done; do you think anyone . . . ?" but as Woods raised her head, she corrected sadly: "No, that's right darling! Don't say it! I put the catch up on the outside door of the anæsthetic-room, so that nobody should come bursting in on him."

"Besides, it's all hooey about giving him an injection of something," said Gervase flatly.

"And especially as this does look as if there was something in McCoy's story of the masked figure taking the theatre key . . ."

"And that was before midnight, and before midnight *def*initely only Major Moon, and us three, Esther and Woody and I, and Gervase and Bates could have known about Higgins having been brought in."

"Perhaps Bates killed Higgins," suggested Woods, suddenly sitting up straight.

"But then who killed Bates?"

"God knows," agreed Woods, giving way immediately.

"And, besides, Bates was killed because she had proof about the murder, and how it was done or who did it or something. I mean, obviously in that case she wasn't the murderer, was she?"

"We had better begin looking to our alibis for this evening," suggested Eden, with bitter humour.

"Well, I haven't got one for a start," said Woody, cheerfully. She sat on a window-sill in the stuffy little room in a favourite attitude, her long legs thrust out in front of her, ankles crossed, her arms folded lightly across her chest, and said to Eden, smiling: "You said you'd come back to the party and see me home, and I hung about for a quarter of an hour at the Mess and you never came, so I went on by myself. Now I shall probably be hanged for a murderer, because of course I took care to keep well out of sight, being a mere other-rank and having no right to be there 'unattended by an officer.' "

"I went after Bates," said Eden. "I thought she was much too whistled to go across the grounds by herself, and that she'd soon repent of her refusal to let me see her to her quarters. She must have run like a lamp-lighter, because I never caught her up; I went by the path round the hospital, right across to the Sister's

Mess, and waited there for about five minutes, but she didn't turn up, so I suppose she must have gone in; I came back the other way, in case she should have gone up the avenue and through the hospital. . . ."

"So she did," said Major Moon. "I met her legging it up like a bird afraid of the dark. She said something was following her; of course I thought it was all imagination; she'd obviously had a little too much to drink."

"And now it turns out that it wasn't imagination," said Freddi.

They glanced at each other uneasily, and hurriedly looked away, only to find their eyes travelling again to those well-known, those pleasant, familiar, everyday faces. One of them had followed her up the avenue, crept after her, poor fluttered, terrified, panic-stricken girl, like an animal, in the dark; crept up the long avenue of trees, like a beast of prey, pausing, hiding, standing alert and motionless, moving on again in horrible pursuit. . . . Impossible, horrible, grotesque, and fantastic thought! Little Major Moon, pink and chubby, creeping on his neat small feet with his mild blue eyes gleaming with predatory madness . . . or Woody, moving catlike on her beautiful legs; or Eden a grey wolf, head thrust forward, hunting down the quarry with re-lentless ease; or Esther, following with unhurried stealth, quiet, cool—deadly; or Barney, dear Barney, driven by God knew what compulsion, blotting out from his heart the pathos and helpless-ness of the trembling creature fluttering ahead; or little Frederica, neat, impersonal, fastidious; implacable . . . Barney, shuddering, put out his hand to her: "At least you're safe, darling; at least it couldn't have been you! You were on the ward, and nobody can question your movements."

"Except that they consisted largely of sitting in the bunk, darling, with everybody sound asleep all round me, and not having the faintest idea of what I was up to!"

"And the theatre so handy, just across the hall," said Woods, grinning.

Barney's face fell. "This is beginning to look rather awkward," said Major Moon. "I went back to my room in the Mess after I met Sister Bates in the avenue; but I can't prove that. Where were you, Barney, my boy?"

Barnes looked uncomfortable. "I'm afraid you'll think it was cheek, Eden, especially as you've just said that you did go after her—but I thought it was wrong to let the girl go off on her own. I thought she was a bit tiddled and over-excited, and she might do something silly or, anyway, get frightened or upset. I'd taken Esther to the party, but she said she'd find Woody and go back with her, and anyway be all right, so I went along to see if I could catch up with Bates, only I took a few minutes explaining to Esther, and I must have missed her."

"Which way did you go?" said Eden.

"The same way as you went, along the path round the hospital."

"*I* didn't see you," said Gervase.

"Well, for that matter, *I* didn't see *you*, old boy," said Barnes apologetically. "I expect you'd hurried on ahead; and it was awfully dark."

"What did you do after that, Barney?" said Woods. Barnes replied that he had come straight back to the Mess and gone to bed; and added, ruefully, that the truth was often a bit lame.

"Well, I think this is fun," said Woody, who did not think it was fun at all. "Every single one of us was lurking about the grounds last night, except Freddi, and she wouldn't have had to lurk. What about you, Esther, darling? I suppose you looked around for me, decided that I'd gone on with—someone or other—and went over to quarters all by your little self?"

"Yes, that's exactly what I did do," said Esther wearily.

"No one saw you come home, I suppose?" suggested Moon.

"No, of course not: Freddi was on duty and Woods was in the hospital, making her great discovery."

"So there isn't one of us that couldn't have been the murderer!" cried Woody gaily.

Esther moved restlessly on her hard office chair, leaning back against the white-washed wall. "No, darling; it's charming."

"Well, I don't want to go all grue," said Woody, somewhat abashed. "But there's no use sitting round having inhibitions about it. Look what good's already come of discussing it."

"You've established that any of us could have murdered Bates, you and Frederica between you; that's about all the good so far!"

"Not all of us; Major Moon couldn't have done it, now that I come to think of it," said Woody, smiling at him.

"Thanks very much," said Major Moon. "But why not me?"

"Because you had no motive."

"What motive did the rest of us have?" said Eden irritably.

"Well, good lord, that's obvious. She knew who had murdered Higgins, and she had the proof and she was going to tell the detective; so, of course, we murdered her to keep her quiet—at least whichever of us murdered her did it for that reason."

"You don't for a moment believe that any of us did it, Woody," said Esther, "or you wouldn't be talking like this about it."

Woods laughed, wagging her head, half defiant, half ashamed. "Well, I do and I don't; my logic tells me that one of us must have; my sentiment tells me that it's quite ridiculous that any of us could have; and my curiosity makes me go on probing about to find out which of us did! Now, for example, we all heard Bates saying she has proof about the murder. . . ."

"Except Freddi," said Barney.

"She dropped into the ward to tell me all about it, darling," said Frederica, laughing.

"Yes, so she did! Well, I mean, she could have; we don't *know* that she didn't. But we do know that Major Moon wasn't at the party when she made her speech. He was doing his round."

"Actually he was talking to me in the bunk," said Freddi.

"Well, all right, darling, it doesn't matter where he was; the point is that he didn't hear what Bates said about her having discovered the murderer."

"As it happens I did hear it," said Moon mildly; "I heard it from her afterwards; she told me when I met her in the avenue. I thought it was just nonsense."

"So did we all think it was just nonsense," said Gervase wearily. He fished out his case and wordlessly handed round cigarettes.

"Only, of course, it wasn't nonsense, after all," insisted Woods, "and the murderer knew that, and he followed her up the avenue and got ahead of her and hid in the theatre. . . ."

"How did he know she was going to the theatre?"

"My dear, she *told* us she had it hidden in the theatre! When she went in and got it, he—well, he stabbed her, poor little thing, and took the proof away. . . ."

"And where is it now?" said Frederica.

The "proof" was at this moment in the operating theatre, right under Cockrill's nose, if he and they had but known it; Gervase said, bursting out with it angrily, as though his nerves would stand no more of this talk and discussion and argument: "You're being very clever and constructive, Woody, my dear, but there's one thing you haven't explained. What were *you* doing, going to the theatre at midnight? You hadn't left your knitting there, I suppose, or forgotten a book, like they do in the sort of novels women write about country house-parties?"

"Darling—most acid!" said Freddi; but she, too, looked rather strangely at her friend.

"I—I discovered the murder," said Woody uncertainly.

"Yes, we all know you discovered the murder; we're sick of the sound of it," said Eden, with irrational irritation, for she had only told the story once and that under considerable pressure from himself among others. "But that isn't what you originally went to the theatre for, is it? Or is it?"

She looked at him with the oddest expression in her shrewd, dark, mascaraed eyes. "Well, no, Gervase, that's not what I went for."

"Why did you go?" he insisted.

She would have to explain this to the detective too. She improvised hurriedly: "I—I was curious. I couldn't think what the proof could be and I thought it would be fun to see what she was doing there."

"*Woody*—do you mean to say that it was you, following poor Sister Bates up the avenue?"

Woods looked about her wretchedly; but said at last: "Well, yes, it was me."

"So you will have seen me speaking to her?" asked Moon.

"Yes. Yes, I did, Major Moon."

"Whereabouts was I when I met her?"

Woody gave up the effort. "Under a mastic tree," she said, laughing.

"There isn't such a tree in the grounds," said Frederica.

Woods went off into a cackle of brittle laughter. "Honestly, Freddi darling, you're *per*fect. You have no sense of humour, have you?"

"No," said Frederica placidly. "I never have had." But Barney could feel the little quiver that ran through her, of hurt surprise at Woody's cruelty.

"She's quoting the Scriptures, darling. Susannah and the Elders."

"Oh, the *Scrip*tures," said Freddi. After all, nobody could be expected to see anything funny in the Scriptures.

There was a miserable silence. Woods was stricken with remorse at having been betrayed by her exhausted nerves into such uncalled for sarcasm. Frederica opened her mouth to say once more that she did wish the Inspector would come and get it over with, and let her go back to her drip saline, but shut it again, abruptly. Esther, however, put the same thought into words: "If only he would come and ask us his questions and let us go. . . ."

2

Cockrill came, casting his hat down on to the desk in the centre of the room, shrugging off his mackintosh, feeling in his pockets for tobacco and papers, his bright eyes all the time searching their weary faces. They stared back, anxious and appealing, and he met their questioning glances with a cold hostility. There was none of the "old pet" about Inspector Cockrill now. He said, at last, grimly: "So Higgins *was* murdered after all! And now we have a second murder on our hands!"

They had spent half an hour convincing themselves of this; but it did not make it any the less horrible, to hear it put again, bluntly, into words. Shakily and miserably, they recounted again, piece by piece, the history of the evening: of the disastrous party, of the scene at the end of it, of the final departure of Bates into the dark night. He said at last, thoughtfully: "If she knew murder had been committed—why didn't she tell me earlier in the day?"

Nobody appeared to know the answer to that. He asked suddenly: "Does anybody know anything whatsoever about this crime that they haven't yet told me? Because, if they do, I should strongly advise them to speak up now. Sister Bates was obviously killed because she had this knowledge and it wasn't too late to stop her from telling it. Be advised and say everything you have to say, *now!* That at least would be one danger averted."

"For God's sake, Cockie," said Esther, white and trembling; "there isn't any *more* danger? This thing isn't going on and *on* . . . ?"

He looked at her briefly but did not reply. Instead he said to Major Moon: "What constitutes a lethal dose of morphia?"

"Morphia?" said Moon, bewildered. He held a little consultation with his feet. "Well, I don't know; what would you say, Eden? Four grains? Five grains?"

"There've been lots of recoveries from that and more," said Barney. "But that would be with treatment."

"Would two grains be fatal?"

"Well, I don't know, Inspector; not necessarily, I shouldn't think."

"Especially on a healthy subject," suggested Eden. "On the other hand there've been deaths from half a grain. . . ."

"And recoveries from twenty grains," said Barney.

Cockrill shook his head impatiently; there should be a lethal dose of a drug and a harmless dose and an in-between dose, and none of this vagueness. He felt disappointed in the medical profession which failed to keep its knowledge in neat little boxes;

and said with some asperity: "Have any of you got any morphia in your possession?"

"Oh, hell," said Frederica.

"I *beg* your pardon, Miss Linley?"

She fished in the recesses of her respirator case and, after some fumbling, produced a small white tablet and laid it on the table before him. "I *thought* that was coming; and I didn't want to give it up!"

"What is this?" said Cockrill sternly.

"Well, morphia, of course," said Freddi; she put out her hand to take it back: "Don't you want it? Good!"

"Yes, I do most certainly want it; what are you doing with it in your gas mask?"

"Most of us keep a small dose handy in case of being buried in an air-raid," explained Barney, glancing uneasily between Cockrill and Frederica. "If you were trapped and in pain, it would be comforting to have some, and might save another person risking their lives to give you a shot of something. I gave Miss Linley some, and I keep half a grain myself." He produced a tiny box and emptied two little white pills on to the table.

"Here's mine," said Eden, following suit, and as Major Moon also handed over two tablets, he added, grinning: "Come on, Woody—cough up!"

"Must I give you mine?" pleaded Esther, white to the lips.

Her mother had died after three days under the ruins of their home; Cockie looked at her from under his eyebrows and his look was full of pity, but he said, firmly: "I'm afraid you must, Esther, but I'll let you have it back the moment this affair is concluded." He added, looking round at them with an ironical lift of the eyebrow: "I presume your being in possession of this stuff is—unofficial?"

"Just mildly unofficial," agreed Eden, smiling back.

Cockrill gathered up the eleven little tablets and placed them in an envelope in his pocket. "Each of these is a quarter, is it? What's the normal dose?"

"A quarter of a grain," said Moon.

"What *is* this, anyway?" said Eden suddenly. "What's morphia got to do with Marion Bates? She was stabbed, wasn't she?"

"Yes, she was stabbed." He ground out his cigarette stub on the floor with the heel of his shoe, and immediately began rolling another; intent on the work of his fingers, he said evenly: "She stood with a look of—I think it was incredulity—on her face; and the murderer stabbed her in the breast, striking a little bit downwards to the heart."

"Did you say '*incredulity*'?" said Woods, and her voice shook.

He looked at her sharply. "You saw the girl yourself; didn't you notice it?"

She stood like one in a dream, staring at him. "Incredulity! Yes, that was it! That was her expression!" and it seemed as though a great load was lifted from her heart. "She was—astonished!" she said. "She—she looked up and she couldn't believe what she saw!"

They all looked at her curiously. "Would Sister Bates have died at once, Barney?" said Frederica, in that little endearing way she had of asking such questions of him with a childish confidence in his ability to reply.

"If she was stabbed right through to the heart I should think she would," said Barney. "Practically at once, anyway." He glanced at Moon and Eden for collaboration.

Esther started to say something, but stopped. Instead, she asked: "What happened next?"

Cockrill had finished the cigarette, and he sat with his head on one side, watching it smoking wispily between his brown fingers. He said slowly: "What happened next was this. The murderer was dressed in a clean surgical gown, from the linen cupboard, and a mask of the more elaborate type, the kind that covers the whole head and leaves just a slit for the eyes. He had with him, or he went back to the laundry basket and fetched a soiled gown and a small, oblong mask. He took the girl's body and dressed it up in the gown and the mask, and he pulled rubber gloves on to the hands and thrust the feet into rubber boots; he laid the body out on the operating table and then . . ." He paused for a moment and added deliberately: "Then he stabbed the dead body again."

"Oh, Barney!" said Frederica. He took her little hand and held it warmly in his own.

"Stabbed her a second time—when she was dead?" said Woods, recoiling.

"Yes, she was dead," said Cockrill, drawing on his cigarette. "The second wound was smaller and closer than the first; and it hasn't bled at all."

"How can you know which was first?" said Freddi.

"I happen to be a detective," said Cockie, raising a sardonic eyebrow. "The smaller wound was made after the gown was put on. The first wasn't—there's a big, ragged hole in the gown, and they've tried to make it look as though both wounds were made when she already had the gown on; but I don't think they were. I think the gown was put on after she was dead; and then she was stabbed again."

"But why?" cried Woody, shuddering horribly. *"Why?"*

Cockrill wished he knew; and because he did not know, because he was so anxious and uneasy, so helpless in face of the appalling absence of tangible evidence that confronted him, he grew, as always, nervous and irritable, staring at their pitiful white faces with a sort of irrational enmity. To-morrow there would be work to do, fingerprints to be checked, photographs to be pored over, innumerable answers to be noted and sorted and digested and compared; the whole, familiar, satisfying paraphernalia of police routine. But to-night—to-night there was nothing to be done. He must dismiss these people to their beds, and for all he knew, one of them was a murderer. He said suddenly and harshly: "The killer took two grains of morphia out of the poison cupboard; you'd better look out for yourselves!" and took an almost sadistic pleasure in seeing their faces grow even more white, even more taut with strain.

"The cupboard in the theatre?" said Woody stupidly.

"Yes, the poison cupboard in the theatre. Bates had hidden the 'proof' there. She still had the keys in her hand as she lay dead on the table; but the cupboard was open and there was no morphia there." He swung round upon Woods. "The poisons book shows that there should have been two grains of morphia in the cupboard; is that correct?"

"I suppose it's correct, if it says so," said Woods. "I know we were pretty low in morphia; we'd have been stocking up again to-morrow."

"Perhaps that was the 'proof,'" suggested Eden. "The morphia phial, I mean."

Cockrill had finished with them; he turned away to the desk to pick up his mackintosh and cram the old felt hat on to the back of his head, preparatory to another plunge out into the night; and said, giving them only half his attention: "No, no, the morphia wasn't the 'proof.' The morphia was kept on one of the middle shelves. The proof, what ever it was, was hidden on the bottom shelf under some lint and bandages and things; she stooped down to get it . . . she had her back to the room, all unconscious that she was being watched. But she was. Somebody was standing, masked and gowned, with one gloved hand on the lintel of the door, watching her quietly; and when she turned. . . ."

Esther screamed once; screamed out horribly, and burst into peal upon peal of laughter, hardly less horrible. They stood appalled, staring at her: Eden shuddered and closed his eyes as though he could hardly bear to see the blankness of her eyes and her mirthless, laughing mouth: Moon swayed in a daze of intolerable weariness, Barney put his arm round Frederica, and she turned away her head and stood against his shoulder, erect, but trembling from head to foot; Woody—Woody walked over to Esther and, as though all this terrible evening of fear and horror and suspicion and uncontrol were concentrated in this one action, hit her with all her strength across the face.

The silence that followed was most terrible of all.

3

ESTHER awoke with a headache, after only a couple of hours' sleep. "What with gin, excitement, and then hysterics," she confided to Woods, as they stood at either side of their room in the cottage, their foreheads butted against the walls, arranging their caps. . . . "I feel like absolute death. I'm sorry about the outburst, darling; thank you for your rather drastic measure—it certainly did the trick."

"I put all I knew into it," said Woody, laughing. "I was a trifle frayed myself by then with, as you say, gin and shock. Actually the atmosphere at the party was a bit off to begin with, smoke and beer and what not."

"Much you know about it," said Esther, smiling at her. "You weren't in the room more than half an hour all told."

"I was pursuing the plan," said Woods, a trifle shamefaced.

"It begins to look as though the plan were pursuing you. Do go carefully, Woody darling; don't get yourself into a mess. I'm afraid Frederica will take this the wrong way, you know. I really do think it's unwise."

Woods was beginning to think it unwise, also, but not entirely on account of Frederica. She shrugged her plump shoulders, however, and busied herself with their breakfast, confining the conversation to the murder of Sister Bates. "You simply can't *believe* it, my dear! When I woke up, I had that hideous sort of cloud hanging over me that you do when something ghastly has happened and you can't quite remember what it is. . . . Then suddenly it absolutely hit me like a hammer. . . . I mean, who could have dreamt that old Higgins was really killed—*mur*dered—and here in the hospital; and now poor little Bates. . . . It's simply fantastic!"

"How on earth can the detective have known all that about what went on in the theatre?" said Esther, pushing aside a plate of untouched food. "It was just as if he'd been there."

"Good lord, no! Utterly elementary, my dear Watson; they work it all out from where the blood was and the direction of the wound and things like that."

"Well, but how does he know where the 'proof' was hidden? I still think it might have been the morphia."

"He said it was on the bottom shelf; if you get a thing from a very low shelf, you squat down and steady yourself with one hand by gripping on one of the upper shelves. These shelves are glass; I expect he could easily see Sister Bates' finger-prints bunched together on the edge of one of them."

"How terribly clever of you, Woody," said Esther, quite impressed.

"Oh, my dear, I'm brilliant. S. Holmes in person. Hell, the gas is running out!"

Esther stood aghast. "My dear, it was my turn to get a shilling and I've quite forgotten!"

"Well, never mind, ducky, I can cope. We'll just have to give Freddi a rather mingy hot-water bottle, that's all." She filled it up from the water remaining in the kettle and trudged upstairs with it.

It was agony to Esther's tidy soul to go away and leave cups and saucers unwashed, but she had adjusted herself to Woody's slapdash habits, and she now tidied the breakfast things neatly away and stacked them on a tray until their return from duty. Woody bundled the knives and forks into a jar of water. "Come on, sweetie, we're terribly late; it's half-past seven."

"All right, half a second." She ran upstairs but reappeared again in a moment. "I thought I'd just shut the window to warm it up a bit for Freddi; but I see you've done it."

"Yes, of course I have; come *on*, darling!"

Eden and Barnes were both standing at their bedroom windows, in the Officers' Mess, Barney shaving, Eden apparently fully dressed. "They're up early this morning," said Woody, waving to them as they ran in through the main gate to the park.

"I suppose they couldn't sleep either," said Esther. "Heaven knows how any of us are going to get through our duty to-day."

"Thank goodness I'm off this afternoon," said Woods.

They met Major Moon puffing round the park in a vest and running shorts. "You look like a heavenly little steam-roller!" said Woody, laughing at him.

"Got to keep the boiler down," said Major Moon, patting it.

"You don't happen to have a couple of bob for a florin, do you, Major Moon? We've run out of gas, and Frederica won't be able to get her breakfast."

"As if he would in a vest and pants!" protested Esther, laughing. "Don't worry, Major Moon, Frederica can easily get her breakfast in the Mess for once. Oh, gosh, we are late! Come on, Woody...."

Freddi looked tired and nervy and was rather cross. "You're awfully late, Esther, and I'm simply worn out."

"I'm so sorry, pet; and another awful thing is that I forgot about my turn for a shilling in the gas, and we've run out, so you'll have to have your breakfast in the Mess. We've done your h.w.b."

"Oh, well, all right, don't worry; I can manage. I'll get in two or three hours' sleep before I skip up to town."

"I'd forgotten you were going to-day; that's why Barney's up so bright and early."

"He's got to go down to Heronsford and get the car; they're doing something or other to it in the garage and he doesn't think they'll ever have it ready. He's calling for me at half-past eleven."

"Would you like me to come over and wake you up at eleven?"

"It'll be all right. I've got the alarm."

"Well, no alarm would wake *me* after only two or three hours' sleep on top of night duty; not to count a slight matter of investigation into murder during the night. By the way, will the detective let you go?"

"We won't ask him," said Freddi coolly.

"My dear, he'd be simply livid."

"I couldn't care less," said Frederica. She added: "Don't remind

Woody that I'm going. She always thinks I'm going to fade away if I don't have my quota of rest, and she'll get hold of Barney and tell him not to take me. I'm as tough as old boots," said Freddi, wriggling her tiny frame into her hideous outdoor coat; "but Woody likes to think of us both as shrinking violets. It does something cosy to her mother urge." She tripped off out of the ward and across the garden to the V.A.D. Mess.

Gervase Eden was not a man who liked early rising; but he was up and dressed and walking up and down the drive by the main gates, when she went across, after her breakfast, to the cottage. She stopped short in her tracks at the sight of him, but after a moment's hesitation, went steadily forward. He came quickly up to her, putting out his hands in a familiar gesture, but hurriedly drawing them back. "Freddi—I wanted to talk to you for a minute."

"Well, I don't want to talk to you," she said, stonily.

He looked at her, astonished, and said rather sharply: "That hasn't always been the case."

"It's like you to remind me of it, Gervase," said Frederica.

He was obviously puzzled and hurt, but he went on doggedly: "Well, all right, if you feel that way, Freddi, it makes it easier to say what I was going to, or perhaps I needn't say it at all."

"Well, don't then. I don't want to hear it," said Freddi who would, nevertheless, have liked, from sheer curiosity, to know what it was.

His dark eyebrows met together in a frown, half-humorous, half-hurt. "Have it your own way, my dear," he said, and stood aside for her to pass through the gate.

She remained uncertainly on the other side. "Well, come on," he said, surprised. "Aren't you going to your quarters?"

"Yes, I am: when you've gone back to the Mess," said Freddi, remaining where she was.

"My dear, good child—you don't think I'm going to attempt a seduction scene here in the middle of the main high road, at eight o'clock in the morning, do you? Or what on earth's wrong with you?" His face cleared suddenly, and he burst out laughing. "Oh, my lovely Freddi! You couldn't possibly be afraid that I was going to leap upon you with a hypodermic full of morphia, filched from the theatre last night . . . ?"

"Of course not," said Freddi, tossing her head; but she came forward, nevertheless, and, keeping well away from him, passed on towards the cottage. He stood looking after her, still laughing, and the sound of his laughter followed her into the house. "Damn him!" she said, slamming the door after her; and she took off her stiff white cap and flung it on to Woody's bed, and chucked her coat after it, and, unpinning her apron as she went, made her way wearily upstairs.

The window would not open. She struggled with it, standing in her pyjamas on the bed, and finally gave it up. "After all, I shall only be here two or three hours and I can't get up much of a fug in that time." She crawled under the blankets, and the moment her golden head touched the pillow, was sound asleep.

Woods returned to the cottage an hour later. Without hesitation, she went to the kitchen mantelpiece and took a shilling from under the clock there; put it in the meter, and made herself a cup of tea. She sat at the table drinking it, staring ahead of her, with an expression of pain and weariness, a sort of desperate resolution on her face; and, after a quarter of an hour, cleared away the things and, moving very quietly, left the house and walked across the park without a backward glance. The heavy, musty smell of escaping coal gas crept after her down the stairs and was barricaded in by the closing front door. Frederica tossed and muttered in her little bed, and fell back again on her pillow and lay motionless.

4

THE patients had been washed and tidied by the time that Esther came on to the ward; they lay dozing in their beds, trying to sleep away a few more minutes of their interminable day. She whisked up and down among them, taking temperatures, counting pulses, measuring out doses, examining dressings. The up-patients in their blue linen suits, were tidying beds or making toast on the gas-cooker in the little kitchen outside. Chalk and Cheese were in a fever of activity at the other end of the ward. The fractured tib. and fib. announced that his behind was aching abominably, and that he would very much like it rubbed.

The oldest patient in every ward is known as "Pop"; anybody tall is invariably addressed as "Lofty," anybody short as "Tich" and anybody bald as "Curly"; for the rest the patients are called by their surnames, or in the case of sergeants, by their rank; but there is no accounting for the vagaries of the British soldier, and the fractured tib. and fib. was known, for no apparent reason, as William. He had lived down the stigma of his pansy voice, and was popular in the ward; there was a certain amount of competition among the V.A.D.s to attend to him, for, though every strata of society has been absorbed into the ranks of the Army, the vast majority of soldiers are still drawn from the so-called middle and lower-middle classes; and, as a sophisticated, well-to-do and extremely personable young man, he was vastly interesting to

Chalk and Cheese. Esther effectively concealed, even from herself, that she shared in this rivalry but she could not prevent a small sensation of pleasure at observing her colleagues so very busily occupied elsewhere. She advanced with a bottle of methylated spirit in her hand, and, lifting him on one arm, slid away the air cushion, and began to rub his thighs and back.

"That's *quite* comfortable now," said William with complete truth, seeing that it had never been otherwise.

"You haven't got a trace of bed-sores," she said, unsuspiciously, lowering him again and tucking in his bed-clothes.

"Thank you so much," he said; and as she stood by the bed, he took one of her hands in his. "Look at your poor little fingers!"

They were beautiful hands, small and narrow, with tapering fingers and the perfect filbert nail; but rough work and hard water had chafed and stained them, and, with all her care, the nails were broken and blunt. "I'm ashamed of them," she said, putting them behind her back.

"You should be proud. They got that way in a very good cause."

"Well, I suppose so, but—look!" She spread them out in front of her, frowning down on the callouses on her palm. "A hideous great scar where I burnt my finger last week, and a bruise on my wrist, and a horrible black stain round my thumb nail. . . . I used to keep them looking so lovely and now they're just a disgrace; my poor little hands!"

"Could you take them very quickly somewhere else?" said William abruptly.

She stared at him in astonishment. "Why on earth?"

"I'm seized with an irresistible desire to kiss them," said the fractured tib. and fib, "and I'm afraid you might not be pleased. . . ."

She would not have been pleased, and she picked up her bottle of meths. and walked hurriedly away: but a small, bright ember began to glow very warmly in the depths of her desolate heart. She left Chalk and Cheese, however, to attend to the rest of William's needs.

At a quarter to eleven she made an excuse to the Sister, and, hanging her outdoor coat over her shoulders, ran across the grounds to the cottages, where Freddi would be in bed upstairs. At the door she paused and sniffed, in the sitting-room she paused and sniffed again, and a moment later she was running up the narrow stairs.

Frederica lay on the little truckle bed; her short heavily curling hair was spread over the pillow in a network of deep gold; her face was scarlet, her arms flung up over her head, the fingers tightly clenched. There was a strong, choking, sickly smell of gas.

5

PANIC. The hospital hummed and buzzed and seethed with rumour. Linley's been murdered. Frederica Linley's dead. Somebody left the gas on in the Woodites' quarters, and Freddi was found nearly dead. Esther Sanson saved Frederica's life. Freddi Linley saved Esther Sanson's life. Esther's dead. Freddi's dead. Sister Bates is dead. We're all going to be murdered in our beds.

Cockrill sent for Miss Woods. "I want you to come down to the cottage with me. Miss Linley's too ill and Esther Sanson is sleeping off the shock. Can you get away from your operating theatre for half an hour?"

"I dare say it'll manage to stagger along," said Woody, who was, in fact, off duty.

They walked together across the rough grass, under the tall, bare trees, and along the drive to the gate; a strapping, deep-bosomed woman, and a little brown old man in a droopy mack-intosh and a perfectly enormous hat. "I must have picked up my sergeant's by mistake," said Cockie irritably, pushing it up from over his eyes for the fifth time. "I'm always doing it." He was perfectly indifferent to anything but the discomfort involved by this accident. Woods gave a fleeting smile at the thought of the sergeant's probable feelings, but such distractions could not last for long, and she said, vainly trying to steady her voice: "This is all really rather awful, Inspector, isn't it?"

"Getting the wind up, are you?" said Cockrill.

Woody considered. "Well, yes; I think I am."

"You women are all arrant cowards," said Cockie contemptuously.

Woods looked about her at the bomb-scarred landscape and the blast-pitted buildings where she and a hundred other women were voluntarily spending the days of their service to their country; at the fields, pitted with craters, at the gaunt white limbs of the trees broken down by a bomb the night before; at the ruins of the Navy, Army, Air Force Institute where a girl called Groves, whom she had hardly known, had been killed by falling masonry; at the patches of dry grass all round her, blackened and scorched by innumerable incendiary bombs; at the jagged fragments of bomb-casing littering the ground at her feet. For a moment she felt the earth shudder and rock beneath her, for a moment the guns thundered in her ears, and the drone of the bombers was torn by the shriek of a falling bomb. . . . Six months of it. Six months of it, day and night, almost incessantly—and in all that time she had not known the meaning of fear; had not seen in the faces about her, the faces of middle-aged women or young girls, a shadow of panic or failure or endurance-at-an-end. One felt it, of *course;* some people had a queasy sensation when the sirens wailed; some people's tummies turned over at the sound of a falling bomb; most of them would go through life with a humiliating tendency to fling themselves flat on their faces at any loud noise; but that was all. They were all much too busy and tired to be afraid. She smiled outright this time, and said with a lift of her strong black eyebrow: "Oh yes, we're terrible cowards, there's no doubt of that."

Cockie had followed her glance, but he remained unimpressed. "You can take the blitz in your stride; but a couple of unexplained deaths, and you all get the jitters."

" 'Unexplained' is the operative word," said Woody coolly. "Personally, I'm much more petrified of the blitz on the nights that it *does*n't come; once it's there, it's there, but I don't like the uneasy waiting for it to begin, and I don't like waiting to be murdered—or to have my friends murdered."

"What makes you think they may be?" said Cockrill.

"Two successful murders, one attempted one, and somebody running around with two grains of morphia in their pocket," said Woody succinctly. As they passed through the gate and turned right towards the row of cottages, she added: "Here's our slum— the one this end, nearest the gate. Pardon the squalor, but this is the best that a grateful nation can do for its Florrie Nightingales in the year 1940."

"It looks all right," said Cockie ungraciously. "What are you grumbling about?"

"I'm not grumbling. I haven't got a word to say against it. But I thought you might be a bit surprised and I was being the complete hostess."

"It depends what you're used to, I suppose," said Cockie, standing in the narrow doorway, politely averting his eyes from a line of solid-looking underwear hanging across the little kitchen.

"Well, *I'm* used to a streamlined flat in town," said Woody abruptly.

"Oh! Are you? Town-bred girl, eh?"

"Mostly," said Woods, automatically picking up a hairbrush and an outsize brassiere and pushing them under a cushion.

"I see. I only wondered," said Cockie, "because there were some people of your name living in these parts once."

"My father did have a house down here once, ages ago, when we were—when I was a child."

"How many ages ago?" said Cockie, lighting a cigarette before getting down to work.

"Well, actually—I mean *that* was ages ago, when I was a child, of course; but they lived here till—oh, I don't know, four or five years ago."

"I see," said Cockie again. "Quite a short age, really. And where are your parents now?"

"They're dead," said Woody. She dived under the line of washing, holding up a garment for the Inspector to follow her. "Excuse the Jaegar coms and things, but chiffon and *crêpe de chine* don't quite suit the life of a V.A.D. Sorry about the fug; it's not us—it must be the results of the gas."

"Let's have a look at the meter," said Cockrill.

She opened a cupboard door. "Here it is. . . . Good lord, somebody seems to have been dusting it. It hasn't looked so clean for months."

"My sergeant has been going over it for fingerprints," said Cockrill. "He always clears up after himself."

"We must get him down for the spring cleaning," said Woody equably.

He examined the meter carefully. "I see that there's six shillings in here," he said, peering at the little dials. "Would that be about right, do you know?"

Woods considered this, muttering calculations to herself. "Me and then Freddi and then Esther, and twice three's six, but last week Freddi put in two. . . . Yes, that's right; we put in the shillings in turns, and it was Esther's turn this time. Actually I suddenly remembered that I had put a bob under the clock for emergencies, only I'd forgotten it, so now Esther owes me a shilling."

"It boils down to this, that nobody but yourselves has put any money in the meter since it was last cleared?"

"No such luck," said Woods.

"Well, now, let's go up to the bedroom, shall we? I want to look round up there."

The window had finally been got open and most of the fumes had blown away from the little room. "The tap of the gas fire was turned on," said Cockrill, pointing to it with the toe of his shoe. "The fire wasn't lit, and of course the gas was pouring into the room. I wonder how the tap can have been turned on?"

"Not by accident, for a start," said Woody decidedly. "That tap was always frightfully stiff; and besides, it's very un-get-at-able, isn't it? I mean, nobody could have pushed it on with their foot by mistake, or anything like that."

"Exactly," said Cockie, scattering cigarette ash all over the bedroom floor.

"I came up just before we left the house," went on Woody, "and it certainly wasn't on then, because the gas had only just petered out downstairs, and if it had been on before that, there would have been a smell of gas which there wasn't. Esther came up a few minutes afterwards to close the window, only actually I'd already closed it, but she didn't know that; and *she* says there wasn't any smell either."

"You both seem very thoughtful of your friend," said Cockie.

Woody smote her large bosom a resounding thud. "Under our mountainous exteriors, we have hearts of gold."

"Oh yes?" said Cockie politely. He produced a little wooden object from his pocket. "I wonder what heart of gold it was that thought of wedging up the window with this, so that it wouldn't open."

Woods stared at it, electrified. "Do you mean to say that that was stuck in the window? It *can't* have been! It's one of our clothes pegs, out of the kitchen."

"I noticed that one pair of coms was hanging a bit skew-wiff," said Cockrill.

She took the peg from him and stood, leaning back against the dressing-table, turning it over and over between her fingers, looking down at it as though she could not believe her eyes. "I don't understand. This was jammed in the window . . . ? But *why?*"

"It would take a very long time to gas a person in a room with an open window," said Cockrill, sitting on a corner of the bed, looking up at her.

She dropped the peg, as though it had suddenly become contaminated with evil. "It's too horrible . . . it's inconceivable! Are you telling me that somebody deliberately jammed up the window so that poor little Freddi would be gassed to death? It's too . . . I . . ."

He looked at her curiously. "You're so surprised? Yet you knew this was an attempt at murder; you said so yourself, just now."

"Well, I suppose I knew in my mind that it was, but one can't sort of rea*lise* it, one doesn't really face it . . ." She broke off and said wretchedly: "But who could have done such a thing? Who put the shilling in the gas meter, for a start?"

"Well, as for that—you did, didn't you?" said Cockrill, still watching her.

"I? *I* did?"

"Of course," said Cockie.

"But, Inspector . . ."

"Miss Woods," said Cockrill patiently, "let's get this straight. At twenty-past seven this morning, the gas died in your meter; we know that the tap up here was not turned on then, because there was no smell of gas. Very well. After that you came up to this room to put a hot-water bottle in Miss Linley's bed, and you closed the window. Later still, Miss Sanson came up to close the window, but found it already shut. At half-past seven you both left the house.

"At about ten to eight, Miss Linley came back and went to bed. She found that she couldn't open the window. That is to say that in the half-hour between the time the gas ran out in the meter, and the time she came back to bed, somebody had jammed up the window, and it's only reasonable to assume that the same person had turned on the gas-tap in here."

"But Freddi would have smelt the gas," protested Woods.

"No, she wouldn't," said Cockie. "There was no gas to smell; there was none coming through the meter—yet."

"My God!" said Woody.

"Yes, it is rather 'my God!' isn't it?" said Cockrill calmly. "It's a very old dodge, of course. At a quarter to nine, by which time Miss Linley would be fast asleep after her heavy night's work, you yourself were all scheduled to come across and make yourself a cup of tea; and that necessitated . . . ?"

"Putting a shilling in the meter," finished Woody obediently.

6

COCKRILL finished his cigarette, and ground out the stub in Freddi's little ash-tray. "Do you usually come over and make yourself tea?"

"Yes, I do," said Woody, at once. "I'm the theatre V.A.D., as I suppose you know by now, and I go on duty at half-past seven like the others, and clean up and check instruments, and all the rest of it; but operating doesn't begin till half-past nine, in the ordinary way, so a bit before that I come over and make myself a cuppa, and have a cigarette and put up my feet for twenty minutes or so before the dog-fight. It's all quite fair and above-board; everybody knows I do it."

"Everybody?" said Cockrill.

"Well, actually I meant Theatre Sister and so forth; but now I come to think of it, everybody else does too. All the theatre staff, I mean. . . . Major Moon and Barney, and Gervase—Major Eden, that is. I often walk back with them when they're going on duty after their breakfast. And of course Freddi and Esther; I don't know that anybody else knows."

"Well, those are the ones we're interested in, anyway, aren't they?" said Cockie smoothly.

She leaned back against the dressing-table in her favourite attitude, her lovely long legs stretched out before her, her arms crossed over her breast; and her friendly, intelligent face was drawn with worry. "I suppose they are: Frederica and Esther, and Major

Moon and Barney and Gervase—and me. . . . Nobody else can have known that Higgins was in the hospital; nobody else knew that Sister Bates had the 'proof' of the murder; and now there's this; just those five people knew that I could come across and make myself some tea. It can't be true—and yet it must be true. One of us—one of *us!*" She was silent for a moment, thinking deeply; but at last she cried, raising haggard eyes to his: "But, Inspector, *why?* Why should any of us have done these things? I don't see who would want to. Who would want to kill Higgins, for a start? None of us had ever set eyes on him before; he was just a country postman, and as far as we know, he'd never been out of Kent. Sister Bates came from a London hospital. Frederica had always lived abroad. What was the connection? What was the sort of a—the common denominator between these three? Why should any one person want to kill these three particular people?" She added, suddenly, struck by an idea: "There couldn't be a maniac involved, Inspector Cockrill? You don't think it could be a maniac, or something like that?"

"No, I don't," said Cockie. "Maniacs don't plan murders; at least they don't plan deaths that will take place when they're not there to see. They like killing people; not just having them die. A maniac wouldn't shut anybody up in a gas-filled room and go away. He'd want to see the fun."

"Well, then, all I can say is that it's utterly hideous," said Woody, desperately. "You suggest that one of us, one of my friends, has killed, or tried to kill, three absolutely unrelated people, for no apparent reason. . . . I mean, supposing for the sake of argument, that Higgins had been blackmailing Major Moon or Barney because he'd been delivering feelthy postcards from Paris at their doors—what could that have to do with Sister Bates? What could it have to do with Freddi?"

"As far as Bates is concerned, we know that she was murdered because of what she could reveal about the original murder," suggested Cockrill, reasonably.

"Well, all right, but that doesn't explain this business of Frederica? What's the connection between her and Higgins?"

"There's one connection that you don't seem to have thought of," said Cockrill, looking up at her from under his eyebrows; "Higgins talked of 'goings-on' in the sisters' bunk that night that he was brought in . . . there was one other person who could have witnessed those 'goings-on'—and that was your friend Frederica."

The rouge stood out very pink and blotchy on Woody's cheekbones, as the natural colour drained away from beneath the skin; she said, breathlessly: "But—but Freddi herself was mostly connected with the 'goings-on'; I mean, she and Barney were talking in there. So if Freddi's killed—I mean if anyone tries to kill Freddi . . ."

"I believe Major Eden and Sister Bates were also talking in there."

"Oh, good lord, that was all nothing," said Woods, brushing it aside. "Gervase had a slight affair with Bates, everybody knows that; and he was tired of it and she was full of lamentations and reproaches. . . ."

"And threats?" said Cockie.

She caught her breath; but went on, earnestly, almost at once: "She may have threatened to make a fuss; she was jealous and miserable and perhaps a bit hysterical—but what could she have done? Nothing very dreadful. He's already divorced from his wife, or anyway, separated. There was nothing to be wrecked by a scene with Marion Bates."

"Except his practice," suggested Cockrill. "I understand that Major Eden had a great many women in his practice?"

"He's a general surgeon," said Woods stoutly.

"Largely patronised by women," insisted Cockie; "and though I don't suggest for a moment that Major Eden consciously exercises his charm over these ladies, well, I dare say they wouldn't flock to him if he were old and ugly and disagreeable."

"He *is* old and ugly and disagreeable," said Woody, impatiently; but she added, ruefully: "At least *rath*er old, and *rath*er ugly. . . ."

"And not at all disagreeable," said Cockie, smiling.

"No, he isn't," admitted Woods, smiling too; a little, affectionate, reminiscent smile that she immediately checked.

"And so I say that, supposing there had been a sordid breach of promise case, or something of that kind—it would have done Major Eden's private practice no good; no good at all."

"What would that matter? He's in the Army now."

"He won't always be," said Cockrill.

She jerked her head impatiently. "Good lord, Inspector, are you seriously suggesting . . . ? It's nonsense. People don't murder people for things like *that!*"

"People have been known to murder people for a great deal less," said Cockie, grimly ironical.

"But I . . . But he couldn't . . ." She said, with belated caution: "I don't know why I should take it upon myself to defend Major Eden like this, but the point is, you're all wrong. He just couldn't have done it. He isn't that kind of person."

"Well, that's a most rational defence, I must say," said Cockie, mockingly. "He isn't that kind of person! Isn't that just like a woman! Now, look here, Miss Woods. . . . I don't say for a moment that Eden killed Bates and Higgins; but he's one of six equally unlikely people, and he had some sort of motive, which is more than can be said for the rest of them, as far as I can see . . . and he *could* have done it. He's accounted to me for the time after he saw Higgins in the ward; but he has no alibis for the time between his seeing the man carried through the hall and the time that he visited the ward."

"Oh, good heavens," cried Woody, impatiently; "what rubbish all this is! Saw the man carried through the hall! We saw a bundle of rags carried through the hall, huddled up on a stretcher with his face all covered with dust and filth and his poor old toes sticking out through the remains of his boots. Are you suggesting that on the strength of that, Gervase made up his mind to commit murder, concocted a deep and elaborate plot, and started the whole thing going? It's nonsense, of course it is. Of course it wasn't Gervase."

Cockrill got up from the bed and stood at the window, looking down at the cold greyness of the park. "Of *course* it wasn't Gervase," insisted Woody anxiously, frightened at his thoughtful silence.

"Then who was it?" asked Cockrill, turning back from the window. "Who else do you suggest it was? Which of your five friends?"

"I don't know," said Woods helplessly.

"It wasn't you yourself, for example," said Cockrill with a twinkle. "You would hardly be likely to make these elaborate arrangements for gassing Frederica Linley, and then come and put the shilling in the meter yourself! Similarly it couldn't be Miss Linley, could it, for she was one of the victims, or Miss Sanson, because she saved Miss Linley; and it wouldn't be Captain Barnes, for whatever else he may be, he is definitely very sincerely in love with Miss Linley and would never attempt to harm her. You insist that it isn't Major Eden, so that only leaves Major Moon."

"And it couldn't be Major Moon," said Woods, smiling at the bare idea. She added anxiously: "You *don't* think it could be him?"

"Ah, that would be telling," said Cockie. He flapped with a corner of his mackintosh at the cigarette ash scattered over the window-sill, and suddenly turned and stumped out of the room and down the narrow stairs.

Woody followed him; she said urgently, her hand gripping the thin wooden banister: "Does that mean that you know? You know who did it?"

"Of course," said Cockrill. He picked up the hat from the kitchen table and thrust it rakishly on the back of his head.

She stood transfixed, staring at him. "You know, Inspector? But how on earth? I mean, how could you . . . what can you . . . when did you find out?"

"Oh, just a few minutes ago," said Cockie gaily, and was just in time to wink at her before the hat fell like an extinguisher over his bright brown eyes.

Chapter VII

1

THE fractured tib. and fib. lay in the corner bed where Higgins had spent his single night in the hospital; the screens round the bed next door cut him off from the rest of the ward. He complained rather plaintively that his leg was hurting a lot; and added incautiously that this time it really was.

"What do you mean?" said Esther innocently. "Doesn't it always?"

"Oh yes, of course, always, abominably," said William hurriedly; but again he could not help laughing and adding, "Though oddly enough, only when *you're* on duty!"

Esther, having slept off the effects of her rescue work, had, as she had expected, been put on night duty in the ward until Frederica should be fit to work again. She said, uncertainly, standing at his bedside: "Are you trying to flirt with me again?"

"Yes," said William, and caught her hand and kissed it, and turned it over and kissed the palm and each of the fingers, and then lay still with his cheek against it, holding it very closely in both his own; for a moment they were silent in the sweet, warm, infinitely peaceful joy of emotional surrender.

It was true that his leg was hurting more these days; and his back ached and he was bored and miserable and out of sorts, and his ship would sail without him while he lay here in hospital, and all the friends and companions he had made aboard her would sail with her, out of his life; he would be stuck in this gloomy ward for weeks and weeks, and God knew whether, when he finally got out, the Navy would ever take him back again. But, meanwhile, he held this small, slim hand in his own, and looked up into brown eyes suddenly alight with tenderness, and he smiled and said, "Oh *dar*-ling!" and pulled her down to him and held her close to his heart.

Chaos reigned in St. Elizabeth's that evening. "Hey, nurse, you haven't given me my hot drink! Have one of mine, mate, she's given me three! What's this, nurse?—there's nothing but 'ot water in my mug? Oi, nurse, there's only a bit o' cocoa powder in mine!" They laughed and grumbled and argued and pulled her leg. "You must be in love, nurse; that's what it is! Nurse Sanson's in love!"

Nurse Sanson's in love. How warm and comfortable and safe and *final* it felt, after all the pain and bitterness of the past. William would look after her; she would put her hand in his and wrap herself about in his love and find a refuge there. "I will begin again," she thought; "I won't worry and agonise and crave after Mummy any more. She would want me to forget now, and be safe and happy and contented, and so I will. William will look after me. . . ." And she went back to him and said, "Oh *dar*ling!" and gave him her hand again, and they gazed for a quite ridiculous length of time into each other's eyes.

"Oh, darling!" said William.

"Oh, *dar*ling!" said Esther.

"As I can't go on calling you Oh-darling indefinitely," suggested William at last, "I think perhaps, sweetheart, you had better tell me your name."

"Darling, you *can't* want a girl to marry you when you don't even know her name!"

"Well, tell me your name quickly then," said William.

"My name's Esther, dearest."

"Now, isn't that a coincidence," said William; "I never was in love with a girl called Esther before!"

She sat by his bed for a long time in the darkened ward, jumping up now and then to attend to a patient, sleepless or in pain, but always coming back to sit with her little roughened hands in his; to talk, not of the past, but of the future; not of her mother and the air-raids, but of their life together when the blitz should be a thing of the past. By the time the Orderly Officer was due on his round, they had brought the war to a successful conclusion, had built themselves a white house on the hill overlooking Godlistone, had furnished themselves with three children, two boys and a girl, and were changing the honeymoon two-seater Chrysler for a sedate family Daimler. Esther dragged herself away at last. "You're supposed to be an invalid, my sweet; you really must go to sleep. . . ."

"Talking about sleeping, Esther . . . have you ever given any serious thought to the double-versus-twin-beds controversy?"

"Oh, William!" she protested, laughing and blushing.

"I think I'm definitely anti-twin," said William, pulling her back to him by the corner of her apron.

2

Night Sister came round with the Orderly Medical Officer. "We had three new operation cases to-day, Major Jones; will you prescribe for them? And one of the hernias that was done yesterday is having a good deal of pain still. The fractured tib. and fib. seems to have been complaining that his leg is hurting him more than it did; how is he to-night, nurse?"

In the brief intervals during which he had had time to notice it, William had said that his leg really was a bit troublesome; he might as well have a good night, anyway, thought Esther, and reported that a sleeping draught would be welcome. The O.M.O. scribbled prescriptions and Sister handed out morphia and sleeping powders from the poison cupboard. Esther, going off up the ward with a syringe in her hand, heard her say to the doctor: "I suppose it's all right to let her give the injections? After all she *is* one of 'them' . . ."

Major Moon arrived in the bunk at half-past ten. "Got any tea going, Esther, my dear?" As she assented, smiling, he came up to her suddenly and took her chin in his hand, turning her face to the light. "What's happened to you, child? You look positively lovely to-night!"

"Do I?" she said, foolishly happy.

He took his hand away, but his fingers seemed to linger over the smooth, soft skin. "You always were a beautiful creature, Esther, with that perfect oval face of yours, like a madonna in a church; but to-night the madonna seems to have gone all—fey."

"The madonna's fallen in love," she confessed, laughing.

He caught his breath sharply, but almost at once he said gaily:

"In love! You're in love, Esther; that's what it is, it's written all over your face. Tell me about it and who is the lucky young man . . ."

She told him all about it. William slept peacefully in the bed next door to the bunk and she poured out the happy story of their love affair, of all that it meant to her. "Don't think that the—the security and money and all that mean *anything*, Major Moon, compared with just being in love with him; but of course they do count, they must. I was so frightened of the future, because after the war I'd have had to keep myself and I just wouldn't have known where to begin. Mummy had a pension and she lived on that, and—well, you know what mothers are, she didn't want me to work and she always thought I would get married and not have to. . . . I never had any training, and being a V.A.D. doesn't get you anywhere, though I used to think it would help, that was why I took it up. . . . But it doesn't does it . . . ? I just don't know how I would have lived. But now . . . and, oh, Major Moon, he *is* so sweet and I *am* so much in love. . . . It's quite absurd, I know, we've only known each other a week or so, but—well, there it is, these things happen. . . ."

"I'm very glad for you, my dear," he said and he put his arm round her and kissed her on the lips.

It was a tiny shock, for it was not the kiss of an elderly man, saluting a young girl with her heart engaged elsewhere; but of a lover. He released her at once, however, and said humbly: "I'm sorry, Esther; I meant to give you just a fatherly peck and my blessing, and it got out of hand a bit. . . . You must forgive me; it's your fault—you're so very lovely to-night!"

Woods appeared at the door with her arms outstretched before her, moaning, "Unclean! Unclean!" At sight of Major Moon, she dropped her hands to her sides and said, laughing: "Oh, I'm sorry, sir; I didn't think anyone would be here. But still, you're one of us, too . . ."

"What *is* the matter with you, Woody?" said Esther.

"My dear, the inmates of our shelter have petitioned that when there are air-raids, I shall sleep somewhere else; they think I'm going to rise up in the night and set fire to their palliasses with oil from the paraffin lamps!"

"Oh, nonsense, darling. . . ."

"They do really. Can I have some tea? No, honestly, Esther, you and I and Freddi, when she gets well, have got to use the little Anderson shelter outside the cottages. Com thinks we shall 'feel more comfortable' there."

"What happens if we slaughter each other? Nobody cares about that, I suppose?"

"Well, we're all potential criminals and we're supposed to be hardened to attempted murder. Are you an outcast too, Major Moon?"

"There's a tendency to allow Barnes and Eden and me to monopolise the ante-room fire undisturbed," confessed Major Moon. "But everyone is very polite and friendly, and they do make great efforts not to let us feel our position too acutely! The Press is seething round the hospital, and the C.O.s put a sentry on the main gates, and on the gates of the Mess with orders to let nobody in without a pass. . . ."

"What fun we do have," said Woody. She stood with her elbows on the mantelpiece, staring down unhappily into the fire, and repeated what was uppermost in her mind: "The Inspector says it's one of us; and he knows which!"

One of us. One of *us!* "Of course Frederica's out of it," continued Woody, as though it did them any good to narrow the circle even further down, "because she'd hardly have tried to gas herself. . . ."

"No, of course; Freddi's right out of it," said Esther, glad of that, anyway.

"On the other hand, she might have, knowing that she would be rescued; I mean, then all of us would have said, just as we're doing, that of course Freddi couldn't be suspected. For that matter, Esther, so might you have fixed the gas tap, knowing that you would be able to save her, and throw us all off the scent."

"So I might," acknowledged Esther, much struck.

"But how could any of us have wanted to kill Higgins?" cried Major Moon impatiently. "That's the crux of the matter. The attempt on Frederica was probably made because she 'knew too much' as they say in the novels; and the murder of Sister Bates was almost certainly for that reason. But why should any of *us* have wanted Higgins to die?"

Woody did not repeat her theory of the feelthy postcards. Instead she suggested that perhaps Sister Bates had killed Higgins and somebody had killed *her* in revenge.

"Oh, nonsense, darling," said Esther. "Why should Bates have wanted to kill Higgins in the first place?"

"Well, because he'd heard a scene between her and Gervase, in here, and he was going to publish it all round the hospital."

"Even if that could have been a motive for either of them, Woody," said Major Moon gravely, "it would be more likely to be Eden."

"Yes, but we know it can't have been Gervase, anyway," protested Woods, "because he certainly wouldn't have tried to kill Frederica, later on. He was terribly keen on Freddi—he'd never have tried to harm her."

"Why do you say he *was* fond of her?" said Esther.

"Well, is, then, if you like."

"I don't think your defence would cut much ice with Inspector Cockrill, Woody," said Major Moon quietly. He finished his cup of tea and got to his feet and his mild, blue eyes were full of anxiety and distress. "I like Eden," he said, rather inconsequently. "I have always liked him; he's a—he's a charming fellow. I wish . . . I don't think . . ."

Esther wished that the conversation might end, for she was dying to tell Woody about William. She said, firmly: "Gervase couldn't have had anything to do with the murders of Higgins or Bates, for the simple reason that he couldn't have had anything to do with the attempt on Freddi, whether he likes her or not. He was nowhere near the cottage this morning; he couldn't have wedged up the window and turned on the gas tap. He didn't know that the meter needed a shilling."

"No," said Major Moon; "of course." But he still stood, looking down miserably at his toes, and he seemed to be on the brink of a resolution. He said at last: "I don't like to say this but. . . . You girls must look after yourselves. . . . Esther, you must look after yourself, my dear. I don't want to say a word against Eden, not a word, but . . . well, after I met you girls in the park this morning, I saw Eden, you know. When I run around the grounds of a morning I take an old tweed coat with me, just to put round my shoulders when I cross the road, back to the Mess. This morning I dropped it down beside a bush; and as I stood there putting it on, Eden came out of the Mess. He—well, Esther, he looked carefully up and down the drive; I don't like to say it, my dear, but he did. Then he went over to your cottage and—he glanced up at the window, stood looking up at the window; and then he pushed open the door and went in. A minute afterwards he came out again and looked about him; by that time I was at the gates of the Mess and I suppose he didn't see me. But I saw him. Eden may not have known about the shilling, my dear girls, but two minutes before Frederica came off duty and back to her bed—I saw him coming out of your house." He added, heavily, turning to the door: "What worries me is—why hasn't he mentioned it?"

3

WILLIAM had a visitor on the following afternoon. Detective Inspector Cockrill arrived at the door of the ward, and stood peering in rather nervously, his felt hat crushed into a shapeless bundle under his arm. Cheese appeared at his elbow. "Inspector— how lovely to see you again!"

"Have I ever seen you before?" said Cockie, bleakly.

"Oh, Inspector! The first night you came here, don't you re-member? My friend and I talked to you in the Com's office, over at the V.A.D. Mess; you were so sweet to us!" said Cheese with a girlish wriggle; and added that she and her friend had been wondering ever since if they could ever dare to ask him for his autograph.

"You'd better not," said Cockie in a fearful voice. "What do you take me for—a film star?" He suddenly waved his stick: "Hallo, my boy! Coming to have a talk with you . . . !" and marched over to William's bedside, leaving Cheese flat. "Got out of his bed the wrong side, this morning," she confided to an equally disappointed Chalk.

Cockrill had known William's father, as he knew most of the personalities of North Kent. "Hallo, Cockie," said William, struggling up to an almost sitting position. "How ripping to see you!"

"Don't *you* start asking for my autograph," implored Cockie; he chucked his hat on to the floor beside his chair, and took out a tin of tobacco. "I suppose I can smoke in this vale of antisepsis?"

"Yes, rather, of course you can. Here," said William, producing the three cigarettes remaining out of his daily ration of five; "do have one of mine."

"No thanks, I prefer my own." His nicotined fingers packed and rolled; he said, not looking up from his work: "How's your leg, my boy?"

"Oh, it's quite all right," said William, breezily. "Getting along like a house on fire."

"Are you all right in this place? Do they look after you properly?"

"Good lord, yes," said William devoutly. "It's marvellous."

Cockrill raised an eyebrow and looked about him. It did not seem so particularly marvellous. The tables down the centre were brightened by a few flowers in an assortment of rather hideous vases, and the up-patients lounged round them in their blue linen coats and trousers, doing jig-saw puzzles or writing letters; or clustered round the beds of those not yet up, playing Housie-housie or Whist. Large notices on the walls forbade gambling for money, under pain of death, so the pennies and ha'pennies were kept tucked away under pillows. A man only just out of bed was being led slowly and with infinite patience and kindliness, by a great lout of a guardsman, up and down the ward. "There you are, mate! Doing fine, you are. . . ." The Red Cross librarian came round with a trolley-load of books. They scrabbled in their lockers for last week's. "Give us a nice bit of blood and thunder,

Miss." "You give 'im a love story, Miss, that's what 'e wants . . . a nice bit of romance. . . ." A man lying drowsy from his pre-operative injection was loudly consoled by his friends. "Won't be long now, old boy. Have a nice ride, mate; give our love to the operating theatre." A couple of robots in long, green gowns whisked in with a wheeled white trolley, and bundled him on to it; covered with blankets and with his head wrapped in a rug, he was wheeled out of the ward. "Good luck, chum!" cried the men, and went back, apparently unmoved, to their Housie-housie. On a bed stripped down to the rubber sheet, a man lay without pillows, coming-to from his anæsthetic. A scarlet face was raised for a moment, two bright eyes looked vacantly into space, and the head dropped back with a heavy thud. "You lay still, mate," yelled half a dozen voices; and a man got up and went over and held the man's wrist for a moment, bending over him. "You lay quiet, boy, and don't keep shoving yer 'ead up." He called down the ward: "Here, nurse; 'e's coming round," and went and sat down to his game again. "Pore beggar; I wouldn't be in 'is shoes! Thank 'eavens, I've got mine over." A man with a broken back lay on a high, S-shaped bed, staring up at the ceiling as he had lain and stared for six weeks and must lie for many weeks more. Number seven, who still had asthma, inhaled Friar's Balsam in sickly wafts, peering out balefully from under a woolen shawl. Cockrill finished his first cigarette, ground out the butt with his heel, and then respectfully picked it up and put it in the ash-tray on William's locker. He said, without preamble: "I suppose you know about these—deaths? Higgins, and the Bates girl."

"Yes, I know about them. News travels like wildfire in a place like this, and poor old Higgins was a pal of mine."

"How did you come across him—up at the brewery?"

"No, I worked under him in the A.R.P.," said William. "He was leader of a rescue squad, you know. I didn't get called up for about a year after war broke out, so I thought I would do a bit of voluntary work while I waited, just to prevent the girls from handing me white feathers in the streets, you know. He was a marvellous old boy, was Joe. I went through all the raids with him; we never missed a blitz and we had a lot of fun. When I came back on leave I dropped down to the Town Hall to see him, and got caught in the raid there; we were sitting talking and listening to the radio while he waited to go out on a job, when— whang! a bloody great bomb hit the place smack in the middle and the whole roof caved in. The other three chaps copped it, but Joe and I were protected by a beam or something, I suppose, and lay there trapped by the legs. He asked me if I was O.K. and then I must have passed out, I think; when I came to again we were still there, but he was unconscious. Then the chaps got down to us and hauled us out; they took him first, of course, because I was more or less all right." He added, grinning: "I'd like to be able to tell you that I implored them to leave me and save the old boy and I would stick it out till the end, but I didn't have a chance, because that's exactly what they were going to do anyway! The fantastic thing was that the radio went on working all the time; we'd been listening-in to the German broadcast, and while I lay there in the dark—with water dripping all round me, a gas-escape somewhere not too far away, and my leg caught under a girder and giving me hell—some filth-hound was droning away about how effete and rotten I was, and how we all ought to make friends with Germany before it was too late. There was a frightful din going on outside, and the bombs were dropping down like ripe apples. . . ."

Once, when Cockrill was driving along the Heronsford Road

in his car, an incendiary had hit the roof and gone right through to the back seat and set the whole concern on fire; he would dearly have liked to tell about it and about the time he had driven slap into a crater that hadn't been there half an hour before—how if he'd been only twenty minutes earlier, if he hadn't called in at the Black Dog in Pigeonsford village and had a glass of beer with the landlord, if he hadn't stopped to offer a lift to three Auxiliary Territorial Service girls, and gone a few miles out of his way to take them to their station, he might easily have been killed. . . . But William, having got his own bomb-story off his chest, had returned to Higgins. "I can't think who on earth could have wanted to bump the old boy off; I mean, he was an awfully good fellow, really, one of the best, never did any harm to anyone; you can't go through the raids working for a man, and not know what he's really like." His own part in going through the raids, humbly working "for" William Higgins, postman, did not appear to impress him as anything particularly praiseworthy.

Cockie started a small conflagration at the wispy end of a new cigarette. "Do you know any of the other people concerned in this case?"

William drew deeply on his own cigarette, and replied that he knew Esther Sanson; she—well, actually she worked in this ward. "And I know little Linley; she was on night-duty here, before she got her head put in the gas-oven; and I've seen Eden in the ward, looking at his cases, and Barnes, of course; and Major Moon looked at my leg this morning, as the surgeon who originally did it is away on leave. He seems a nice old boy. My father used to know him on various committees and things, and Dr. Barnes too—this chap's father."

"Do you know Miss Woods?"

"No, she told Esther—she said she was coming to see me one day and make my acquaintance, but she hasn't turned up. I used to play with some children of that name when I was so-high; I wonder if she'll remember me?"

"I doubt it," said Cockie dryly. As William looked surprised, he added rather quickly: "Tell me about little Miss Linley; you saw a good deal of her, that night you were brought in, I suppose?"

"Yes, she was marvellous to me," said William, at once. "I must have been a frightful nuisance having to be rigged up with this thing in the middle of the night, but she went about it quite calmly and coolly as if she had nothing else to do all night, and of course she was frantically busy really, poor kid. Even Higgins had to admit that she was wonderful, though he didn't have much use for her, having seen her necking with her boy-friends earlier in the evening, in the bunk next door; but he had a terrible night, poor old boy, in a lot of pain, and not able to get any sleep, and he said that she was terribly good to him; she never left the ward for a moment, and he didn't know how she kept it up, a fragile looking little thing like her. She's a funny girl, though; I heard her talking to old Moon, night before last, in the bunk; he was telling her about his child being knocked down and killed by a man on a bicycle; and all she could think of by way of sympathy was to ask him politely what colour the bicycle had been! Esther says it's because she's really shy under all that poise; and rather inarticulate and that she would like to be friendly and sympathetic, but she can't."

Cockrill would never have thought Frederica devoid of self-possession. "She seems rather—hard," he suggested. "Is she a good nurse?"

"Oh, the perfect article," said William immediately. "She talks to you as though you were a naughty and rather mutton-headed little boy, and quite convinces you that your leg doesn't hurt at all, really, and that, if you only knew it, you have a passionate desire to eat your nice ground-rice pudding. She hasn't got any use for weakness or self-pity, but when things are bad . . . gosh! She's too sweet. The chaps simply love her. Of course she talks as though it were all a perfect bore, and she simply didn't know *what* she was doing here anyway! But that's just because she doesn't like slop. I must say, I like Frederica. I think she's grand."

A man groaned horribly in a bed half-way up the ward. Cockie shuddered, reaching under his chair for his hat. "Poor devil—what's wrong with him?"

"He gets attacks of pain," said William cheerfully, with the strange, protective indifference that grows up round the hospital patient, against the sufferings of others. "You get used to it. I used to groan a bit myself, and nobody shed tears over *me*. It's awful at night, though; we had two emergency operations yesterday, and the poor devils kept us awake till morning; however, we've got the day to sleep in if we want to. It's extraordinary how you get acclimatised."

A case was brought back from the theatre, having crossed with the gentleman who had just gone up. Cockie blenched slightly as a sickly wave of anæsthetic wafted itself to his nostrils. The head lolled, scarlet faced, on the rubber sheet, mouth open, eyes closed. In a cocoon of blankets, the limp figure was lifted on to the bed and there left to its own resources, a kidney shaped bowl placed handily at one side. The stretcher was just being wheeled off when one of the green-robed figures suddenly jerked itself away and advancing in a dreadful eddy of ether, cried lustily: "Hallo, Inspector! What ever are you a-doing-of here?"

"Oh, hallo, Miss Woods," said Cockie, faintly.

"Keep an eye on him, will you?" said Woods to William, nodding casually in the direction of the prostrate victim in the opposite bed. "If he tries to sit up or anything, yell to him to lie down, and pipe up for the nurse." She ran off after the departing trolley, crying gaily: "Oi! Wait for me!"

Cockrill was much relieved to find that the patient was not to be left entirely to the limited ministrations of William, for Chalk—or was it Cheese?—emerged from the bunk and stood over him for a few minutes, flexing an apparently boneless arm, before tucking it away under the blankets, and arranging a couple of fresh hot-water bottles in the bed. He sat silent for a moment, staring down into the crown of his hat, trying to formulate a question to put to William; for he was made very anxious by something the boy had said—or not said; and, finally, looked up suddenly with the query on his lips. But it was never made or answered; for William was sitting erect against his pillows with his hand to his mouth, staring into space, and muttering feverishly: "Oh, my God! Where on earth have I heard that voice?"

Chapter VIII

1

GERVASE Eden sat on the great wicker laundry basket in the lobby of the operating theatre, and waited for Major Moon. "Where is the silly old beezer? He said he'd be here at seven. . . ." The swing doors had been hooked back, and through the doorway he kept his eye on the main entrance across the hall.

Woods came out of the theatre and locked the door behind her. She pretended not to notice Gervase, sitting in the half-light smoking his cigarette. The act was over. Freddi was, for some reason, refusing to have anything more to do with him; she had seen nobody since her escape from the gas, but Barnes; and Barney had come back, radiant, from their first interview, and confided to Woody that Frederica had, all on her own initiative, suggested that they should get married very soon. There was no longer any need for Gervase to be distracted; she could lapse back into her former indifference and never bother to speak to him again. . . . But out of the corner of her eye she saw the turn of his head, the line of his thin, angular body, the movement of his nervous fingers as he fumbled his cigarette; and when he said, "Hallo, Woody!" her heart leapt and she said softly: "Hallo, Don Juan!" and went over to him.

"Oh, heavens!" thought Eden, appalled by a note in her voice that he had heard in the suddenly exultant voices of too many women. "Oh, gosh! Don't let *her* start!" He informed her as roughly as he could that she had a dirty mark on her face.

Woody went rather pink. "Oh, Gervase, have I?" She rubbed at it with her handkerchief, standing rather uncertainly before him.

"Yes, you have," he said. "And it looks awful." But it looked very sweet, really, and a little bit pathetic, and he drew her to him and took the handkerchief out of her hand and wiped the mark gently away. "Now you look a clean girl," he said; and he gave her a little shake and added, quite involuntarily: "Oh, Woody—I do like you!"

Woody's heart melted within her. "*Do* you, Gervase?"

"Yes, I do," he said. "You're so. . . ." He broke off and improved the shining hour by improvising: "You're such a good *friend*, Woody. You don't get sentimental and silly and take things too seriously; you can have a little petting party in the evening and just be ordinary again, next day. And if a man kisses you, you don't go off the handle and run round screaming that you've been robbed of something above rubies."

"It would be a bit comic if I did," said Woods dryly; "at this stage of my career."

"And above all, you don't let your emotions get tangled up with just having fun," said Gervase, earnestly, in his gratitude persuading himself that this was really so.

"No, darling," said Woody, and she bent forward and kissed him lightly, so that he should not see the tears in her eyes.

Major Moon appeared at a trot, advancing towards them across the circular hall. "Sorry I'm late; hasn't Esther turned up yet?"

"Here she is now," said Eden, as Esther came in at the main door, pulling off her little round outdoor cap.

She came and joined them. "Did you call me?"

"Yes, child, come here. We wanted to catch you before you went on night duty," said Moon, taking her hand and tucking it warmly into his own. He looked at her with troubled blue eyes. "We have a little bit of news for you that you're not going to like very much . . . no, Woody, you stay, my dear, we're glad to have you. . . . Now, this isn't serious, Esther, and you mustn't upset yourself; but Eden and I have been talking over your young man's fracture, and we don't quite like the way it's going. We think we ought to have him along to the theatre and open up his leg."

She stared at him, horrified. "Oh Major Moon—no!"

"I'm afraid we must, Esther," said Eden definitely. "There's nothing to worry about, ducky. We think there's a bit of pus there, that's all, and it would be better to take out the stitches and drain the wound."

"Do you mean he's getting an infection?"

"Just a spot, Esther, it so often happens; but we can clear it up all right."

Cockrill passed through the hall still bent upon his ceaseless investigations. He saw Woods among the little group, and, recollecting William's half-recognition of her voice, decided to enter into conversation, in the vague hope of surprising something out of her. In the dim light he did not notice the distress upon

Esther's face until it was too late to draw back; Major Moon passed it off with a casual explanation: "She's a little bit upset; we're going to do a small job on her beloved and she doesn't like it; she'll be all right in a minute. . . ."

"It's very silly of me," said Esther, gulping back her tears.

"It's nothing at all to worry about, darling," insisted Woody. "I've seen thousands of them done in the theatre—well, at *least* four or five—and it's quite a small operation, isn't it. Major Moon?"

"It's not the danger; it's just that I—I can't bear to think of him being ill or in pain. . . ."

"He'll be much more comfortable after this, Esther," promised Gervase.

Cockrill had been putting two and two together. "Is it young Will Ferguson that you're talking about? I was down there seeing him this afternoon. . . ."

"Miss Sanson's engaged to him," explained Eden.

Cockrill turned round upon her. "Are you indeed, Esther? I congratulate you; I've known him since he was a boy—he's a very charming fellow."

"He's a darling, Esther," agreed Woods enthusiastically.

She looked up in surprise. "Have you been to see him at last, Woody?"

"Yes, I introduced myself this evening, after operating had finished in the theatre; he's sweet, darling. He told me he'd been having a chat with you, Inspector."

"I was asking him about Higgins," said Cockrill, who did not think that this was the time to ask Woods if William had remembered where he had heard her voice.

"He didn't know Higgins," said Esther. "He was brought in after him."

"Yes, but only because he took longer to get himself dug out. He used to work for Higgins—they'd been through all the blitzes together, and they were sitting talking about the old days, when the bomb hit them."

"Listening to the German radio," said Cockrill.

"Yes, he was telling me about that," said Woody, rather breathlessly. "It was extraordinary how—how the wireless went on and on talking when everything else all round them had been shattered. I mean, a bit off to have to lie pinned down by debris, heroically waiting to be rescued, while Lord Haw-Haw tells you how effete you are!"

"Was it Lord Haw-Haw?" said Cockrill.

"Well, so William says," replied Woody indifferently.

"Those fellows ought to be hamstrung!" exploded Major Moon. "Of all the filthy treachery, I think that is the worst. A good honest spy is a brave man; he's working for his country in the enemy's country, and if his methods aren't very charming, well it doesn't make him any the less a hero, from his own point of view; but to stand safely in Germany and pour out abuse of your own country . . . dis*gus*ting! *Filthy!* I only hope that at the end of the war we really deal with them as they deserve."

"I feel sorry for their relatives and friends," said Eden mildly, "having to sit here and listen to them telling their German lies!"

"Their relations and friends are probably just as bad as they are," said Major Moon roughly. His kind blue eyes had gone stupid with the natural, unthinking welling-up of his disgust and contempt.

"Not necessarily," said Cockie thoughtfully; "but I dare say a good many people in this country would agree with you." There is nothing like just indignation for fostering unreasoning hate.

161

Woods looked at her. "Esther, isn't it time you went on duty, my pet?"

"I suppose it is," said Esther, who had been standing by, taking no part in the conversation. "I'd better go. I—I don't know how I'm going to face William!" She stood for a moment with her head bent, her hands pressed against her forehead.

"We've explained everything to him, my dear," said Major Moon. "He's not worrying a bit; it's only a little thing, nothing to be anxious about."

"Higgins' operation was nothing to be anxious about," said Esther suddenly, dropping her hands and staring at them, white faced, with burning eyes. "But *he* died. Higgins died!"

"But my dear child . . . !"

"I'm afraid," cried Esther. "I'm terrified! Supposing William were to die too?"

"Oh, nonsense, Esther darling," said Woods. "Why should William die? Who on earth would want to kill him?"

"Who would have wanted to kill Higgins?" said Esther.

"Perhaps you would like to get someone else to do the operation, Esther?" suggested Major Moon gently. "Perkins did him originally, of course, but he's on seven days' leave. We could fix up for Jones to do it, or Colonel Greenaway would if you like."

"No, no, Major Moon, of course you must operate; of course you must! Gervase, you'll be assisting, *won't* you?"

"I was supposed to be," said Eden.

"Yes, do; do assist. You must. Please don't think . . . it's awful of me even to seem to suggest that I don't trust you to do the very best for William. I know you will; of course I do. Do forgive me, everybody; it's only that . . . I'm sort of upset. . . . If anything should happen to him . . ." She left them abruptly and ran off to her ward.

"Poor child; she's so much in love," said Major Moon, looking after her.

"Is the operation really nothing serious?" asked Cockrill, deeply interested.

"Not serious at all; it would be if it were left, of course. He's developing osteomyelitis, and we must drain the wound, that's all."

"Osteo-what?" said Cockrill crossly; he hated to be ignorant of what other people clearly understood.

"Osteomyelitis—infection of the bone, Inspector. We take out the stitches and pack the wound open so that the pus can't collect; and cover the whole thing with plaster of Paris, instead of having him strung up to an extension."

"Why is he strung up anyway?" said Cockrill.

"Well, the bones are fractured and they were overlapping; that usually happens. The extension pulls them out so that the broken ends can meet and unite again. I think that about explains it, eh, Eden?"

"A most masterly exposition," said Gervase.

"So you see it's all very simple, Cockrill. There is a little infection, pus is forming, and it mustn't be allowed to collect, so we arrange matters so that it can drain away."

"It may sound simple to you, it's double Dutch to me," said Cockie; he added, gently probing: "I can't even visualise how you go about it."

Major Moon fell innocently into the trap. "Come along to the theatre to-morrow and see for yourself."

Cockie affected great astonishment. "Goodness gracious—could I really?"

"Well, of course; we'll rig you up in a gown and you can stand and look on. You'll probably enjoy it."

Cockrill thought it extremely unlikely that he would enjoy it, but he was anxious, for his own reasons, to get into the theatre, and he said cheerfully: "I'll be there!" and as soon as they had dispersed hurried over to his office to give orders to his men. He had known for some time Who; and now he knew Why; but he could not make an arrest until he knew How. It was taking a risk, but perhaps to-morrow would show.

2

ESTHER had thirty-six hours' leave on the day of William's operation, so as to be ready to switch from night duty to day duty on the following morning. Frederica was by now sufficiently recovered to go back to work. They assembled for one of their rare meals all together, lining up at the serving hatch in a queue of V.A.D.'s.

"*Stew!*" said Frederica.

"What's for pudding?"

"Rice and some rather sordid looking prunes."

Forty girls were already at their lunch, elbow to elbow, round two inadequate tables. Knives screeched against china as they scooped up the thick gravy and scraped it on to their forks, heads poked forward to lessen the distance between their plates and their open mouths. Tongues wagged unceasingly. "Pass the salt, Mabel. Ask Mrs. Brown to shove the bread up this way. . . . I tell you, Simpson, I simply can't swap duty with you. . . ." There seemed no apparent reason why some should be called by their surnames, some by their Christian names, and some with the added Mrs. or Miss. The Commandant sat at their head looking rather forlorn.

"What about going back to quarters?" said Woods.

"Yes, let's. I can't take this."

The cooks obligingly served all their stew on to one plate and the pudding on to another. "You Woodites! Don't you ever eat in the Mess?"

"No, we'd rather go to the parrot house in the zoo; if we can't get that, we go back to our quarters."

"Well, we don't blame you," said the cooks who, by nature of their calling, ate by themselves when the rest had finished.

"Those Woodites are too toffee-nosed for words," agreed the V.A.D.s, closing up the queue after them when they had gone.

Esther and Freddi and Woods did not care two hoots if the V.A.D.s thought them toffee-nosed. They emptied their plate of stew into a saucepan on the gas-stove in their own little house, and heated up the savoury mess. "It looks too revolting, darling, but it smells all right. What shall we do with the prunes?"

"Put them down the huh-ha," said Frederica.

"Now, Freddi, nonsense; you *must* eat them—they're good for you."

"They look like little old, old negro gentlemen," said Esther, holding one up on a fork and making it do a little shuffling dance on the plate.

"If only we had some black treacle to heat them up in!"

"And a dollop of Devonshire cream. . . ."

"Well, we haven't," said Woods cheerfully. "And we're not likely to for another million years. . . ." She was glad that Esther had made the little joke about the black gentlemen, for it showed that she was pulling herself together a bit. She seemed to have the willies about this mere little operation on William.

"Well, work again for me to-night," said Freddi, tucking into the stew. "How are my suffering patients, Esther? Tell me the worst."

"Edwards and Smith have gone out. Johnson's up and that old gall-stones, the one Colonel Greenaway did, is getting up to-morrow . . . what's his name, I never can remember? There's a retention of urine, but perhaps he won't still be retaining it by the time you go on this evening, it'll be an all-time record if he is, that's all I can say; and there's an appendix for to-morrow and a hernia. The two hernias Major Moon did the other day seem to be all right. They had a lot of pain, I think; they're always grumbling, so don't take too much notice. Pop's getting on marvellously—he *is* so sweet; and there's a rather heavenly sailor-with-the-navy-blue-eyes come in for observation, query appendix. . . ."

"And a perfectly di*vine* fractured tib. and fib. in the corner bed," said Woody, laughing.

This was a trifle rash, however, for at mention of William's name Esther's face clouded over; she did not respond, but jumped up from her chair and asked what Freddi had done with the rice.

"It's on the kitchen table. Woody, darling, *need* I eat these dreary prunes?"

"Yes, Freddi, you must; they're good for you. Esther, you've hardly had any of your stew."

"Well, I can't take it, darling; don't badger me."

Barney appeared at the door. "Hallo, my divinities; can I come in?"

"If you think you will ever be able to love Freddi again, after seeing the squalor in which she eats," said Woods.

"I can just about bear it. Would it be a good idea if I took the saucepan off the table for you, before I sat down?"

"Hoi, no, that's our sweet," said Woody, grabbing it.

He sat down on the edge of the bed and Frederica left the table and perched herself on his knee, putting her arms round his neck and rubbing her golden head against his cheek. "*You* won't make me eat prunes when we're married, darling, will you?"

"Not if you ask him like that," said Woody, laughing.

Esther sat at the table pushing the prunes around with her fork. "Are you giving William's anæsthetic this afternoon, Barney?"

"Well, that's what I came to ask you about," said Barney. "Would you like somebody else to do it, Esther? Perkins could give it."

"No, no, of course not; I *want* you to."

"I thought you might prefer it if we didn't have all the original crowd," said Barney carefully.

Esther stopped chivvying the prunes and put down her fork. "Well, Barney, I would have preferred it, in a way, but I couldn't say so, could I? Major Moon and Gervase both offered to arrange for other people to operate, but it seemed so awful to accept. I do genuinely want you to give the anæsthetic, darling. I mean, I know Captain Perkins gives them sometimes, but he's not really an anæsthetist, *is* he, and I'd much rather you did; but the others . . . oh, dear, I know I'm being silly, I know Woody and Frederica think I'm making a fuss, but I can't help it. . . ."

"No, we don't darling; we perfectly understand."

It was possible that Frederica, with that unflurried detachment of hers, "understood," but Woods, though she would not have acknowledged it for the world, was irritated by all this display of nerves and hysteria. She had always thought that Esther tended to dramatise her sorrow and sense of loss at her mother's death, and really it was absurd if she were going to get all intense about William and spoil their happiness by developing an anxiety-complex. Woody's mind worked in a direct, straight-forward line of solid common sense; she made very little allow-ance for superabundance of imagination.

Esther turned upon her sorrowful and reproachful eyes. "I know I'm annoying you, Woody; but if you'd been through what I have. . . ."

Woods was overcome by remorse. "Oh, Esther, sweetie, *don't!* I do understand, honestly I do; and I haven't forgotten a bit about all you've suffered. It's only that it's such a little thing, darling, and it's foolish to get so het up about it and make yourself ill over nothing. You ought to be cheering poor old William up, not going to him with a face like a ghost. . . ."

"I went in and had a look at him this morning," said Barney. "He seemed quite full of beans. Have you seen him, Esther?"

"No, I've only just got up from sleeping-off my night duty. I—I don't seem to want to see him, Barney; I'm afraid of burst-ing into tears or doing something silly."

"Oh, nonsense, ducky, go along and visit him now. He'll be having his pre-operative injection soon, and I expect he's won-dering where on earth you are."

Esther dragged herself to her feet. "Well, all right. I'll see you in the theatre then, Barney?"

"Oh, Esther, you're not coming in?" said Woods.

"Of course," said Esther. "I couldn't let him go all alone. I may not stay while Major Moon's doing him—I can go out to the waiting-room; but I must see him before he goes off. Major Moon won't mind if I come, Barney, will he?"

"Not a bit, I don't suppose," said Barnes. "And if he did, you can wind him round your little finger."

"Yes, I believe the old boy's got quite a crush on her," said

Woods, as Esther departed. "It was that night that she and William fixed things up. I went in afterwards and she was in the bunk with Major Moon, and he was looking at her as though she were made of—of treacle and Devonshire cream," said Woody, laughing, harking back to their supper. "I'm not surprised, because she really did look perfectly lovely that night, all lit up like a Christmas tree. Well, I must push off to my arduous duties and leave you two love-birds alone."

Barney could not appear broken-hearted at this suggestion. He sat on the bed with Frederica held closely in his arms, and thought that he had never been so happy in all his life. Even on the night that she had consented to marry him, she had sent a stab of pain and jealousy through his heart with that odd little, sly little glance at Gervase Eden. But now—she refused to have anything to do with Eden, she had promised to marry him, Barney, as soon as they could arrange the wedding. . . . He took her head in his hands, tilting it back to kiss the long line of her throat. "Oh, Frederica, my little love. . . ." Elusive, detached, inarticulate, it was only in moments such as this that she would ever be entirely his; but now he held her in his arms and kissed her warm throat and the little round chin and the beautiful Burne Jones mouth. "Frederica, I love you, I need you so. . . . My sweet, my adorable, my desirable one. . . ."

Here was language Frederica understood.

Chapter IX

1

WILLIAM was lying on a wheeled stretcher when Cockrill arrived and, losing his way, blundered into the anæsthetic-room. Sergeant Bray was sitting in a corner in a white coat, counting over instruments with an air of deep concentration and apparently only for the pleasure of jumbling them up together and sorting them out again. He favoured the Inspector with a reassuring nod of the head. Cockie cast his hat and mackintosh into a corner and stood rather uncomfortably looking down at the patient. The etiquette of an operating theatre was outside his sphere of experience. William lifted his head from the pillow, smiled wanly and said: "Hallo!"

"Hallo, my boy," said Cockrill.

"Come to see the execution?" mumbled William. His mouth was dry from the pre-operative atropine.

"That's right," said Cockie. On second thoughts, however, this did not seem the most appropriate reply and he added with a rather ghastly cheerfulness: "That's a fine pair of socks you've got!"

William wriggled his feet in their vast white woollen stockings. He was dressed in a grey flannel nightgown and covered with blankets and looked indescribably helpless and pathetic.

Esther came into the room, thrusting her arms into the sleeves of a green surgical gown as she walked, and looking very white and strained. Barnes followed her, also gowned, his mask hanging by its tapes round his neck. He said, smiling: "Hallo, Inspector."

"Major Moon arranged for me to come in and—watch," said Cockie, glancing apologetically at William.

"Yes, he told me; come along and we'll get you fixed up with a gown."

In the washroom was Woods, assisting Major Moon and Theatre Sister to scrub up. Cockrill scoured his nicotined fingers and submitted to having a sort of green nightgown tied on to him and a mask over his mouth and nose. Stumbling slightly over the gown, which was much too long for him, he meandered back to the operating theatre, his bright little eyes peeping over the mask, very bright and alert. Esther came in from the anæsthetic-room; she said, in a low voice: "Thank you for letting the sergeant come up from the ward with him and wait there. . . ."

"William will never be out of his sight or mine," promised Cockrill.

"I can't say 'thank you' enough; I'm being foolish, I know; it's good of you to humour me."

"That's all right; nothing to thank me for," said Cockie brusquely.

"I'm getting them to put out everything fresh," she said, moving restlessly about the big, green, shining room. "Then nothing *can* go wrong." As Woods came in carrying a cylinder of gas, she said irritably: "Do hurry up, Woody. They'll be starting soon and you simply must have everything ready."

"All right, all right," said Woody equably, balancing on one foot to close the door behind her with the other. "I'm coping."

Cockrill relieved her of her burden and held it while she unclipped one half-used cylinder from the anæsthetic trolley and put the new one in and connected up the tubes. He watched her carefully, checking over in his mind the points of Barney's lesson a few days before. Esther said, fidgeting: "Have you opened a new drum, Woody?"

"Yes, Esther, darling, I'm seeing to all that. I promised I would and I will."

"And fresh bundles of swabs."

"Yes, of course, darling; we would in any case."

"And a new bottle of iodine, Woody; open a new bottle. Have you done Barney's trolley?"

"I'm coming to that, Esther," said Woods, her patience fraying a little. "I can't do everything at once."

"What is it you want, Esther?" asked Barnes, coming into the theatre.

"Oh, Barney, I do want to have everything *fresh* on your trolley. I want everything brand new so that it can't possibly have been tampered with. I asked Theatre Sister and she said it would be all right. It doesn't involve very much and the other stuff can be used up afterwards. Of course the instruments come straight out of the steriliser—they must be all right, don't you think so, Barney? Don't you think they must be all right?"

"Yes, of course, Esther."

"And the needles and gut and knives and things are in

antiseptic. . . . It's just the bottles, Barney, and your stuff. You don't mind, *do* you?"

"No, I don't mind in the least, my dear, if it makes you any happier."

"Well, it does. I know I'm foolish," said Esther miserably; "but it just makes me feel better to know that there *can't* be any mistakes."

"I quite understand, Esther. It's perfectly all right with me."

She stood irresolutely beside his trolley, fingering the various bottles and jars. "You won't be using any of these, will you?"

"Not unless anything goes . . . not for the regular anæsthetic." corrected Barney hastily.

"And no ether or chloroform or anything?"

"No, no, just the ordinary gas and oxygen."

Woods came staggering across the theatre with a second cylinder and Barnes helped her to fit it into its holder. "I'm sorry to give you all this extra trouble, Woody," said Esther humbly.

Cockrill watched the tubes fitted up to his own satisfaction. He said suddenly, darting a finger at the three glass jars suspended over the trolley: "These bottles—the gas and oxygen mix in the first one, above the surface of the water, and pass along a single tube to the patient . . . ?"

"That's right," said Barnes.

"Could anything go wrong there? Are we sure this is water in the bottom of the jars?"

"I don't see what else it could be; but we can jolly soon make sure," said Barney, without excitement. He took down the jars and sniffed at them each in turn. "They seem all right; but still, just in case, you could empty them out, Woody, and put fresh water in."

Cockrill satisfied himself that the jars were replaced with

nothing more perilous in them than a little sterile water, and returned to the trolley. He ran over the various points in his mind, trying to eliminate anything irrelevant. "Nothing involved except this one cylinder, black, of nitrous oxide; and this one, black and white, of oxygen. The green cylinder of carbon dioxide in the middle is duly switched off, and so are the spares of gas and oxygen. Everything is connected up properly. The patient has nitrous oxide first and then oxygen as well, and you can judge from the first and third tubes in the clear glass jar over the trolley how much of each he's getting. The gas and oxygen mix in the jar and pass along the single tube to the mask over the patient's face." Put like that, it seemed very simple and straight-forward; he could not see where there could be room for accident. After a moment, however, he said suddenly: "Will you be using this air-way tube?"

"I expect so," said Barnes; "I usually do."

"Didn't you tell me that you dabble the end in lubricant first?"

"Yes, to make it slip into the throat more easily."

"You haven't given us a fresh pot of lubricant, Miss Woods," said Cockie, raising an eyebrow.

Woods came over to the trolley. "No, so I haven't; but surely . . ."

"I said *everything*, Woody," said Esther fretfully.

Woods shrugged her shoulders and went to a cupboard just outside the theatre. "Let's have this pot," suggested Cockrill following her, pointing with a crooked finger at a jar other than that which she was lifting down. "And while we're about it—let's have a different bottle of iodine, shall we, right from the back row. . . ."

Esther put an unsteady hand to the lintel of the door. "Inspector—what are you suggesting?"

"Nothing, nothing, nothing . . ." But he dropped his air of false jollity and said, glaring at them all from under his eyebrows: "We want no clever tricks; easy enough to force a doctored bottle on us, wouldn't it be? Like a conjurer forcing a card. What else have you put out new, Miss Woods?"

"Only the adrenaline," said Woody, rather shaken. "And of course I've opened a fresh drum of dressings and things."

Cockrill pointed to a bottle of adrenaline still in the cupboard. "Well, take this one instead. We needn't trouble about the dressings."

Woody obeyed, but she said doubtfully: "I don't know what on earth you're suggesting, Inspector. After all, only Esther and I knew that we were going to have everything fresh."

"I'm suggesting nothing," said Cockie irritably. "For all you know you've been playing into the murderer's hands, arranging to have everything new." His hand went to his side in search of papers and tobacco, but found no pocket in the green gown; the atmosphere of the theatre, the bright light and the heat, and the knowledge that, though he did not really think that there was serious danger, he was taking a risk with a man's life, made him jumpy and on edge. He wished that they would get on with it.

Major Moon, in khaki shirtsleeves, came in from the washroom. "Will you be starting soon, Barney? Eden's here. I'll begin changing now. Oh, hallo, Inspector; everything all right?"

"Well, it's all *right*," said Cockie grudgingly, "except that I want a cigarette."

"We won't be long now," promised Moon, grinning briefly. "Carry on, Barnes. Esther, my dear, you're not going to stay?"

"No, I'll wait outside, Major Moon, if that's all right with you. Frederica's coming to hold my hand." She smiled at him wanly.

He gave her his gentle smile, and disappeared. Esther went

out to the anæsthetic-room; they could hear her speaking quietly to William, and after a minute Sergeant Bray, in his white
coat, fastened back the doors, and she wheeled the trolley in;
Bray glanced at the Inspector for instructions and, receiving a
jerk of the head, assisted her in lifting the stretcher on to the table; she jerked out the crossbars, and slid away the steel supports.
Woods arranged blankets and cloths. Esther said shakily: "Well,
William, I must go along."

"Yes, darling," said William, essaying a smile.

She seemed unconscious of them all, standing there under the
big, mirror-lined white light, looking down at him; her eyes were
lit by a sort of glory that transfigured the pure, rather colourless
oval beauty of her face. She bent down and kissed him gently on
the lips and walked away, not looking back; and suddenly terror
welled up in Cockie's dry little heart. "Supposing I'm wrong," he
thought. "Supposing I've made a mistake. Supposing I've watched
the wrong person, and all this time somebody else has been working secretly . . . and this boy dies. I ought not to have left the
place unguarded for a minute last night; I should have stayed here
and sent for a man, not gone to fetch one. As it was, there must
have been ten minutes after we stood talking in the lobby outside, when anyone could have slipped in. . . ." On the other hand,
Barnes and Moon had known for some hours, then, that William
was to be operated on next day; and Eden too, probably. Any of
them could have made their dreadful arrangements during the
morning or afternoon, before he, Cockrill, had known. But what
arrangements? He himself had superintended the pre-operative
injection in the ward; he, himself, had chosen the jars and bottles
of anything that might conceivably be used on the patient in the
theatre. The apparatus for anæsthesia was correctly connected

up; and he was satisfied that it would be physically impossible to introduce the wrong gas into any of the cylinders. William had been guarded and watched from the moment he left the ward. It was impossible for anything to go wrong; and yet. . . . He remembered Esther's face as she had kissed her love good-bye; and fear hammered at his heart, driving out reason and responsibility and efficiency, a nameless, uneasy terror of he knew not what. He stared about him at the impersonal, shining room, at the rows of steel instruments, gleaming sadistically, sharpened and hooked and curved to bite into the shrinking flesh; at the writhing red rubber coils of tubing, at the swabs and needles and bundles of sterile gut, at the delicate bubbles playing so innocently up and down the narrow silver tube in the clear glass jar, at all the bright, unfamiliar impediments of surgery; and felt very helpless and very much afraid. There was a little roughness on the palm of his hand; he picked at it nervously with a nicotined fingernail.

Barnes was sitting on his stool, the square of gauze pulled up now, over his mouth and nose, his left hand holding the mask a little away from William's face, the right, passing under the left arm, fiddling with taps and valves. His voice said steadily: "Just breathe normally. Just relax and breathe normally. That's right. No hurry. Just breathe in and out. . . ." Woods stood at the side of the trolley, looked down at the patient quietly. Theatre Sister hovered over her instrument trolley. Eden and Moon came into the theatre pulling on their thin brown gloves, dusted with boracic to a dull grey. William closed lack-lustre eyes and his head fell to one side of the pillow. The line of bubbles increased in the clear glass jar.

Nobody spoke: but outside the theatre they could hear the tap-tap-tap of Frederica's little heels on the stone floor as she joined Esther in the waiting-room. William breathed deeper; his face, at the edges of the rubber mask, was an ugly red. "Is that all right?" asked Cockrill of Barnes, standing behind his shoulder.

"What, his colour? Yes, he's quite normal. It's time for the oxygen." He turned another tap; bubbles appeared at the surface of the water from the third tube in the jar, and crept slowly down. The colour increased and deepened.

"Are you sure he's all right?" said Cockrill in an agony of apprehension, picking nervily at the dryness of his palm.

"Just needs more oxygen," said Barney steadily.

Moon and Eden stood absolutely silent, staring down at the table; Woods' face was lined and heavy; the sister turned back from her instruments to glance at the patient and away again. She was new in the theatre since Sister Bates had died, and the mounting tension of fear and unreason passed her completely by.

The bubbles crept steadily down the third tube, dying away to a pinpoint on the first, as Barnes cut down the gas and poured in more oxygen. A line of sweat appeared across his brow. His face grew suddenly grey. He said in a low voice, but very clearly and distinctly in the silent room: *"My Christ!"* It might have been an oath or it might have been a prayer.

"What's happening?" whispered Moon. "I—I don't like it, Barnes; I don't like his colour . . ."

Eden said urgently, putting out a hand to steady the jerky legs: "He's starting jactitations."

Cockrill could not bear to look. His mind, usually so keen and clear, was a dark confusion of terror and self-questioning and hideous anxiety. He had made an experiment, thinking it was all so safe; had taken a terrible gamble with a man's life; and suddenly everything was going wrong. He jerked out abruptly: "Stop giving the anæsthetic! Don't give him any more!"

179

"I'm not giving him any," said Barnes in a sick voice. "He *must* have oxygen."

Cockrill wiped damp hands on the sides of his gown, fighting down his panic, fighting to regain his ordinary grim composure, and glanced down, unthinking, at the roughness inside the palm. A little black speck.

A little black speck.

The room reeled about him in a swirl of green and silver, with a small black speck growing larger and larger and larger; blotting it out, blotting out sight and sound and sense and reason, muffling his brain in soft dark velvet, hammering at his memory with a drumming, thudding, throbbing insistence . . . a sliver of steel pierced the blackness for a moment, thrust quivering into a bloodstained, torn green gown; his own hands loomed at him out of the mist, pink and clean from the surgeons' washbasin; Woody came staggering towards him, a heavy iron cylinder clasped like a child to her breast . . . and he was on his knees at Barney's side, clawing like a madman at taps and reducing valves. "Cut it off! Cut the oxygen off! Use the spare cylinder . . . the spare cylinder of oxygen . . . give it to him from that . . ." As Barnes took over, brushing his hands aside, he caught up a pair of scissors from the trolley and ran the blunt outside edge down the black and white oxygen tube. A curl of soft black paint peeled away under the steel. Beneath the black was a layer of shiny green.

2

CARBON dioxide. A cylinder identical, but for its colour, with an oxygen cylinder. A colourless, odourless gas. A cylinder of carbon dioxide with a coat of black paint over its green, placed where an oxygen cylinder should be. Nothing to show, no way of telling; nothing but a speck of sticky black paint on a pair of clean hands; on the front of a surgical gown.

Ten minutes later Barney was saying shakily: "All the time I thought I was pouring oxygen into him, it was CO_2!"

"I remember you told me," said Cockrill, mopping his brow, his brown hands very shaky but his eyes bright again and his brain quite cold and clear, "that if it could have been possible for Higgins to have been getting gas and carbon dioxide instead of gas and oxygen, he would have died in very much the same way."

"Of course; asphyxia. He was getting no air."

The terrible colour was fading from William's cheekbones; the jactitations had ceased, the bulging neck muscles relaxed and he began to breathe more normally. They stood motionless gazing down at him; gazing at the livid green scar on the black cylinder. "This doesn't concern you, Sister," said Cockrill going over to the staring woman behind the instrument trolley; "perhaps you'd leave us, would you? And not a word about this outside. Do you hear?" Nobody else moved or spoke. Barnes continued to sit with his right hand heavy on the mask over William's face.

And suddenly Esther was standing in the doorway, with Frederica at her elbow. She looked at their ashen faces, at the quiet form on the table, at the unused instruments and the trolleys pushed aside, and cried in a voice of dreadful despair: "He's dead!"

Woods ran across to her. "No, darling. It's all right. He's safe."

"He's dead," repeated Esther, not even seeing or hearing her, staring straight past her into some private inferno of her own.

Barney looked up for a moment from his work. "No, no, he's perfectly all right, Esther; really he is, he's perfectly all right."

"There has been a little—accident, my dear," said Moon, gently, going over to her and taking her by the arm. "But it's all over now; he's quite all right now."

"An accident?" she said faintly.

"Someone accidentally painted a carbon dioxide cylinder black and white to make it look like oxygen," explained Cockie sweetly.

"Painted. . . . Carbon dioxide. . . ." She looked at him, trembling, but suddenly burst out, turning on him violently: "Inspector Cockrill—*you* did this! You let him in for this! You knew it was going to happen. . . ."

"No, I didn't, Esther," said Cockrill coolly. "I was quite sure it wasn't going to happen. He had to have the operation—that was out of my hands, and I thought an attack might be contemplated; but I'd taken every possible precaution. . . . I didn't think it could be attempted."

"The Inspector saved William's life, Esther," said Major Moon gravely. He moved over and stood beside Cockrill, a little, plump, pink and white old man, looking earnestly into the face of a little, thin, brown one. "You did a marvellous job, Cockie; thank God we had you here."

William breathed steadily and quietly, a million miles away in some dim, dreamless land outside the recollection of man; they talked across him as though he had been a log of wood; but Esther moved over to the table and stood very close to him. Woody said eagerly: "You were terribly quick, Inspector. I saw you suddenly glance at your hand; and it seemed only a second before you had snatched up the spanner and were opening the spare oxygen. You realised it was black paint on your hand, and then . . . ?"

"Well, then, I knew it must be the cylinder," said Cockie

gruffly. "That's all. I hadn't touched anything else since I washed my hands outside; but I did help you carry the cylinder."

"Still, even so . . ."

"And then there was Sister Bates."

"Sister Bates?" they echoed foolishly, gathering round him, all but Barney who continued steadily to tend his patient.

"There were two things that really interested me about the murder of Sister Bates," said Cockrill. "Two things seemed to hold out some sort of clue to what had happened; and they'd both been done after her death."

"She was stabbed a second time," said Woody. This macabre detail seemed always to hold a special fascination for her.

"Exactly," said Cockrill. "And?"

"And her body was rigged up in the mask and gown and boots."

"Precisely," said Cockie.

Frederica had been standing quietly by, making a little Swiss roll of a corner of her starched white apron, and automatically trying to smooth it out again. She said in her rather dense way: "I don't see what anybody could tell from that."

"Anybody who gave it a moment's thought could tell a great deal from it," said Cockrill. While appearing to watch them all, he studied one face in particular. "First of all—to dress her up like that! That was either the act of a lunatic, or it was done for some reason—some reason worth all the risk of spending extra dangerous minutes on the scene of the crime."

"Perhaps this person's a lunatic then," said Freddi, intent on the little roll.

"No," said Cockrill. "The murderer is not a lunatic. I think he has what they call an *idée fixe* on just one subject but in everything else he's as sane as—as you or me." He gave a grim little smile, for in addressing them, he was addressing the murderer. Nobody responded. He continued: "Higgins and William were attacked for the same reason; Frederica because the murderer was afraid of being caught; Sister Bates because she held tangible proof of the murder . . . some proof of the murderer's identity or of how the crime had been committed. There was no secret as to how *she* had died; therefore all the flummery with the mask and gown, and the second stabbing must have been connected, not with her murder, but with this missing 'proof.' That's obvious, isn't it?"

"Clear as daylight," said Eden ironically.

Cockrill caught him suddenly by the shoulder and pushed him in front of the poison cupboard against the wall of the theatre. "Just stand there a minute, Major Eden. That's where Bates was, taking out her 'proof.' The murderer stood here." He went over to the doorway and paused for a moment. "You turn and see me. . . . I take three paces forward. . . ." He raised his hand dramatically poising an imaginary knife. "You stand staring at me, terrified and incredulous . . . and I strike!"

"I think this is horrible," said Esther in a low voice.

"I dare say it was horrible at the time," said Cockie briefly. He turned back to his victim who still stood very much alive, in spite of the blow having been struck, with his back to the poison cupboard. "Now—he's dead. What do I do? Do I snatch the proof out of his hand and clear out? No, I don't. I dress the body up first and lay it out on the table. Major Moon—that wound from the knife: it wouldn't have bled very much?"

"Not externally," said Major Moon.

"And the second wound—it would have had to be made very shortly after death, to have bled at all?"

"Almost immediately."

"Yet there was blood all round the edges of the tear in the gown; that means that the gown was put on almost immediately the girl was dead. It wasn't a clean gown; it had been used before. Miss Woods—where would a soiled gown be kept?"

"In the laundry basket," said Woods; "out in the anteroom, waiting to be collected."

"It would have taken a little time to go and get it then?"

"Yes, a minute or two; and the basket would have been fastened . . . you couldn't get it open all in a second."

"So I should think we might say that the murderer didn't go to the basket for the gown."

"You told us before that the murderer was dressed up in a gown," put in Eden, coming forward from the cupboard. "Perhaps he had also brought a gown along for Sister Bates."

"No, he was wearing a fresh gown and mask from the linen cupboard; we checked that up afterwards. This one was soiled. Besides, I don't think he knew that he was going to need a gown for Sister Bates."

"Well, when did he find out?" said Freddi, impatiently.

"When he saw her standing there with one in her hand," said Cockrill, triumphantly.

There was a startled silence. Woods blurted out at last: "You mean—*that's* what she had hidden away in the poison cupboard? A surgical gown?"

"Your surgical gown, Miss Woods."

"*Mine?*" said Woody stupidly.

"I only saw Sister Bates once, for a few minutes' interview," said Cockie, turning it over in his mind. "I thought she was a foolish creature; but that's a different thing from being a stupid creature. She saw something that day, after Higgins died, that gave her the whole clue to what had happened. . . . I dare say she didn't really believe in it, in her heart; she just played about with the idea, pretending to herself that it meant more than she really believed, pretending it was a story to be stored up, to be trotted out one day when it suited her. . . ."

"Why should it ever have suited her?" said Eden, half-contemptuous, half on the defensive.

"I wonder," said Cockrill, lifting a sardonic eyebrow.

Gervase shrugged his shoulders angrily. "The whole sugges-tion is absurd. How should Bates have noticed anything wrong with the cylinders? She'd have had to see that it had been painted, to understand what had happened. Well, how could she? She wouldn't have been fooling about with it. It isn't the sister's business to deal with the cylinders; the V.A.D. does that. . . . And anyway, after Higgins died, the cylinders must have been practi-cally full; they wouldn't have needed changing. Why should she have been touching them?"

Esther spoke suddenly, quietly, from her place at William's side. She said: "You're wrong, Gervase. Sister Bates could have noticed the cylinder that day. Don't you remember that Woody took Higgins down to the mortuary and left me to clear up for her? I didn't know the routine of course, and Sister Bates helped me. She may easily have touched the cylinders, or even changed them."

"In fact she must have," said Barnes, who had been sitting si-lent all this time. "Otherwise the next patient would have died too." He went a little grey again, at this dreadful possibility.

"So you see!" said Cockie.

"I don't see what it had to do with the gown," insisted Woody, who seemed to take it as a personal affront that her gown should be involved.

"Ah, the gown," said Cockie, rocking gently backwards and forwards from his toes to his heels. "The gown was the clue to it all; the really substantial clue. Miss Sanson has shown us that Sister Bates *was* fussing around in the theatre that morning, after Higgins died; she may have noticed the gown then, or later; we don't know . . . but at any event, she hid it away in the poison cupboard on a shelf that wasn't much used; and when the murderer found her she was standing there by the cupboard with the gown in her hands. He killed her to get it, but having killed her, he couldn't take it away; he couldn't go marching about the hospital with a soiled surgical gown under his arm, without somebody noticing it. He had to leave it in the theatre; and since he had to do that, he had to leave it in such a way that we should not notice it; or noticing it, shouldn't understand its significance. He dressed the body up in it and he added the mask and boots and he laid the poor girl out on the table, to look as though it were some sort of crazy afterthought . . . some sort of rite or ceremonial that only a lunatic would have thought of. . . ."

"Lunatic's the word," broke in Freddi, impatiently. "Who but a lunatic would have killed Bates to get the gown from her and then gone away and left it. It doesn't make sense. I don't believe a word of it." She dismissed the whole business and marched over to Barney, leaning over his shoulder to look with professional interest at William's face. Barney moved the mask away for a moment, to let her see the improvement in colour, and lifted with a delicate third finger, one of the eyelids. "He's doing *fine*," said Frederica, smiling up at Esther reassuringly.

Cockrill entirely ignored this slightly bossy display; but it relieved the tension a little, brought them all down from their high horses of self-defense. Woody smiled indulgently and winked at Gervase; she always adored Freddi when she was showing off. Major Moon pulled off his little, round Chinaman's cap and twiddled it round quite gaily, holding it by its centre. Even Esther faintly smiled. Cockrill brought them all up with a jerk, saying coolly: "And then of course, having laid the body out as we've seen—the murderer stabbed it a second time—through the gown."

Woody recoiled, as ever, from this ugly thought. "But *why*— that's what I just can't see."

"To make us think that the hole in the green gown had been made when the body was stabbed."

They stared at him. "But wasn't it? When was it made then? And why—why was it made? Surely—surely it must have been made by the knife . . . ?"

He picked up a piece of lint, gingerly fished a surgical knife from a tray of instruments in the trolley, and, with a single gesture, thrust it through the lint. It left a tiny, almost imperceptible slit.

"So what?" said Freddi, remaining unimpressed.

"So the hole in the gown was quite a big, jagged hole. It was made—not by the stabbing; but to cut something away."

Freddi had lost all pretence of interest in the patient now. She came forward slowly from the table, fixing the little Inspector with her big grey eyes. "To cut what away? I don't understand. What did he want to cut away from the gown?"

"A smear of black paint," said Cockrill and Eden and Moon and Barney and Esther and Woody, all impatiently.

3

BARNES announced that William might be taken back to his ward. Cockrill summoned sisters and orderlies and despatched him on a wheeled stretcher; he sent for the Matron and the Commanding Officer and talked to them at length—neither of them had felt so young for years. Finally he withdrew to the anæsthetic-room and went into a consultation with Sergeant Bray. "These six people must be guarded night and day; separately or together; they must never be allowed out of our sight. Never mind if they don't like it—all the better in fact. I want a confession. I've got everything but absolute proof and I must have a confession. Nobody can stand this pace for more than a day or two longer; we must break them down."

"Is it safe to leave it, sir? With all that morphia . . . ?"

"There's more morphia than you know, Bray. No, of course it isn't safe; it's very dangerous, but it's all that I can do. I haven't got a shred of proof, that I could make an arrest on, let alone offer to a jury. There's the motive, of course; there's the half-hour unaccounted for on the night that Higgins was brought in; there's that look of astonishment on Bates' face; there's the fantastic reason for Linley's being gassed; there's the wakefulness of certain patients in St. Elizabeth's ward; and finally there's that strange conversation in the lobby outside the theatre last night. Put them together, and the case is as clear as daylight; separate them, and they fall apart in your hands. I've *got* to wait!"

Bray thought it over, pulling the lobe of his ear. "You couldn't work on a process of elimination, sir? For instance, the Linley girl: she didn't know last night that the operation was to be performed on this chap to-day. The theatre's been watched, sir, from ten minutes after that talk in the lobby, to this very moment. She couldn't have got in and painted the cylinder. She *must* be out."

"You're working too fast, Sergeant. Barnes met the girl-friend on his way back to dinner in the Mess, told her what was in the wind and went straight on. She *says* she came over to see Esther Sanson and comfort her, but didn't find her; Woods *says* she looked for her also, but didn't find her and went back to her quarters; Esther *says* that was because she crept away to a dark corner somewhere to get herself back under control before she went on duty, which sounds feasible enough; but you see, this way, none of them has an alibi. Barnes and Eden and Moon, of course, had ample opportunity earlier in the day; they knew all about the suggested operation, naturally, and could have slipped into the theatre . . . it would only have taken a few minutes to coat the thing over with paint. They'd got it all taped; it wasn't the first time. . . ."

"S'awkward, isn't it?" said Sergeant Bray, his ear by now very pink.

It was a full hour since Cockrill had remembered his desire for a cigarette.

Chapter X

1

BARNES and Eden and Moon presented themselves at the cottage that afternoon, for tea. "We thought the band of murderers had better stick together," explained Gervase, sliding a plate of bread and butter from the crook of his arm to the table, and producing a couple of biscuits out of a pocket. "The Mess was sitting around uneasily, jiggling their teaspoons in their saucers and jumping whenever we spoke to them, so we made ourselves scarce. We brought our rations with us." He fished three more biscuits out of another pocket.

"Some rather doubtful sandwiches," said Barney, unwrapping them from the lace paper doyley off a plate.

"And a whole cake," said Major Moon gleefully. "I just picked it up off the table and marched out, and nobody dared to say a word."

Esther lay on the narrow bed in the sitting-room looking very ill; but she smiled gratefully at their rather forced jollity and struggled to her feet. "*I'll* make tea, Woody."

"You'll do nothing of the sort," said Woods, pushing her down again. "Come on, Freddi, we'll cope."

Frederica would rather have stayed perched on the edge of Barney's chair and twiddled his soft, fair hair into two little horns to make him look like Pan; but she trotted off obediently and they could hear her plaintive voice saying: "But I don't know where we *keep* them, darling. . . . But I never can cut it *straight*, Woody. . . ." as Woods clattered about among the cups and saucers and issued instructions. Moon sat down on the edge of the bed beside Esther. "How do you feel, my dear?"

"Oh, I'm all right, Major Moon. I had a bit of a shock, that's all. I—I stood there in the doorway, and you were all so still. . . . You were all standing so still. . . . I knew something must have gone wrong. I thought he was dead . . ." She broke off, leaving her sentence in the air.

"Is it true that Cockrill won't let you see William, Esther?" said Barnes.

"He won't let anybody see him. He told me he was going to have him watched night and day, and that it would be better if none of us went near him, even me. It's all so terrifying, Barney!"

"It's over now, Esther," said Eden soothingly. "Now that he knows how it was done, it won't be long. . . ." But that was not a happy thought either, and he went off on a slightly different tangent. "Anyway, we've all got a holiday. Officer Commanding Surgical Division is taking over all the operating lists for the next few days. . . ." He blew out his cheeks in a lightning sketch of Lieutenant Colonel Greenaway taking over the operating lists with much pomp and ceremony: ". . . and Perkins is giving the anæsthetics. Heaven help the patients, that's all I can say."

"Isn't Colonel Greenaway good, Gervase?"

"Oh, he's all right, I suppose. He's so *slow* he drives you to drink, though. . . . I assisted him in an emergency appendix the other day. . . ." He drifted off into hospital gossip, and they were deep in reminiscence when Woods and Frederica returned with a large, chipped earthenware teapot and an assortment of cups and plates.

"By the way, are *you* being followed about by coppers, too?" asked Woody, dumping a jug of tinned milk on the table and rummaging in a drawer for knives and spoons.

"Yes, a chap came over here with us; he's walking up and down outside, now."

"Poor pet," said Woody. She filled a cup with tea and tinned milk, grudgingly added some sugar, and went out to the back door. "Oi! You—mister! Want a cuppa?" They could hear her assuring him cheerfully that there was no arsenic in it.

"As far as we know," corrected Freddi, under her breath.

Barnes heard her. He said tenderly: "Darling—it isn't getting you down? You're not frightened?"

Frederica was practically incapable of being unnerved. It pleased her, however, to parade his little show of tenderness; to demonstrate to Gervase how very much she and Barney were in love. She was uneasily ashamed of her infatuation for Eden and was now seeking, subconsciously, to throw the onus on to him. She sat on the arm of Barney's chair and allowed herself to be made a fuss of. Esther lay on the narrow bed with Major Moon's hand on her wrist. Woody dispensed tea. Nobody made a fuss of her.

Conversation waxed and waned. How long would their enforced holiday last? How would the theatre get on without Major Moon and Barney and Woods? How could St. Elizabeth's survive without Esther and Freddi? How could the surgical division plod along with nobody left but Greenaway and a general duties officer and the orthopod? But they could not keep away for ever from the subject that was in all their minds, and it was Woods who finally said, breaking in upon an impassioned defence of Chalk and Cheese and how marvellously Esther thought they would manage in the ward: "Well, don't let's talk about inanities any longer. Let's talk about black paint."

Perhaps, after all, it would be rather a relief to talk about the black paint. "It was so incredibly simple," said Barney, still apparently lost in astonishment at the trick that had been played on him. "You can't alter the gas in a cylinder; so you alter the cylinder. The gases are colourless and odourless—in a thousand years one couldn't possibly tell."

"Doesn't carbon dioxide prickle, Barney?"

"If you get a strong enough concentration it does; if you could put your nose right into a bowl of it, you'd get a faint sort of creeping sensation like soda water bubbles; but you don't get it through a mask. I couldn't have got it by sniffing round the trolley. Besides, I never even tried. An oxygen cylinder is an oxygen cylinder; one just doesn't doubt it."

"Methinks the gentleman doth protest too much," said Woody.

"I don't protest at all," said Barnes, not too pleased. "There was not the slightest reason to suppose that Higgins had been murdered; and under the circumstances no anæsthetist in the world would have dreamed of questioning the contents of the cylinders. Even if I'd known he'd been killed, that would have been the last thing that would have occurred to me—or to anyone in my position."

"All right, sweetie, no offence meant," said Woody pacifically.

"Cockrill has been doing experiments," said Major Moon. "He

seems to have proved to his own satisfaction that the cylinder must have been painted well before midnight, on the night before Higgins died, to have allowed it to dry in the time."

"Of course the theatre's hot . . ." said Eden.

"He's allowed for all that. He says definitely about twelve hours. That would bring it to about ten o'clock in the evening, or a bit later."

"Which couldn't be more significant," said Freddi.

"Significant—in what way?"

"Only that it proves all over again that it *must* be one of our lot," said Eden, interpreting Frederica's vague assertion. "At ten o'clock, or even eleven, to be on the safe side, there were definitely only the six of us, and Bates, who could have known that the man was in hospital. . . ."

They knew it; and yet their minds would not accept it; reason told them that one of themselves was a killer but sentiment rebelled against reason. For, after all, *who?* Not dear old Moon. Not Gervase, with his ugly charm, his bright intelligence, his impatient honesty. And, God knew, not Barney! And not Esther, the gentle and dignified, or Freddi the exquisite, or Woody with her big, warm, generous, laughing heart. "What I can't make out," said Eden, drawing their attention away from these painful thoughts, "is how anyone can have worked it out in the time. Dash it all, Higgins was only brought in at about half-past nine. How can the murderer have made up his mind and evolved the whole plan, all in an hour or so? What gave him the idea?"

"Oh, it was the salvage tins, *was*n't it?" said Freddi, as if this must, surely, have been obvious to all.

"The *sal*vage tins? What *are* you talking about?"

"She's talking about Colonel Beaton having had all the rubbish bins repainted," said Esther. "Ever since he came we've been tripping over tins of black and white paint in the hall and the corridors! Of course the murderer noticed one, and it put the idea into his head. He just took a tin and went into the theatre with it, and then put it back where he'd found it."

"Or rather two tins, because, of course, an oxygen cylinder has a white collar, so he must have used black and white. Well, I think that's brilliant of you, Freddi, to have thought of that, really I do!"

"Good gracious, Woody, I thought of it the minute I knew about the paint having been used."

"How could he be certain it would be used on Higgins, though?" said Esther.

Woods took Barney's cup and filled it; she said, standing over the little table with the tea-pot lolling, forgotten, in her hand: "That would be easy. The more you think of it, the more you see how easy it all was—if it came off. Higgins was second on the operating list. The murderer released some of the oxygen out of the cylinder on the trolley, so that there would be just about enough for one more operation—one long operation like a duodenal ulcer; and he knew we'd be bound to put in a fresh cylinder for the next case. Of course the cylinders come up from the Reserve Medical Store; but we have three or four in the storeroom off the theatre according to what sort of list we have for the day; and he simply put the repainted one on the rack so that I would take that next; naturally I'd choose the one nearest to hand."

"How on earth could he know how much oxygen the duodenal ulcer would take?" said Barney. "I'd be very sorry to have to estimate it, myself."

"Well, he made a guess at it then; and it was a jolly good guess because I remember that the oxygen had run right down after the duodenal was finished. That's why I started off on the new cylinder and didn't just switch to the spare. Of course if it was anyone in the theatre, they could have released the rest of the oxygen while nobody was noticing. . . ."

"And we were all in and out of the theatre between the two operations," pointed out Eden.

"Except Frederica," said Barnes.

"Does that make me a non-suspect?" said Freddi. "How lovely!"

"Wouldn't there have been one too many used oxygen cylinders, Woody," said Eden, "and one too few carbon dioxides?"

"Oh, lawks!" said Woods, pop-eyed. "I wonder if there were!"

"You can bet your life there weren't," said Barney, laughing at her startled face. "Cockrill checked the whole lot over next day. I expect a black one had been painted green, to tally."

"But there isn't any green paint anywhere," said Frederica.

"Well, then, the black paint may have been removed, afterwards; before the empties were counted. Easy enough in a theatre where there's lots of acetone and turpentine and things about; and the stuff wouldn't have hardened yet. It was only just dry."

"Not even quite dry," agreed Eden, "since it left a black mark on the front of Woody's overall."

"Wouldn't the turps have taken off the underneath paint as well?"

"No, it's that hard, shiney, baked-on enamel; it may have marked it a little bit, but those cylinders get awfully shabby and knocked about. Nobody would ever notice it."

"Woody, darling, do put down the tea-pot," said Esther, mildly exasperated. "You're baptizing everything with tea."

"So it couldn't have been me, *any*way, Barney, could it?" said Frederica suddenly, having evidently been thinking things over in her mind. "Because all the time the cylinder was being doctored, I was in the ward with my suffering patients."

"Any of the rest of us could have done it, though," said Major Moon reluctantly. "It was such a hell of a night, and nobody would be noticing what anyone else was doing. Woody says she was sitting in the cottage; Esther says she joined her there as soon as she left the ward; Barney was out of the theatre for half an hour or so, soon after Higgins came in, and Eden was doing his night rounds. . . . I was in Reception, but not solidly all the time."

"Any of us could have done the first murder," said Gervase impatiently; "All right, Frederica, not you! And any of us could have killed poor little Bates; but none of us could have tried to kill Freddi with gas, that day. Take me, for example; I couldn't possibly have known that they were short of a shilling; and only anyone who knew that the gas had run out in the meter, could have thought of rigging up the turned-on gas tap and all the rest of it."

There was a short, uncomfortable pause. Everybody remembered that Gervase had been seen coming out of the cottage that morning, and had never acknowledged his presence there; but nobody liked to put it openly into words. He looked round at them with a little, puzzled movement of the eyebrows, but since nobody spoke, he went on: "The same applies for Barney and Moon—they might have done the other things, but they couldn't have tried to kill Freddi. I suppose Esther could have; but it was she who saved Freddi's life; and anyway, she obviously wouldn't have wanted to kill William, later on. As for Woody . . ."

"What about Woody?" asked Woods, as he paused.

He glanced up at her with his quick smile. "Actually you could have done them all," he pointed out, laughing.

"So I could," said Woody equably.

"*Could* you, darling?" said Freddi, staring.

"Well, of course. I was sitting here all alone waiting for Esther to come off St. Elizabeth's while the oxygen cylinder was being got ready for Higgins, so I've got no alibi for that time; in any case, I'd have endless opportunities for mucking about in the theatre by myself. I was alone while Sister Bates was being killed, and I could easily have pretended to 'discover' her after she was dead. I knew all about the gas shortage on the morning that Frederica was put to sleep, and though it's true that I did know Barney was taking her up to town, that day, I might easily have forgotten about that, or thought he would be too late to save her. As for William—well, it would have been money for jam; above all, as I said before, I have lots of time all to myself in the operating theatre—for substituting repainted cylinders and seeing that they don't get used again and things like that. . . ."

"*So* you have," said Frederica.

They glanced at her uneasily, and then at Woody's face, and then at everything or anything in the untidy little room, rather than meet those bright, dark eyes again. Out of a friendly, idle discussion, in mutual confidence, something sharp and ugly had suddenly raised its head. After all, *some*body had committed these crimes; and Gervase had just illustrated that it could be none of the others. A look of incredulous pain crossed the plain, lined face, and was replaced by one of defiant pride. She said harshly:

"And since you all seem so ready to believe that it was me, I'd better give you the motives, too."

Eden flung out a hand. He said sharply: "No, Woody!"

She hesitated for a moment, but took no further notice of him, and said, loudly and crudely: "Higgins and William . . . when they were buried under the debris, during the air-raid—what was the last thing they heard?"

Esther roused herself from a sort of terrified stupor. She said urgently: "Woody darling; don't tell us anything. Don't say anything. Of course we don't believe it was you. Don't say anything you'll be sorry for afterwards. . . ."

Woods was beyond reason. She repeated violently: "What was the last thing they heard?"

"The radio," said Freddi, gazing with uncontrollable curiosity at Woody's face.

"The *Ger*man radio," said Woods. "Don't forget that! The German radio, telling them Goebbel's lies. And Higgins when he was going under the anæsthetic—when he was losing his consciousness, when he was in the same mental condition as he must have been in when the debris was falling on him—he heard my voice, he heard me say something about 'Churchill' as I dare say the radio did then . . . and what did he do? What did he say? Esther, you were there, and you, Barney, and Gervase, and Major Moon—you were all there; what did Higgins say when he heard my voice?"

"He called out that he had heard it somewhere before," said Esther, deliberately quiet and calm.

"William did the same thing afterwards. I passed his bed in the ward and stopped and said something to the Inspector, sitting by his side. I had just brought a case back from the theatre; I was probably smelling of ether—it may have been association of ideas, it may have taken him back to his own operation in the theatre on the night of the blitz when they did his leg, and so back to the time when he lay under the debris listening to the voice . . . it may have been just my voice, but William sat up in bed and called out, like Higgins had: 'Where have I heard it before?' "

"Well, don't be silly, Woody," said Frederica impatiently. "He hadn't heard *you* giving out the German broadcasts, I suppose?"

"She once had a very favourite brother," said Major Moon, softly, and Woody sat down at the cluttered little table and put her head in her arms and burst into tears.

2

ESTHER was up from her bed in a flash, and Frederica off the arm of the chair. "*Dar*ling Woody . . . ! *Sweet*ie pie . . . ! Woody, *don't* cry, darling . . . ! Woody, it's terrible for you, pet, but as if it would make any difference to *us* . . . !" Major Moon broke into their affectionate twitterings, pointing out in his reasonable voice: "This is tragic for you, Woody, my dear; but it needn't have been—your brother—that was talking that night. It might have been Lord Haw-Haw. In fact William said it *was* Lord Haw-Haw. You told us so outside the theatre, last night."

"I asked William to say it," said Woods, not looking up. "I wouldn't go and see him at first, in case he should recognize my voice—my brother and I have a sort of—family likeness; a sort of way of saying things. . . . I forgot all about it when I spoke to Inspector Cockrill on the ward; but after William had recognised me, I went and talked to him. I told him—all this, and I asked him not to give me away."

"You talk as though *you* had done something discreditable, child," said Major Moon.

She lifted her head then and looked at him with her tear-stained eyes. "You're a funny person to talk, Major Moon! It was you who said last night that all such traitors should be hamstrung, and that their relatives and friends were probably just as bad as themselves. . . ."

"You're eye-black's all running, Woody, and you look most pec*u*liar," said Freddi, into the ensuing silence.

Woods got up without a word and blundered out into the kitchen. Eden gave her two minutes and then followed her. She turned away from the cold water tap, holding a wet cloth to her eyes; he smiled at her and took the cloth away and mopped gently at her face with a dry towel. "My poor old Woody," he said, as though he were speaking to a child.

"So now you know my ugly secret, Gervase," said Woody, smiling bleakly.

"You shouldn't have borne this burden all by yourself, my dear; you should have told your friends."

"*Told* you?" cried Woody. "Good God, I'd have done anything to keep it secret!"

"Except murder," suggested Eden, his head on one side.

"That was silly of me," she confessed abruptly. "But for a moment you all looked as though you really thought I had done it. Of course I didn't murder Higgins: he could have given me away and it would all have been horrible and unpleasant and I'd probably have had to leave here. . . . But it wasn't a motive for murder. And even supposing I *had* killed him, and tried to kill William for the same reason—why Freddi?"

"And why Marion Bates?" said Eden.

"Ah, well, Bates was different," said Woody honestly. "Of course I could have got hold of the gown any time without having to kill her for that; but I couldn't get rid of the knowledge in her head. If the paint on my gown had been any proof of my being the murderer, it would have been no use my destroying the gown if the knowledge were still in her head."

"Yes, but—well, all right, pretend that you had to kill her that night. What would you have done then? Just put the gown back in the linen basket; picked off the worst of the paint, perhaps, and put it in with the rest. Only *you* knew how many gowns had been used, how many were to come back clean and all that kind of thing. You could wangle the lists. Was it likely that you were going to spend dangerous minutes dressing her up in the gown, laying her out on the table, adding the boots and the mask to draw attention away from the gown; and stabbing the poor girl a second time, when she was dead . . . when all you had to do was to dispose of the gown in some other way, which you could easily account for—you being the only person, especially now that Sister Bates was dead, who knew anything about the routine? No, no, Woody; you were the very last person of any of us who could be suspected of having killed Bates." He added curiously: "All the same—I *would* like to know what the devil you went to the theatre for that night!"

She propped herself up against the little sink, as she so often stood, legs stretched out before her, ankles crossed. They could hear low voices in the adjoining room. She said, looking into his eyes: "Do you really not know that?"

"Well, of course not," he said blankly.

She faced him squarely. "I thought you had killed Higgins!"

"*I?*" he said incredulously.

She turned away her eyes. "Well, Gervase, I didn't know. I couldn't make up my mind. But if you didn't—why was Marion Bates protecting you?"

"Protecting *me?*"

"Darling, don't go on and on saying 'I?' and 'Me?' and things. Surely you must have known that she'd only hidden her precious proof because she thought it was implicating you?"

"I don't know what you're talking about, Woody," said Eden.

"My dear, that night of the party—she said she knew who'd done the murder; and that she had proof. Well, so she had. Then why hadn't she told the detective? Who was she protecting? Not me, for example! And not Frederica—she had no love for our Freddi! And not Esther, you can bet your life; and why should she go out of her way, make herself accessory after the fact or whatever it's called, to shield Major Moon or Barney? Of course it could only be you. As Inspector Cockrill said, she really only half believed the evidence of her own reason, but she hoarded the 'proof' up so that she could make a scene with you about it one day; and then you were unkind to her on the night of the party and she was angry with you, and decided to give you up to justice! I followed her to the theatre that night to see what she was hiding there."

"You followed her?"

"Oh, not actually. I mean, it wasn't me creeping up the drive after her. I really did wait for you, as I said; and then I decided to go home, but on the way I thought I'd drop in and see what she was up to in the theatre."

"Why on earth?" said Gervase.

Woods fiddled with the tap, running little spurts of water into the sink and turning it off, and running it again. She said, off-handedly: "*I* don't know—just curiosity."

"Why didn't you tell the Inspector all this?" said Eden.

The tap gave an extra big squirt, deluging her sleeve with water. She said, busily mopping her arm: "Oh well, when he talked to us that night—after she was killed, I mean—I saw that it couldn't have been you."

"Why not?" said Eden.

"Because of the look of astonishment on her face when she died. He said that she looked—incredulous."

"So would you, if you saw a masked and gowned figure standing in the doorway at one o'clock in the morning."

"Yes, in any other doorway. But not in the doorway of an operating theatre! You expect to see masked and gowned figures there. You might be surprised, because you didn't think there was anything going on in the theatre, but you wouldn't be as*ton*ished; you wouldn't be in*cred*ulous."

"You would if you realised that this was the murderer."

"Well, she probably did realise that this was the murderer; and that's my point. She was terribly surprised to see who it was."

"You mean . . . ?"

"I mean that she expected it to be you; and if she was astonished, it was because it wasn't."

Eden was silent; after a while he said: "So that convinced you that I wasn't Slayer Eden, the Butcher of Heron's Park?"

"That and—well, next morning it all looked different. It was one thing to have monkeyed about with the anæsthetic in the theatre—or whatever it was that had been done, because of course I didn't know then what had killed Higgins, but quite another to have stabbed poor, silly little Bates; and above all, to have stabbed her the second time, after she was dead. That was so—so cold-blooded and dreadful: I didn't think you could have done a thing like that. Then, afterwards, there was the Freddi affair; and I got all tied up again."

"For heaven's sake, Woody—you didn't think I'd tried to murder Frederica?"

"Well, what were you doing in the cottage that morning, then?" said Woody bluntly.

"In the cottage? Here? That morning? Of course I wasn't. . . ." His face cleared. "Oh, good lord! So I was! At least I wasn't in the cottage at all, actually; but I wanted to speak to Freddi and I watched for her from my window in the Mess; when she didn't appear, I thought I must have missed her—I realised afterwards that she was a bit later than usual because she'd have to have breakfast at the V.A.D. Mess, as the gas had run out in your quarters—anyway, I went to the door, here, and put my head in and called out to see if anyone was in. I didn't get an answer, so I came back to the gate and waited and met her there. I wanted to talk to her about—well, I just wanted to talk to her."

"You must have been very much in love to want to talk to anybody at that hour of the morning," said Woods, with bitter jocularity.

He looked at her, weighing her up, and said, after a moment: "I had some—reparation to make, Woody, I—I like Barney, you know. I think the world of him; and I—well, I lost my head a little a couple of nights before and—and said something to Freddi; and I wished I hadn't. Freddi didn't respond, of course," said Gervase loyally, "but I felt I'd let Barney down. He'd gone off to Heronsford to get his car fixed up and he was taking her to lunch in town, and I thought it would be a marvellous opportunity for them to get really engaged; to buy the ring and all that, you know. It sounds as if I were trying to crash in where angels fear to tread," said Gervase wretchedly; "but I don't mean it like that. I just wanted to apologise to Frederica for having kissed— for having talked to her like I did, and ask her to forget all about it, and say how much I wanted to see her and Barney happy." He broke off miserably.

"In other words you wanted to tell her that you were out of the running, and leave the path clear for Barney," said Woody coolly.

"No, it wasn't that, of *course.* . . ."

"All right, darling, don't bother to put on an act for me. I understand. So then what?"

"Well, then, when Freddi arrived, she wouldn't have anything to do with me anyway; I suppose she'd arrived at the same conclusion as you had, my clever one, and thought I was the big, bad wolf, and she was next on the list."

"It was because of what she overheard between you and Bates, in the bunk," explained Woody. "Bates was threatening you with breach of promise and various other reprisals, and of course Freddi knew Higgins had heard."

"That might have been a motive for my murdering Marion, but hardly for my killing Higgins!"

"Well, our Frederica is not exactly overburdened with the grey matter," said Woody, smiling.

"You all seem to have been very ready to suspect me," said Gervase, bitterly.

"And to protect you," said Woods.

He put his hand under her chin and turned her face so that her eyes met his. She looked plainer than ever, now that the make-up was wiped away by her recent tears; with little smears of mascara still under her eyes, and the crows' feet etched deeply at the outside corners; there was a faint streak of rouge down one cheek. He pulled her to him and held her for a moment close to him, his head thrown back so that he could still look into her eyes. "You're rather a splendid person, aren't you, Woody? All through this hideous time—how loyal you've been!"

"It's easy to be loyal to those you love," said Woody, her shaking hands on his coat sleeves; she felt the twitch of the muscles in his forearms, the almost imperceptible stiffening and drawing away, and added, with hardly a pause: "If you mean that I've been loyal to my brother. . . ."

3

FREDERICA was tired of sitting in the stuffy little room with Esther and Major Moon. She preferred either to be alone with Barney or to have Gervase there to witness their happiness together. She had quite persuaded her blunt little mind that Eden had been madly in love with her and was now being punished for his temerity by the spectacle of her devotion to Barney, whom he would have betrayed; so did she cast out the uncomfortable memory of her own temporary disloyalty to her love. She said restlessly: "Can't we go for a walk or something, darling? It's so fuggy in here."

"I'll take you for a little run in the car," said Barney immediately.

"Oh, yes, that would be heaven!" She jumped down off his knee and wiggled herself into her long, blue coat, pulling the round V.A.D. cap over her springy gold hair.

"You look like something out of an orphanage," said Barney,

laughing at her; "I've never seen anything so pathetic." He hastened to add: "But something quite adorable out of an orphanage!"

Frederica laughed ruefully, rolling up her hair over the edge of the cap, twitching into prominence the scarlet lining of the coat collar. "Well, I *know* it couldn't be more frightful; sometimes one just can't believe it's oneself in this awful scruffy coat, can one, Esther?"

"It seems like another life, that one had nice tailored coats, and silk frocks and funny little hats with flowers and feathers and things; I've forgotten how to put on anything except this wretched little round cap. . . ."

"What a girl does for King and Country," sighed Frederica. She hitched down a respirator case and tin hat from a hook on the door. "I suppose I'd better take the old gas mask and tin hat."

"That's mine, darling," said Esther.

"No, it isn't. Oh well, it may be; we really must mark these new haversacks, Esther, we're always getting them mixed up. However, I can soon tell." She fished in the recesses of the canvas respirator case, and produced a small glass phial with one white tablet in it. "Yes, it is mine, here's my what-not of morphia."

Esther looked shocked. "Freddi—you didn't get some more? I thought Cockie said we were not to have any."

"No, I didn't get any more; I just kept back half I had," said Frederica, smiling coolly. "I produced a quarter of a grain so smartly that he never thought of asking me if that was the lot. Wasn't I clever? Barney was glaring at me, but he didn't dare to give me away, did you, sweetie? He meekly forked out his own two tablets and so did everyone else; but I only gave up one!"

"I don't know how you put up with her, Barnes," said Major

Moon slightly scandalised, but unable to help laughing at her naïve pride in this achievement.

Barnes would willingly have put up with a great deal more from Frederica. "Well, come along, darling."

Freddi picked up the gas mask and tin hat and swung them in her hand, deliberating. "Oh, hell to it! I *can't* be bothered to take them. . . ." She slung them up on the hook again and took his arm and they went out into the wintry afternoon.

They walked in silence for a minute or two, until Barney suddenly stopped. "Does it look rather rotten to go off for a drive and not to ask them to come? It might do Esther good to go out for a bit; she oughtn't really to mug in there, worrying about William."

Freddi knew that if they were alone, Barney would stop the car somewhere, would take her in his arms and kiss and caress her, would tell her that she was lovely and adorable; emotionally inarticulate, these were the only moments when she could express her very real love for him, and these were the moments she craved. She would not, however, deprive Esther of a little pleasure when Esther needed it so much, and she said immediately: "Darling, of course; go and ask them!" and stood and waited for him while he ran back to the house.

Gervase and Woody were still in the kitchen. Esther was vaguely uncomfortable alone with Major Moon, for though he said not a word that could trouble her, nor, since the night of her engagement, had he ever touched her, there was a helpless and hopeless devotion in his eyes that broke her tender heart; and she was thankful for the invitation to go for a drive. There was a general reshuffle in the little room as Eden and Woods, emerging rather constrained from their conversation at the sink, were informed of the plan. Major Moon went off to fetch the men's gas masks from the Mess having apparently rather more conscience in the matter than Frederica. Barney returned to Freddi, who was walking up and down rather impatiently in the cold park. She was pleased at the information that Gervase and Woody were all going to try and squash in. A policeman, however, stopped them at the gates.

"I beg your pardon, sir; was you thinking of going out?"

"We're going for a drive," said Freddi.

"I'm afraid one of us will have to go along of you," said the policeman apologetically.

"Well, you can't," said Freddi calmly. "There won't be room."

"We can't let you go alone, Miss."

"We're not going alone. We're going with four other people."

"Sorry, Miss," said the policeman stolidly.

They returned disconsolately to the cottage, and the first little murmurings of uneasiness began; the first strange sense of being always watched, of being never alone, of being dogged and harried and badgered, that was to drive them to desperation in the next few days; the first creeping faint irritation of the nerves that was to arise to a hideous crescendo in Cockie's process of "breaking the criminal down." They sat about crossly, staring out of the window at a broad back motionless just outside. Freddi said fretfully: "Esther, darling, even *now* you've gone and got our haversacks mixed up again!"

"I haven't. I took mine out and left yours on the hook."

"Well, this is mine on *your* hook."

"What the dickens does it matter, anyway?" said Woods impatiently.

"Well, I'm sure Esther's put mine on *her* hook."

"Oh, for Pete's sake!" said Woody. She got up and went over to the door and took down the respirator case. "You're quite wrong, Freddi; this is Esther's—there isn't any morphia. And here's yours with the bottle in it, so do for goodness' sake stop fussing about it. . . ." She stood with the haversack in one hand and the tiny bottle held out to them in the other.

But the morphia that had been there ten minutes before was gone.

4

THE three men walked slowly back to dinner at the Mess. "I don't like to leave those girls alone there," said Moon, shuffling along in the centre with his eyes on his boots. "One doesn't know. . . . All that morphia."

"Two grains the murderer took from the theatre cupboard. . . ."

"And now he's got two and a quarter; it all adds up."

"Do you think two and a quarter would be fatal, Moon?"

"I suppose it easily might," said Major Moon, shaking his head.

"Surely nobody could possibly want to kill any of those girls, though. . . . But there," said Eden, shrugging his shoulders, "why go over and over it? Somebody tried to kill Frederica without any apparent motive; and if the creature's mad—why not her again, or either of the others. I suppose he *is* mad."

"All murderers are a little mad," said Moon. He added abruptly: "I've felt like a murderer myself, and I know."

Barnes looked at the old man affectionately. He was indeed

old, aged twenty years before his time. "I can't see *you* a murderer, I must say," said Barney, smiling.

Major Moon left them rather abruptly and went on into the Mess. "There goes one at least that's innocent," agreed Eden, looking after him.

"If this were a detective story, he'd be the murderer for a certainty, though," said Barnes. "They always pick on the benevolent elderly gent, because you'll never think it *could* be him!"

"Ah, but nowadays they're more subtle; they know that the reader's wise to that trick and the older and more benevolent a character is, the more he'll be suspected."

"Perhaps it's gone all the way round and come back full cycle," suggested Barney, laughing; "and elderly gents and paralytics in bath chairs are suspects number one all over again because the reader doesn't think the author would be so obvious. Anyway, this isn't a detective story, and it certainly wasn't old Moon."

"So that leaves you and me and the three girls," said Eden, grinning sardonically. "A charming alternative."

Barney jammed his fist deep into the pockets of his British Warm. "Oh, that *must* be rubbish. . . ."

"Cockrill doesn't seem to think so, old boy."

"It's unthinkable," said Barney wretchedly.

"I suppose you'd really like it to be me," said Gervase, watching him half-humorously out of the corner of his eye. "By a process of elimination, I mean. I can't say I wish it was you, Barney; you're the last person I can imagine as an assassin."

"Thanks very much," said Barney. He added, shrugging his shoulders: "Apart from your intuition on the subject, there's the fact that I had no earthly motive for the murders."

"Well, I don't know about that," said Eden, still half-laughing. "What about your discovery by old Higgins as the slayer of his aunt's cousin's sister-in-law's daughter?"

Barney's face changed. He said shortly: "Oh, yes; I heard you were talking to Higgins about that."

"I should say I was. It took me half an hour to convince the old fool that the girl's death was no earthly fault of yours, and that he was going to get himself into a mess if he started uttering libels about a doctor's work. I frightened him out of his wits! I meant to tell you about it afterwards, but that morning the old boy pipped off in the theatre, and I haven't thought of it since."

Barnes looked at him steadily. "Sister Bates had a rather different account of what you said to Higgins."

Gervase looked startled. "Marion Bates? How the hell could she have heard what I said?"

"She was waiting for you outside the ward."

"Well, all the more reason why she couldn't know what I was saying. I hope you didn't take any notice of her tittle-tattle, old boy?"

"Not when I'd thought it over," admitted Barney candidly.

5

A POLICEWOMAN sat up all night by the fire in the downstairs room at the cottage. When Esther, sleepless, got up for some aspirin, she was up the stairs three at a time, and at her side. "Did you want something?"

"I want some aspirin," said Esther faintly, standing at the dressing-table.

"I see. Very well," said the woman. She took the little tube from the drawer, scrutinised it carefully, and grudgingly doled out two tablets; got the water from the tap in the bathroom, and filled a glass. "You have to commit murder to get yourself waited on in the V.A.D.s," said Freddi, watching them from her bed.

"It's for your own safety," said the policewoman resentfully, and marched downstairs again.

Chapter XI

1

THE policewoman's name was Miss Pine. "I don't know about pining—I wish to God she would fade away," said Woody crossly, after a full day spent under this lady's observation. "The only place you're private in, is the huh-ha and even then she rattles at the door and asks if you're all right."

"It's for your own safety," said Frederica, mimicking Miss Pine.

Moon and Eden and Barnes were under the care of a gentleman called P. C. Willing, and it became the preoccupation of what Woody called Lepers' Paradise, to promote a love affair between Miss Pine and P. C. Willing. "But Mr. Willing won't," said Woody plaintively, after a long evening spent in this exercise.

"Darling, your puns couldn't be more nauseating," said Frederica.

They played interminable games of Rummy, coining new rules as they went, and often growing acrimonious over fancied injuries. Miss Pine and P. C. Willing took turn about in watching over these games, and if any party left the group for any purpose whatsoever, solemnly accompanied them; though whether to see that their occasions were lawful or to protect them from sudden attack, nobody could determine. Frederica and Woody took much pleasure in suddenly announcing that they were going to be sick and rushing off in opposite directions for the pleasure of watching the indecision of the guardian as to which to follow, nor did a gentleman ever rise in the middle of a game and announce a necessity to wash his hands, unless poor Miss Pine were in charge. It was pitiful to see her, hanging miserably about outside the gentlemen's cloakroom at the Mess. Reinforcements put an end to these delights; but anyway, they had already begun to pall.

It was now getting seriously on their nerves. You might treat it as a joke, but after all, it was not a joke. The men ate wretchedly in their Mess, conscious of the strenuous efforts of their comrades to "behave as though nothing were wrong"; the girls lived on top of one another in the close little house, making occasional sorties to their own Mess for their rations, dogged by an increasingly obtrusive Miss Pine. "Harass them," had been Cockrill's instructions to Miss Pine and her new colleague Miss Brock. "Never leave them alone for a second. Get on their nerves; drive them to a frenzy." Miss Pine and Miss Brock unconditionally obeyed. Woody made no more puns.

Cockie came down to the cottage on the second evening to prod his victims into a further fever. He felt a brute when he saw the six white faces turned towards him, lit for a moment with hope, falling back, at sight of his grim face, into grey despair; haggard with the strain of keeping back their resentment and irritation, of trying not to visit it on each other, their fellow innocents. . . . Innocents! Ever there, doubt ravaged them.

218

They looked at each other, uneasily and unhappily. *Some*one had committed the murders. *Some*one must be guilty. They formed into changing camps . . . only faintly inimical, only vaguely suspicious, only unspokenly resentful or irritable or cross. But hostile. Freddi showed off before Gervase, Woody grew annoyed with them both, Barnes was hurt, Gervase himself was not impressed and anything but pleased. Esther was white and on edge; Moon irritated them all with his dotard devotion, following her every movement with dog-like, sad blue eyes. What had seemed to them a rather touching affection, now appeared just the Indian Summer of a doddering old man. They greeted Cockrill with voluble complaint.

"And if you tell us that it's for our own safety," said Frederica, "we shall throw things."

"Well, it *is*; for five of you," said Cockie, rocking gently with his back to the fireplace, his eyes on their twitching hands.

Frederica always rose to Cockrill's baits. She said, not stopping to think: "And what about the sixth?"

"That's who I'm protecting you from," said Cockie, grinning horribly.

Eden was perfectly aware that the Inspector was trying to goad them into carelessness; but his nerves reacted independently of his intelligence and he burst out testily: "Well, why the hell don't you pick out your murderer and arrest him?"

"Don't worry," said Cockrill equably. "I will."

"I can't see what you're waiting for," said Barnes.

"I'm waiting for him to give himself away."

Even when you were innocent, it was dreadful to be watched like this; to be driven into saying and doing things beyond your own control; to have your behaviour studied as though you were a guinea-pig inoculated with some strange disease and reacting willy-nilly to expectation. Even when you were innocent. The guilty sat with blenching knuckles tightening on the covers of a book; and blurted out, despairingly: "But supposing he doesn't give himself away? Supposing it goes on and on and on? How long have we got to endure this?"

"I've no idea," said Cockrill, apparently all ready to lay siege for months.

"You can't keep us here for ever," cried Major Moon.

"I won't have to," said Cockie, coolly self-confident.

Yet another day passed. The O.C. Surgical Division laboured through the operating lists. Perkins gave blameless anæsthetics, Theatre Sister retailed for the thousandth time the drama of William's collapse. Chalk and Cheese fell gladly upon a deserted William and ministered to him; a friendship of fully three months' duration, foundered upon the rocks of his alternating favours; they vied with each other in their knowledge and appreciation of beer. Esther held occasional miserable interviews with him, Miss Pine or Miss Brock, vigilant at their elbows. The leg had finally been operated on by Colonel Greenaway and was, contrary to all uncharitable expectation, progressing perfectly well. A garbled version had been given to William of his unfavourable reaction to the first anæsthetic.

Another day passed.

There was an air-raid that night. Provision had been made for this eventuality, and the three girls found themselves imprisoned in a small Anderson shelter with Miss Pine. They sat huddled each in a corner, on the narrow wooden seats, unable to stretch out their legs without inconveniencing their neighbours, unable to sleep, almost unable to breathe. Miss Pine was on night duty and, required to keep awake, regaled them with improbable bomb stories. A man who was a cousin of a gentleman friend of hers, well, not exactly a cousin but a relation by marriage, sort of cousin-in-law she supposed they would call it, had been thrown right into a vat of molten lead at a printing press, and the corpse emerged encased in metal quite like a knight in armour, if they knew what she meant. She had always heard that if you popped your finger very quickly into a thing of lead like that, it didn't hurt at all, but evidently this could not apply if you put more than your finger in, for this poor gentleman, well, really, they had had to bury him just as he was, metal and all, though they did all they could to try and hammer it off, more for salvage than anything else she supposed. Another case she knew of, well, not exactly *knew* of, but she'd heard on absolutely unimpeachable authority . . .

A bomb fell very close. Miss Pine flung herself into a crouching huddle at their feet. The three girls sat perfectly still. "We're *trained* to throw ourselves flat," said Miss Pine, scrambling back to her corner, flushed with illogical shame.

"How nice," said Frederica, yanking back the sadly disorganised rugs.

Their backs were aching, their knees were stiff, their necks were all of a sudden too slender to support for a moment longer the weight of their lolling heads. "I think we'd better make a pact not to say another *word*," suggested Woody, with laborious tact, "and try and get some sleep." Miss Pine agreed heartily. Nobody else had spoken for the past hour.

The bombers were over their heads again; they could hear the monotonous drm-drm, drm-drm of their engines; they could hear the muffled reverberations of far-off guns, the sharp voices of the men in a neighbouring field, giving the orders to fire.

There was a crack and a crash and a loud reverberation of thunder. "That was a near one!" cried Miss Pine.

"It was a gun," said Freddi.

"My dear, do you think I don't know a gun from a *bomb?* After all the bombs *I've* heard! I remember one evening, patrolling the Heronswater Road . . ."

"Woody," said Esther in a low voice, "I think I'm going mad."

Woods put a hand out and touched her, gently and reassuringly, in the dark. She said, immediately: "Miss Pine, I honestly think we ought to stop talking and try to get some sleep."

"Just what I was thinking myself," cried Miss Pine. A gun crashed in a nearby field and she added automatically: "*That* was a near one!"

2

THE three men, who would infinitely have preferred to face the bombs and remain in their comfortable beds, slept on straw palliasses in the basement of the Officers' Mess. P. C. Willing spoke not a word all night. He just sat and sucked his teeth.

3

IT WOULD have been a relief if, when they all met sick and heavy-eyed after breakfast next morning, they could have let off a little steam by comparing notes; but now Miss Brock was in attendance and a gentleman called Mr. Chinn. Miss Brock was dreadfully bright; she had moreover seized upon one of Frederica's little mannerisms and she used it unstintingly. "I couldn't be more sorry," cried Miss Brock, refusing permission for Barney and Freddi to go for a stroll apart from the rest; and, "I couldn't be more grateful," she assured them when they apathetically fell into line with her commands.

"You want to badger 'em a bit more," insisted P. C. Chinn, drawing her apart. "The Inspector won't like it if he hears you being so chummy like."

"I couldn't care less," said Miss Brock, definitely.

Three days and three nights of it; of Miss Pine talking, of Miss Brock sparkling, of P. C. Willing sucking his teeth. Not a moment of privacy, not a moment to relax in, to speak openly, to speak confidentially. . . . Frederica bore it best, for it was her nature to be placid and self-dependent, and she had, moreover, the glorious power to be mildly rude to their tormentors. Eden was sarcastic, but his shafts flashed over their heads and left him impotently fretting. Moon was too kind, Barney too courteous, Esther too gentle and Woody too depressingly conscious that their guardians were doing no more than their duty, to allow them to seek relief in incivility. And all the time, in the background, Cockrill worked unceasingly to track down all he needed—proof!

On the third day, he put a pair of handcuffs into his pocket, demanded the use of the operating theatre for the very last time, and there assembled his victims. "The time has arrived to strike," he said to Sergeant Bray, as they stood waiting under the now fa-miliar central light, in the hot, green room. "And this is the place for it; we want a bit of atmosphere . . . the spot where the victims died and all that nonsense. Last night's air-raid was a blessing from heaven; they've hardly had a wink of sleep in the last three nights, and they're all at the end of their tethers. The murderer is going to crack to-day, or I'll throw up the case." He said impa-tiently: "What are you grinning at?"

"It's the first time I ever 'eard an air-raid called a blessing from 'eaven, sir," said Sergeant Bray, apologetically covering up his mouth with a large, red hand. Like many another, impervious to greater dangers, his stomach turned to warm water at the sound of a falling bomb.

The hospital stayed for a moment its work of mercy to look without mercy upon the six poor lepers being driven across the grounds and into the theatre. "I am a fugitive from a chain gang!" said Woody, dodging behind a bush and being chased out again by Miss Brock, who laughed gaily but laughed alone. From the tall windows of the wards, patients in their blue suits stared down; here and there a white veil appeared and stayed for a minute or two before virtuously driving them away. An orderly wheeling a stretcher down to the emergency theatre (grudgingly opened up to give Cockrill the freedom of the theatre proper) paused to look back; even the patient peered out from his blankets and shawls and forgot for a moment the sickening fear of his journey into the unknown, of the smell of the ether and the glimpses of tapered steel, the hot, slow, sliding of the hypodermic needle into reluctant flesh. . . .

Cockrill laid the handcuffs quite openly on the operating table beside him, but did not refer to them by so much as a glance. They stood in a shuffling line, with the great white light beating down on them remorselessly on every change of expression, on every line and shadow, on every twitch of exasperated nerves. Six worn out, unhappy, exhausted people, and one of them a murderer. Cockrill began.

4

He began very mildly, just talking to them. He leaned back against the operating table and jingled the money in his pocket; now and again he picked up the handcuffs, absent-mindedly, and jingled them instead. He talked about Higgins and the night he had been brought in, of the next day when he had died. "Just be Higgins for a moment, for me, will you, Captain Barnes? Just lie on the table here, and I'll put the mask over your face. . . . You'd be standing here, Major Moon, and you here, Major Eden? And Miss Woods and Miss Sanson were at the foot of the table, watching him die. Miss Linley—you weren't here to see that, *were* you? You were over in the cottage, asleep in bed?"

"Yes, I was," said Frederica belligerently, for everything sounded like an accusation the way Inspector Cockrill was saying it.

"That's right. You'd only seen him for a minute, in the central hall, while he was being brought to the theatre, when you leaned over him and spoke to Esther Sanson, half an hour before he died. . . ."

It was strange and horrible to Barney to be lying on the table with the rubber mask over his face—held even lightly, over his face. The smell of the rubber, though familiar, was heavy and sickening. He felt stupefied by it, and said, pushing Cockrill's hand away: "You haven't got any gas turned on, have you?"

"Of course not," said Cockrill innocently.

Certainly the water in the bottle was quiet. He kept his eyes on it, but could not rid himself of the panicky dread that he was getting at least a little gas through the mask. He was shaking all over when at last Cockrill let him get up. Frederica stood shakily beside him with huge, grey, frightened eyes.

Cockrill passed on from Higgins to Sister Bates. "She looked so amazed! As if she'd seen something she simply couldn't believe. What do you suppose that was?"

"I *know* what it was," said Woody. She advanced her theory about Gervase Eden, but it did not seem so sane and confident now. Cockrill looked at her with interest from under his shaggy brows. "Oh so you had all that worked out, did you? It has only one snag, Miss Woods; how could Bates have known the masked figure wasn't Eden?"

"How could she have known? She could see, couldn't she?"

"She could see a masked figure."

"Oh, for Pete's sake," cried Woody, "don't let's have that masked figure stuff. Of course she could tell who it was. You always can—you can tell—well, *I* don't know, by the way people walk, by their gestures. . . ."

"But if the murderer was standing in the doorway?"

"Well, I bet she could have told," said Woody stubbornly.

"Let's try," said Cockrill. He chivvied the others into the washroom and mumbled instructions. A figure appeared suddenly, standing stock still at the theatre door. Woody opened her mouth to say that it was Gervase, but closed it again, for it was difficult to judge the height and it might have been Barnes; and then again you really couldn't tell whether it was a man or a woman, and Esther was very much the same height as Barnes. The figure walked forwards slowly, and still she could not be sure. The eyes, which might have decided her, were downcast. She thought it was Gervase; she was sure it was Gervase.

"Say what I told you," said Cockrill, and the figure said: "What have you got there?"

It was strangely moving; strangely uncanny. She knew that it was only one of her friends, dressed up, and yet she could not remain quite calm. The voice was muffled by the mask, muffled by the pounding of her own, overexcited heart. She thought it was Gervase; but it might have been Barney. She said, "It's you, Gervase!" but added honestly, as he pulled off the mask: "I only just knew."

"And you had time to think," said Cockrill, standing in the doorway, looking pleased. "What's more you weren't in a state of terror. Sister Bates was, poor girl."

They all had a dreadful vision of her crouching there, poor silly, pretty little Bates, hugging the stained gown to her breast, staring at her murderer with astonished, wide blue eyes, trembling still from her panic-stricken scuttle up the drive; of the green-gowned figure, the knife in its upraised hand. Woody said, in a strangled voice: "Twice! He stabbed her twice. He stuck the knife into her after she was dead . . ." and went and sat down, trembling, on a theatre stool. Barney pulled up another and sat down beside her. "Don't let it get you down, Woody. He's playing with us like a cat with a lot of mice."

"The big cheese," said Woody, managing a shaky smile.

"You look awfully green, ducky."

"You aren't bearing up so terribly well yourself," said Woods, as though this were an accusation.

"That business of making me lie on the table—does he think *I* poured CO_2 down the poor chap's throat?"

"Well, you did actually, didn't you? I mean, you didn't know you were doing it of course. . . ."

Eden paced restlessly up and down the theatre. "Why the hell should he pick on me to dress up in the gown? Did Woody give him some idea or other, blundering in with her theories? Why *me?* What did he think he was proving?" He wore his customary air of slightly exasperated humour, but his hands were not quiet for a moment.

Freddi came over to him. "Do keep still, Gervase, you're getting on my nerves."

"I didn't know you had any nerves," said Eden, for Frederica's placidity had sorely tried him in the last three maddening days.

"Well, I have, and they're somewhat shaken up this morning; what did he mean by saying in that phoney voice that I had talked to Higgins just before he died?"

"Well, so you had, hadn't you?"

"I spoke to Esther while she was wheeling him to the theatre. I just asked Higgins how he felt or something. There was nothing to it."

"Well, all right, then; you haven't got anything to worry about."

"He said it in such a funny *voice*," insisted Frederica, jerking nervously at her tie.

Cockrill's funny voice had meanwhile succeeded in reducing Esther to the point of collapse. The theatre was desperately hot and stuffy and there was no window. She said faintly: "I simply must have some air."

Cockrill indicated the open door of the anæsthetic-room. "Go and sit down for a minute." He pushed the door wide open so that he could watch her while she flung up the window and stood drinking in great gulps of the cold outside air. Woody made a movement to go to her, but his eyes said: "No. Stay here." He turned his attention to Major Moon.

Major Moon was not very easy to ruffle. There seemed to be a settled melancholy upon him that was far removed from panic or even unease. He kept his troubled eyes upon Esther as she stood at the window. Cockrill said at last, irritated: "It's all right. She won't run away. It's barred."

It's barred! They all looked up, shuddering, at the crisscrossed, heavy iron. Would one of them be thus caged in for ever, when this interminable scene came at last to an end? Would one of them spend the rest of his life behind bars—the rest of his life, his short life, until the day when he was taken away to a place appointed, and there hanged by the neck. . . . Freddi's lovely neck, or Esther's, so long and slender, or Woody's where the deepening "bracelets" gave away her age? Or Major Moon's pink and chubby throat, or Eden's thin one, or Barney's where the little golden hairs grew low at the nape of the neck? Cockrill interrupted their thoughts. He held out his hand suddenly and in it was a tiny glass bottle. "Have you ever seen this before?"

"It's mine," said Frederica. "It's where I used to keep my morphia."

"The morphia you didn't give up to me?"

"Yes," said Freddi sullenly.

"And where is that morphia now?"

"It was stolen," said Freddi, still sullenly. "It was taken out of my haversack the other day."

"Who stole it?"

"I don't know. Anyone might have. We were all in and out of the room."

"Anyone?" said Cockrill.

"Any of us six," corrected Frederica miserably.

There was a frozen silence. Cockrill again broke the tension. He turned and swooped suddenly upon something which he had left in a heap in a corner of the theatre. "Now, Major Moon—have you ever seen this before?"

And suddenly the old man's face was pink and chubby no longer, but a dreadful haggard grey; his hands trembled and his childish blue eyes were full of a stupid wonder. He stammered as though he hardly understood what was said to him: "It's my old tweed coat."

"Which you put on every morning after you run round the grounds? You leave it under a tree and just slip into it while you walk across the main road to the Mess? Is that right?"

"Yes, that's right," mumbled Major Moon.

Cockrill slid a hand into each of the pockets; he placed on the operating table, side by side, a handkerchief, a stub of pencil, a couple of old letters and—two or three coins. "So you *do* carry money, Major Moon, when you run round the grounds?"

From the window of the anæsthetic-room, Esther swung slowly round and stood staring at them. Moon said, mumbling desperately: "Are you trying to suggest that it was I who gassed Frederica?"

Cockrill picked up the handcuffs. He did not reply.

"But why?" cried Major Moon suddenly, and his voice rose almost to a scream, and he moved across the theatre, crabwise, his eyes fixed on Cockrill's hands. "Why should I? What harm had she ever done me?"

"She had it in her power to do you harm," said Cockrill, standing still, following him round with his eyes. "She had it in her power to tell us something—if only she had thought of it. You wanted to silence her before she should begin to guess. . . ."

Frederica stood, open-mouthed with astonishment. "I? What could I have possibly told about him? What did I know about him? What could I have guessed?"

"His child was killed by a man on a bicycle," said Cockrill, his eyes on the old man, now standing mumbling foolishly at the door of the anæsthetic-room. He added, his voice loud and harsh, with a sort of rising triumph ringing through his tones: "You could have guessed the colour of his bicycle!"

"His bicycle?" said Frederica stupidly. "His *bi*cycle? What *was* the colour of his bicycle?"

Esther moved slowly forward from the window of the other room; in another moment she would have spoken, but Moon cried: "No, no! Don't say it. Don't tell them!" and his blue eyes blazed into hers in an agony of supplication, fear and pain. Into the ensuing silence, Cockrill's voice fell like a cold pebble into a sun-drenched pool. He said: "It was a red bicycle."

A red bicycle.

A postman's bicycle.

At that moment Major Moon sprang.

5

Cockrill had been waiting for something, but not for this. As he reached the door of the anæsthetic-room, the key turned in the lock, and he heard the bolts being shot. Esther's voice cried suddenly, filled with terror: "No! *No!* NO!"

"I must do it, Esther," said the old voice, gentle and mumbling. "I must do it. I can't help myself. . . ."

Cockrill battered with small brown hands at the door. "Major Moon! Moon! Open the door!"

Woody screamed, rattling at the handle: "Esther, open the door! Get to the door and open it . . . !"

"The window!" cried Gervase.

"It's barred," said Cockrill.

"Well—my God, there's the other door! Perhaps he's left the other door unlocked!" They were out of the theatre almost as he spoke.

Frederica dropped on to her knees at the foot of the door, prodding through the keyhole with a probe to force out the key. She whispered in a voice of sick horror, peering through the aperture: "He's going across the room towards her. . . . She's standing with her back to the window, with her arms flung out, beseeching him. . . . He's got—oh, Woody, he's got a hypodermic in his hand. . . ."

He had forgotten the second door. Cockrill, bursting in with Barnes and Eden and Sergeant Bray at his heels, flung himself across the little room and, with all his wiry strength, tore the syringe out of the old man's shaking hand. It fell to the floor with a little tinkling crash, and the fluid ran, thin and pale, across the tile. "Thank God we were in time," said Cockrill, staring down at it.

"Thank God," echoed Frederica and Woody, crowding into the doorway after them; and Esther, still standing with her back to the window, arms outstretched, crucified against the cold winter sunlight, said with shining eyes: "Thank God! Thank *God!*" Shrinking away into a corner, trembling horribly, Major Moon also mumbled, "Thank God!" to himself; the tears ran unchecked down his pink and white wrinkled old cheeks, and his witless blue eyes were fixed despairingly on her flushed face.

Cockrill put his hand in his pocket and drew out the handcuffs; and she dropped her arms slowly and came forward smiling a little, quite gaily, and held out her wrists.

Chapter XII

1

COCKRILL slid the steel rings over the narrow hands and clicked-to the catches. He said, turning away his head: "Esther Sanson, I am arresting you for the murder of Joseph Higgins and Marion Bates; and for the attempted murder of William Ferguson; and for causing grievous bodily harm to Frederica Linley. You know that anything you say will be taken down and may be used in evidence . . ."

Esther acceded to it all quite quietly. To their wordless astonishment, to Woody's noisy protestations, she responded only with a strange little smile. Her eyes were bright and tearless, there was unwonted colour in her cheeks; she seemed lit from within as she had been on the night that William had told her of his love. It was unendurable to see her standing there, so straight and slim, so lovely, so—so gay, with the ugly bracelets over her slender wrists. Into the terrible silence Woody cried: "Esther, say it isn't true! Say this isn't true! I can't bear it, Esther; tell us it wasn't you . . . !"

"Oh, but it was me, Woody," said Esther, and turned upon her shining bright brown eyes. She said to Cockrill, smiling at him: "*You* knew, Cockie, didn't you?"

"Yes," said Cockrill. "I knew." He added slowly: "I knew almost from the beginning, but not early enough to prevent Bates being killed. After I understood about the cylinder, of course, I was certain; but I still had no proof."

"It was bad about Bates," said Esther. She passed her tongue over her lips and gave a little shudder. "You—you knew so much about it, Cockie. It was horrible and uncanny the way you kept describing it all, as though you had been there and seen it done. No wonder I had hysterics that night, just afterwards, when you questioned us; Woody explained it all away next morning, but I thought at the time that you must have been watching me . . . that you were stringing me along."

"I wasn't certain," said Cockrill. "It was her look of astonishment that gave me the first clue. She was expecting—if she was expecting anyone—Eden. Well, what told her in those few moments that it wasn't Eden? She couldn't have recognised the figure; she couldn't have recognised the voice . . . supposing it had been Barnes or Major Moon; she would have assumed it was Eden speaking."

"Only it was a woman's voice," suggested Esther, still faintly smiling.

"Yes. It was a woman's voice. There was only one thing that, in that brief moment, could have made her look so amazed and incredulous; the figure that she thought was Eden, stepped forward and spoke with a woman's voice."

Woody looked up at her piteously, with streaming eyes. "Oh,

Esther . . . how could you have *killed* her? How could you have *stabbed* her? And the second time . . . ?"

"Yes, that was bad," said Esther again, but she spoke with a sort of light-hearted carelessness, a sort of offhand irresponsibility. "Higgins was different, of course; he had to die. It was justice. And William, too, when I knew about him. But Sister Bates knew too much; and I couldn't let her speak. I should have been found out and punished—I should have been punished for doing what I knew was right. I couldn't allow that; it would have—sort of cancelled it out. I had to kill her." She said to Cockrill: "I knew it would be fatal if you discovered about the paint. I had to prevent her from showing you the gown."

Gervase Eden was recovering from the shock. He said, in his quick way: "Did you have to kill the girl, Esther, to prevent them knowing about the paint? It couldn't have told them who altered the cylinder?"

"It could tell them who hadn't," said Esther. "For the paint to be dry, it would have had to be put on at least the night before the cylinder was used. About ten o'clock, the Inspector says. But at ten o'clock that night nobody in this hospital knew who Higgins was."

"Except you," said Cockrill.

"Except me. We didn't get his name until the next morning. Gervase saw him, of course, and any of the others might have seen him before he was brought into the ward; but they couldn't have recognised him. I didn't recognise him myself." She played with them for a moment, deliberately holding their attention, tantalising them; it was almost as though she were enjoying herself, but at last she added softly: "Until I washed his face!"

2

"He was covered with dust and grime," said Frederica, her eyes widening with comprehension. "He looked like—you couldn't have told who he was." She insisted to the others, as though proof were necessary. "It's true. You couldn't have told *who* he was."

"But Esther cleaned away the dirt," said Cockrill, "and then she knew. None of you saw him after that until the next morning, when it would have been too late to have doctored the cylinder."

"I saw him," said Frederica. "I looked after him during the rest of the night."

"Yes, but in all that time you never left the ward; you went out for twenty minutes to get your supper, but you didn't leave it afterwards; and that was before you could have recognised who he was."

"And Esther . . . ?"

"Esther left the ward at twenty minutes past ten; half an hour later she was only just joining Miss Woods at your quarters. It takes about five minutes to walk across the park." He added, turning to her: "You made a slip when you mentioned to your William that you had seen him being wheeled along to the ward that night; that was thirty-five minutes after you were supposed to have gone to your cottage. I'm sorry, Esther. This is a terrible thing for me to have to do. I knew your mother, and I remember you when you were a little girl; but I must ask you to come along with me."

"Can I have some water first?" she said.

He glanced at her suspiciously, but it was clear that the first flush of strength and excitement was fast ebbing away; her lips were dry and the colour fading from her cheeks. Woody fetched water from the tap, and she drank it gratefully and sank on to a stool, leaning back with a gesture of terrible weariness against the wall. "Just a minute, Inspector, while I pull myself together." She added, with a last sparkle of laughter in her voice: "You can while away the time explaining to them all how clever you've been."

He saw that she would not be fit to walk very far. "Order a car," he said to Sergeant Bray who had stood all this time very pink and excited in the background.

While they waited, Freddi said, as though struck suddenly by an idea: "But Esther—do you mean to say that it was you who tried to kill *me?*" and stared at her as though she could not believe her wits.

There was no more laughter now. She lifted sad, heavy, eyes and held out her manacled hands in a little gesture that immediately she withdrew. "Oh, Freddi, darling . . . darling little Freddi—not to kill you; not to *kill* you! And after all it was I who dragged you into the fresh air. I wouldn't have let you die. . . ."

"She had to have morphia," said Cockrill, since explanations appeared to be unavoidable. "She wanted you out of the way. She didn't want to harm you, only to get you out of the way for a day or two. . . ."

"For a night or two," corrected Esther gently.

"For a night or two. She wanted to go on night duty in the ward."

"They give out so much more morphia at night," said Esther dreamily.

"No wonder the patients on St. Elizabeth's were restless and in pain," said Cockrill. "That first night, after she knew who Higgins was—she kept back his morphia. I think she only wanted to torment him, to have him suffer, but it gave her a quarter of a grain. When she killed Sister Bates, she found more in the poison cupboard. She took that too. She was in danger of being found out, by then, and she wanted it for herself—in case of need. That was two grains and a quarter; but she couldn't be certain that that would be enough; she had to have more. She knew only one way to collect it, and that was to withhold it from the patients. Poor devils—she withheld the doses prescribed for the men on the ward." He pointed with the toe of his shoe to the pool on the floor. "There it is now. Major Moon got here just in time to snatch it from her."

"I saw her just about to use it when you turned your back to pick up my coat," said Moon. He went to Esther and stood by her, putting his arms around her shoulders. She leaned back gratefully against him, closing her weary eyes. Cockrill saw the look on his face and did not interfere. "I—I wanted to save her, even yet," said the old man sadly. "I bolted the door. I didn't have time to think of course, but I had a vague idea of saving her without your knowledge."

She raised her prisoned hands and took one of his and kissed it and held her cheek against it, and said, very softly: "Thank you," and leaned back against him with a little sigh of gratitude, like a child.

Eden pushed forward. He cried eagerly: "William—*William!* Surely, Inspector, you're not going to accuse her of having tried to kill William? She was in love with him. She was going to marry him. . . ." He added in his impatient way, speaking across the silent Esther as though she had not been there: "You don't suggest that that was all false? You don't suggest that it wasn't true that she loved him?"

"Of course she loved him," said Major Moon sadly, looking

down as she sat with closed eyes, her head against his arm. "That night that she became engaged to him—anyone who saw her then must have known that she was happy, and in love. She was transformed. She shone like candlelight in this ugly, grey old place. She forgot the past and looked only to the future, she glowed with gaiety and love and happiness. She was so lovely in her radiance, that I fell in love with her in that one moment; I never knew real love before . . . but I fell hopelessly in love with her like any callow boy." He looked down at her again and added, with terrible sadness: "Twice a murderess, and, God help me, I love her still. . . ."

"What will poor William do?" cried Woody, her big heart numb with misery for all this sorrow and cruelty and pain.

Frederica shook her head with her own little off-hand, contemptuous gesture. "Oh, William'll be all right; he'll look after himself. He's been getting on perfectly well all this time with Chalk and Cheese, if all I hear is true. . . ."

Sergeant Bray's heavy footfall sounded in the lobby outside. As he appeared at the door, Barney, who had remained quietly in the background, came forward. He put into words what they had all been aching to ask: "But *why?*"

Esther sat with bent head and did not reply. Cockrill and Bray stepped forward. Woody cried, as though to hold them back, as though to postpone for just another few moments that terrible moment to come: "Inspector, you *must* tell us that; you *must* explain to us. We—she was our friend. We—we loved her. We knew her so *well.* . . ." She put her hands to her face and burst again into bitter tears.

Cockrill was not sorry to put off, for a little while longer, his ugly duty. He said, pausing: "You should know, Miss Woods, if anyone should. You were there when she told us—almost in so many words; that night when we talked outside the theatre door."

"That night we told her about the operation to William's leg?" said Woody, looking up through her fingers with tear-bright eyes.

"She was worried about the operation," said Cockrill thoughtfully. "She said she couldn't bear to think of him ill and in pain; she said it wasn't the danger—she knew there was no danger. But ten minutes later she was white and trembling, she was saying that William would die under the anæsthetic. She knew he would. She was going to kill him, herself. In that few minutes, she had made up her mind."

"But for heaven's sake—why?"

"Because of something you said."

They had almost forgotten Esther's presence: they spoke of her as though she were not there. Woods blurted out, wretchedly: "*I* said something? What could I have said?"

"I suppose they hadn't talked very much about the past," said Cockrill, not directly answering her. "She and her William, I mean. He told her the important things, of course, about his private life, and life in the Navy, perhaps; but they didn't have very much time together, and I expect they mostly looked ahead into the future. There was a lifetime ahead to discuss the little things—to tell about the time before he joined up, for example. She didn't know, until you told her that evening, that he'd worked with Higgins. . . ."

"In the rescue squad!" said Woods, hardly above her breath.

"In the rescue squad that left her mother to die," said Cockrill; and Esther slid slowly off the stool and lay in a motionless heap upon the ground.

3

"She's fainted!" said Cockrill.

"She's dead," said Moon, and he added softly: "Thank God!" and crossed himself.

Cockrill flung himself on to his knees beside the limp body. Esther's eyes were half-open, the pupils pin-points of black, her skin was cold and clammy to his touch; even as he knelt beside her the laboured respirations faltered and flickered out. He looked about him wildly: "What is it? What's the matter with the girl?"

"Is she dead?" said Gervase, standing over them.

"She's dying anyway." He cried imperiously to Major Moon: "You know something about this! What is it? What has she done to herself?"

Moon did not seem to hear him. Barnes came over and knelt down and took Esther's hand and pushed aside the steel bracelet and felt her wrist. To Cockrill, fuming impatiently, it seemed an eternity before he said slowly: "It's no use; she's dead."

"For heaven's sake, can't you *do* something?" cried Cockrill, frantically. "All you doctors and nurses—isn't there anything you can *do?* Can't you give her artificial respiration?" As they remained unmoving, standing in a silent ring, looking down sadly at the body, he flung himself across her and began clumsily to try to revive her himself. Woods started forward, almost as though in protest; but Frederica crouched down beside the body and, stroking with her little hand the shining, colourless hair, said softly: "Don't worry, darling. He can't do anything. She's dead."

Cockrill gave it up. He left the body lying on the floor and, standing over it, faced them all sternly. "This is *your* doing. You did this! You wanted her to die."

"How could we have borne anything else, Inspector?" said Barnes simply, not contradicting him.

"You knew that she was dying. All of you."

They stood looking down at her silently, Woody with tears running unashamedly down her raddled cheeks, Frederica white and pitiful, Major Moon with bent grey head and shaking hands. Gervase and Barney were quiet and sad, but there was a deliberate determination about their mouths. "This is a very grave matter," said Cockrill, at last. "You've deliberately connived at her death. You've assisted a murderer in evading justice. For all I know you contributed to her death. I can see it now—you've been playing for time. All of you. Every time I tried to speak to her, every time she showed signs of collapse . . . one of you drew my attention away. You knew from the first—from the moment I accused her. . . ."

"Not from the first; not all of us," said Barnes, glancing around him. "But I suppose, finally, all of us recognised the signs. The excitement, the flushed face, the bright eyes, the dryness of the mouth, the gradual torpor. . . ." He said to Major Moon, as though it were a routine matter of medicine: "Death was extraordinarily rapid, though. It can't be more than ten minutes or a quarter of an hour. . . ."

"She got some into a vein," said Major Moon briefly. "Not all of it; there are two puncture marks—it's not very easy to do on yourself, but she's got good veins . . . and she must have got a little in."

"You've been supporting her all this time, Moon," cried Cockrill furiously. "Unless you'd held her, she'd have fallen down, long ago!" He swung round upon them all, dancing with impotent rage. "You are accessories after the fact. I shall charge you all with it. . . ."

Major Moon looked up from a consultation with his shoes. "Oh, no, Cockie—I don't think you'll be able to do that."

A brightness came into Eden's eyes, Barney raised his head, the two girls looked up with an air of expectancy at the tone in the old man's voice. He continued blandly: "You haven't even found out yet what she died of."

Flushed face, bright eyes, exhilaration diminishing into unconsciousness, death ensuing with unusual rapidity because "it" had been given into a vein. Cockrill asked, jerking it out ungraciously, a load of doubt and fear very heavy on his heart: "Very well, then—what did she die of?"

"She died of an injection of morphia—self-administered," said Eden, and could not keep a hint of mocking laughter from his voice.

"Morphia? *Mor*phia?" He pointed suddenly to the pool on the floor. "Then, for God's sake—what's this?"

"That's the antidote, Inspector," said Major Moon; and added with his gentle smile: "And *you* knocked it out of my hand!"

Chapter XIII

BARNEY and Frederica sat in the garden of a pleasant little Kentish pub, drinking shandies and waiting for Woody and Eden to arrive. "Is this one of William's beers?" asked Frederica, holding her glass to the light.

"Yes, I suppose it is," said Barney. He added: "Poor William!"

"I don't think he's 'poor William' at all," said Freddi tartly. "Even before—even while we were still all being suspects, he was flirting with Chalk and Cheese; and I saw him the other day walking down the road from Godlistone with some girl hanging on his arm."

"Well, he's still a bit lame, I expect, darling; perhaps she was holding him up."

"Holding him up my foot!" said Mrs. Barnes.

Barney thought it all over quietly. He said, at last: "You know, Freddi, I doubt very much whether William was ever as serious as all that about Esther. He'd known her such a short time!

I've always wondered, I wondered even then, if it wasn't more a case of William flirting with her, and Esther taking it all to mean more than it really did. Esther was very inexperienced in the ways of the world. If a young man told her he adored her, she probably thought that it couldn't mean anything but that he wanted to marry her. William's a bit of a gay dog with the love-lies; and personally I think Esther took him too seriously. I don't say that he didn't care for her, and wasn't perfectly willing to marry her when he suddenly found himself committed to it; and I may be quite wrong, but I don't believe he was so deeply in love with Esther that he'll never get over it."

"It must have been a dreadful shock to him," acknowledged Frederica.

"Yes, I think it was. Moon had a rotten time breaking the news to him."

"Poor old Major Moon," said Freddi, and now her matter-of-fact little voice did take on a tinge of tenderness, a tear did well up into her wide grey eyes. "Just like him when he was going through hell himself, to take on the job of explaining to William—who didn't care half as much. . . . I wonder if Woody and Gervase have heard about him?"

Woods and Eden appeared, walking along the road from the hospital. "We ordered a couple of shandies for you," said Barney, pushing the big glass mugs across the wooden table. "Would you rather have something else? *We* can use these if you would."

The shandies, however, were just right for a summer evening, after a dusty walk. "Have you heard about Major Moon?" asked Woody, as soon as she had gulped down half her pint.

"Yes, we saw it in *The Times* to-day." Freddi picked up a paper from a neighbouring table. "Here it is again: 'Heroic Surgeon

Decorated. Posthumous Reward for Gallantry in Air Raid.' I should think it was gallantry, though it was useless gallantry. He must have known the woman couldn't be alive."

"Higgins' rescue squad 'knew' Esther's mother couldn't be alive," said Eden.

Frederica stared at him. "Do you think that's why he insisted on going? To sort of . . . ? Well, sort of because of Esther?"

"I should think so," said Barney. He added, "I wish to heavens I'd been there."

"I'm very glad you weren't, darling," said Frederica immediately. "What would have happened to me?"

"That is an extremely typical remark, Mrs. Barnes," said Woody, laughing.

"Well, I don't mean that; I meant that a lot of people had something to lose if Barney died; and Major Moon hadn't got any relations or anything, and I don't suppose he minded dying a bit. He was so terribly unhappy after Esther. . . . It was like seeing a ghost wandering about the hospital, going on doggedly with his work, making his little jokes and smiling his ghastly little smile, and getting paler and thinner and more mumbley every day. Personally I'm glad Major Moon was killed in the air-raid. He died doing something for somebody else, which was just like him, even if it *was* quite useless; and I'm sure he didn't want to live. He loved Esther too much ever to be happy again after—after we knew."

"Poor Esther," said Woody sadly.

They were all silent for a little while. "Do you think Esther was mad, Barney?" said Frederica at last.

"Major Moon told us once that all murderers are a little mad," he said. "I think she was sane enough on every other point but just this one. She thought she had to revenge her mother's death and on that subject she was mad. She killed Higgins and then she silenced Bates and after that I think she was sliding back into being perfectly normal and happy with William, and then she suddenly learnt that he was one of her mother's 'murderers' too—and I think that did knock her right over the edge, into real insanity. Think of her after that—always white and strained and weeping; nervy and hysterical and not able to eat or sleep. . . . Of course we put it down to this obsession about William dying under the anæsthetic, but even that was very abnormal, when you come to think of it. . . ."

"She must have been a very good actress to deceive us all for so long."

"Cockrill says that her mother was a terribly theatrical type of woman; she was never on the stage or anything like that, but he says that she was always acting in private life. I suppose it was 'in' Esther to be able to put on a show. . . ."

"But she was so sweet and gentle and everything I mean, that was genuine enough," insisted Frederica. "How could we ever have known that she was—wasn't normal?"

"We might have guessed," said Woods. "She was very queer when she first came back, after her mother was killed, you know, Freddi. She used to forget things terribly and she was vague and nervy and always crying in odd corners; I'm sure she never slept—I used to hear her tossing and turning all night. It got better, of course, and one thought it was just the shock and sorrow and that she would get over it; but she was terribly devoted to her mother and it must have been the most ghastly experience waiting, literally for days, for her to be rescued. . . ."

"Thousands of other people have had to do the same thing in this filthy war," said Frederica.

"You can't match suffering," said Eden, soberly. "Because

thousands of people have had the same experience, it didn't make it any better for Esther. She must have gone through hell. And then, perhaps, when she was getting over it, getting back to normal again, Higgins was brought in, and she recognised him as the foreman who had refused to go on searching for her mother. He was perfectly right, I expect; he couldn't sacrifice his men for a hopeless cause. But of course she would only think that if they hadn't waited for the proper demolition squad, her mother might have been saved—would have been saved, in fact, because she was still alive two days later. What Esther didn't take into account was the fact that the ordinary rescue squad could probably never have got through to her anyway."

"Why didn't Higgins recognise Esther?"

"I suppose she was covered in dust and filth when he spoke to her; she'd been digging with the rest of them. He probably wiped the worst of it off his face before he went to her. William too—he was working there but they didn't ever see each other except coated with filth from the debris."

"I can't understand how she never realised that William had been brought in with Higgins," said Woody. "Everyone else did. I did. I don't know how I did or who told me, but I seem always to have known that the fractured tib. and fib. was one of the lot who were hit in the A.R.P. centre."

"A pub in Godlistone was hit at the same time," suggested Eden. "I expect she vaguely connected it with William and his beer. Her mind would obviously be entirely given up to the problem of Higgins and what to do about him."

"Higgins kept saying that night that all his mates had been killed," said Freddi. "He didn't realise that William was still being dug out, and William was unconscious most of the night with anæsthetic and morphia; by the time he came to, Higgins had screens round him for X-rays and preparation for operation and all that; I don't suppose he ever saw William. He thought he was the last of his squad."

"That may have put the idea into Esther's head: all the others had been punished and Higgins was not to escape retribution either, especially as he had been the one to give the order to cease digging."

"No wonder Higgins heard all that had gone on in the bunk next door to him," said Barney, who still did not know *all* that had gone on in the bunk. "She withheld the morphia from him. I suppose she just gave him a shot of sterile water, so that he could suffer through a long night of pain as her mother had suffered for three days and three nights. . . . And then as she left the ward, she saw one of the Colonel's tins of paint; and the whole idea popped into her mind at once."

It seemed awful to order more drinks in the middle of the conversation that had grown up round their innocent evening's amusement, but Eden was hot and thirsty, and he got up unobtrusively and returned from the bar with four pint pots held groggily by their handles. ". . . must have been ghastly for her, standing there watching Higgins die," Freddi was saying.

"She looked terrible. I remember during the operation before Higgins, I made her sit down," said Woods. "Of course I thought she just couldn't take it. It was her first abdominal."

"And poor old Higgins was so sort of pathetic with her. He kept calling her 'my dear.' "

"Mrs. Higgins told Cockie that Esther was hard and cruel," said Eden. "The old girl must have spotted what all the rest of us missed."

"But Esther wasn't cruel," insisted Woody, earnestly. "She hated doing it. She just had this—Cockrill called it an *idée fixe* she thought it was wrong not to revenge her mother."

"She didn't kill Sister Bates to revenge her mother. She killed her so that she herself shouldn't be found out."

"Yes, but you can see how the thing worked in her mind. She thought she'd done right; she thought she ought not to be punished. She sort of owed it to her mother *not* to be. You see what I mean?"

"No, I don't," said Freddi.

"Yes, *I* do," said Eden. "It was as if the magic would go out of her revenge if she were found out and punished for it. Of course she was happier, she'd met William by that time, and perhaps she *wanted* to live; but I think the other was the really important reason, the real reason why she went on fighting discovery. That's why she started collecting the morphia; it had become an obsession with her that she shouldn't be caught and punished for her mother's death; she might kill herself—I don't think she would have minded so much doing that; but she would not accept punishment."

Frederica, who was accustomed to refer always to her patients with opprobrium and to her calling with much humorous contempt, was the first to be scandalised at a breach in the ethics or practices of nursing. "To think that she should let the men suffer, just that she could save some morphia! It was too awful; I can't forgive Esther that part of it; it's the worst of all to me!"

"She gave them a little, Freddi; she gave them half doses and things like that. Altogether in the three nights she was on, she must have had, say eight grains to give out. Suppose she kept back four, with the two original grains and then the extra quarter grain she

pinched from your haversack that day we were going for a drive—
of course she hadn't known before that you'd got it—she had six
and a quarter grains, and there was the original quarter that she
didn't give Higgins. That would almost certainly have killed her,
quite apart from her having managed to get some into the vein."

"Of course that's why she died so quickly?"

"Of course. It takes hours of coma and what-not in the ordinary way. I don't think Moon would have saved her anyway, with
his injection of strychnine; but I suppose the old boy did the first
thing that came into his mind. If he could stall Cockrill off for a
bit, he might pull her round. . . ."

"And then when Cockie broke in before he could give her the
antidote they both said 'Thank God!' "

"Well, yes; Moon must have seen then that the game was up
for poor Esther. It was best that she should die."

"But, Gervase, Cockrill obviously knew by then that it was
Esther who had—had killed Higgins and Bates. . . ."

"We don't know that Moon realised that. I believe he thought
that Cockie really suspected *him*. Don't you remember how he
called out to stop Esther from confessing. I believe he'd have
given himself up for the murders, to save her. After all, he didn't
care about life, very much, even then."

"Of course, it wasn't a postman's bicycle that he saw?"

"No, no, of course it wasn't," said Barnes. "Cockrill was just
stringing Esther along, trying to work her up to tell the real truth;
though it's true that ten or fifteen years ago, when Moon's child
was killed, country postmen did have red bicycles. No, this was a
silver-plated thing belonging to a young fellow in the neighbour-
hood; he saw it gleaming in the sun. He's told me about it, often."

Gervase got to his feet. "Well, what about another?"

"No, oi, Eden; it's my turn."

Woody patted her diaphragm. "Well, personally, I should blow up and go off with a loud bang."

"You always have such pretty little ways, my love," said Gervase.

They strolled off down the road, Freddi and Barney arm in arm. "Tell me about the hospital, Woody darling, and how you're getting on."

"Oh, my dear, it's too grim without you; without you and Esther. I'm sharing the cottage with Mary Bell and a frightful new girl called Bassett. Mary's nice of course, and she washes and does all the sort of normal things like sleeping with her window open, but Bassett's too ghastly. Com tried to wish Hibbert on to us, but I said to her, 'Madame,' I said, 'you *know* Hibbert goes to bed in her vest and knickers, because I remember you driving her down to the shelter in them one night. You *must* admit, Madame,' I said, 'that Hibbert would be *too* much for us to bear!' so she very decently said we could have Bassett instead; but sometimes Mary and I wish we'd had Hibbert, vest and knickers and all."

"What's wrong with Bassett?"

"She snuffles at night, my dear, in the most peculiar way; I suppose that's where her family got the name from. I mean they do sort of sniff their way after things, don't they, Gervase?"

"Don't what sniff their way after what?"

"Bassetts, of course, darling, or Bassett hounds or whatever you call them."

"I don't call them anything, Woody," protested Eden. "You know I'm no good at nature study."

Frederica suddenly stood still in the middle of the road. "Oh, gosh, talking about nature study—I forgot to tell you, Woody. I'm going to have a baby."

Woody thought that Gervase would never stop laughing. "You *are* awful," she said to him severely as they branched off alone towards the hospital. "It's most serious that Frederica is going to have a baby. You can see dear, old Barney's as proud and pleased as a dog with seventeen tails. What did you want to go and laugh for?"

"It was so absolutely typical of Freddi, the way she came crashing out with it in the middle of a country road; and six months before any nice girl would give away her pretty secret anyway. 'Oh, talking about nature, Woody, I'm going to have a baby!' " He went off into a fresh fit of laughter.

"Well, personally, I think it's heavenly, and I shall start off right away, knitting it a little woolly vest."

"You ought to have a family of your own to knit little vests for, Woody," said Gervase.

"What me, at my age?" said Woody, laughing.

"Yes, it's time you left off nursing and married and settled down. I think you'd have rather nice babies, darling; comic little things with shiny, boot-button eyes and lots of frizzy little curls like piccaninnies. What's more I think you'd make a very nice mother; and a very nice wife."

"Do you, Gervase?" said Woody, her hands thrust deep into the pockets of her suit because they had begun to shake.

"Yes, I do," said Gervase.

The apples were young and green upon the boughs and all the air was sweet with the scent of a dying summer day. They walked in silence through the country lane, and in the rich fields the rabbits sat up to watch them, rubbing black noses on little, furry paws. The last soft rays of the sun gleamed on the whitened stems of the trees, and foxglove and ragged robin caught at them as they passed, as though to hold them for a moment longer in the magic of a Kentish twilight. Woody repeated softly: "Do you, Gervase?" and her face was young again with light and hope and tender, incredulous joy.

"Yes, I do," said Gervase. "You're so—well, gallant is an overworked word, but I always think of you as a gallant person, Woody. Gay and gallant. Life isn't very good to you, always, and yet you never show that you're disappointed or hurt or afraid. You stick out your old chin and you make a little joke, and nobody would know that there was anything wrong at all." He bent down to pick up a small stone and threw it at a rabbit, who turned a white scut and hopped leisurely out of the way; and as he took her arm and walked on up the lane, he added smiling: "I think the man who finally marries you is going to be a very lucky fellow."

All the light went out of her face; but she did not falter in her step and if there were tears in her eyes, no tears were shed. "I always think of you as a gallant person, Woody. Gay and gallant." She stuck out her chin and made a little joke, and nobody knew there was anything wrong at all.

Laughing and talking they strolled on up the hill, and if the ghost of an old man toiled ahead of them, carrying in his hand a letter signed with the name of his own murderer—they did not notice him.

About the
Author

CHRISTIANNA Brand, who was born Mary Christianna Milne, was considered one of the great writers of mystery fiction. Renowned for her love of language, tight plotting, sense of humor, and surprise endings, she is best known for her Inspector Cockrill series set in Kent, England. She once said that her aim was "to write good, readable entertainment books and above all to write them well."

Born in Malaya in 1907, Brand was the daughter of Alexander Brand, a rubber planter, and Nancy Milne, a housewife. By age four, young Mary could already read fluently, and she was "brought up on the classics." Brand lived in Malaya for several years, until moving to India to attend school at a Franciscan convent. However, the family came upon hard times, and she had to leave the convent in her teens due to financial problems. Apparently her childhood was not always happy. "As a girl I was very poor, cold, and hungry, and I have known a great deal of suffering," she said.

Brand eventually relocated to England and completed her education. Before becoming a writer, she held a wide variety of jobs, including governess, professional ballroom dancer, model, receptionist, secretary, and salesperson. While working as a salesperson, she wrote her first book, *Death in High Heels* (1941), as a way to fantasize about killing a coworker she disliked. During this time, she also married a surgeon, Roland Swaine Lewis, with whom she would adopt one daughter, Victoria.

Brand enjoyed writing mysteries, and the next book she wrote was *Heads You Lose* (1942). This suspenseful story was her first to feature Inspector Cockrill—a character who was inspired by her father-in-law. Next came *Green for Danger* (1944), widely considered her masterpiece and also starring the inimitable Inspector Cockrill. Of the good inspector, one critic summarized, "the reader derives great satisfaction from trying to outwit the Inspector; that he rarely succeeds in doing so is the result of the author's subtlety in planting false clues, dropping apparent red herrings in unlikely places, and providing a cast of convincing Least Likely Persons from which to choose."

In addition to mystery stories, Brand also wrote several romance novels and the amusing Nurse Matilda children's series. Based on tales she heard from her grandfather, the children's books were illustrated by her cousin Edward Ardizzone. The books portray the many adventures and mishaps of the Brown children and Nurse Matilda, their unsightly nanny who changes from ugly to lovely as her boisterous charges eventually benefit from her wisdom, kindness, and quirky teaching methods.

During her writing career, Brand contributed to several periodicals and anthologies, including *The Great Detectives*, *The Saturday Evening Post*, and *Ellery Queen's Mystery Magazine*. She was fond of using pseudonyms and was also published under the names Mary Roland, China Thompson, Annabel Jones, and Mary Ann Ashe. Brand died in 1988.